THE BIG IDEA

I work the room now, making eye contact, pitching, enthusing, using my hands, questioning, teasing, using everything I've been taught and everything I instinctively know, because this is my baby, the Big Idea. Selling it means, at the least, a half-million-dollar test spot for our reels, and, at the most, landing the account. Right now, I don't think about my life, or the fact that the cleaners will be closed when I get home, or the fact that I can't get over my ex-husband who's married to somebody else—I'm just reading their eyes and their body language and I'm dancing and parrying, courting them, and I feel the adrenaline surging until my heart is beating a tap rhythm against the silk of my blouse.

I move in for the kill and I'm balancing my little toe on the stairway to Heaven. . . .

Hype

Liz Nickles

A SIGNET BOOK

SIGNET
Published by the Penguin Group
Penguin Books USA Inc., 375 Hudson Street,
New York, New York 10014, U.S.A.
Penguin Books Ltd, 27 Wrights Lane,
London W8 5TZ, England
Penguin Books Australia Ltd, Ringwood,
Victoria, Australia
Penguin Books Canada Ltd, 2801 John Street,
Markham, Ontario, Canada L3R 1B4
Penguin Books (N.Z.) Ltd, 182–190 Wairau Road,
Auckland 10, New Zealand

Penguin Books Ltd, Registered Offices:
Harmondsworth, Middlesex, England

Hype previously appeared in an NAL Books edition.

First Signet Printing, April, 1990
10 9 8 7 6 5 4 3 2 1

 REGISTERED TRADEMARK—MARCA REGISTRADA

Printed in the United States of America

PUBLISHER'S NOTE
This is a work of fiction. Names, characters, places, and incidents either are
the product of the author's imagination or are used fictitiously, and any
resemblance to actual persons, living or dead, events, or locales is entirely
coincidental.

for Andy

Chapter One

"GAAAAANG-BAAAAANG!"

A ninety-mile-an-hour blur of a swivel chair hurtles down the terrazzo hall, and I dive onto a desktop as six cups of coffee, four storyboards, a Rolodex, an inflatable tyrannosaurus, and two copywriters go flying. Hunched on his back in the swivel chair, yipping in war whoops, is Richard Tetzloff, the brains behind the Atarax aspirin TV hammer demo; steering from behind with the skill of Mario Andretti on a good day is his art director partner, father of that dread social disease Lobster-Claw Hands—which makes the two of them one of the most valuable creative teams in the ad agency, so I'm benevolent about the fact that I'm almost a hit-and-run victim seventy stories above street level.

"Whiplash!" I yell.

Just because I'm making a less dramatic exit from the conference room doesn't mean I'm any less psyched. I'm pumped. I smell blood. We're not talking about a yawn disguised as a meeting, or an overhead projector presentation to glaze your eyeballs opaque, or a pie-in-the-sky storyboard or script. We have just been catapulted out of the gate for the

1

guts and the heartbeat of the advertising business: the new business pitch.

I check my stockings: no runs. And I'd better not find a single snag on my peach-and-olive Armani suit, or there'll be hell to pay. Then again, after ten years in the business, I ought to know better than to put three thousand dollars' worth of clothes at the mercy of the creative department. You never just work here; you *negotiate* your existence, like playing through a miniature-golf course with windmills, tunnels, and a giant mousetrap.

But this is good energy. We've only had the assignment for five minutes, and already people are clustering in doorways, by the drinking fountain and the message center, teaming up, tossing ideas back and forth like the platinum Ping-Pong balls they are. An idea becomes a commercial which becomes a campaign which becomes a pitch which becomes a headline in *Ad Age*, a bonus, a raise, and a promotion. Roughly, that's the way it goes.

"I hate these gang-bangs," says Maeve, a junior art director who is not yet numb to chaos, as she zigzags down the hall with a three-foot stack of magazines. "Hate, hate, hate."

I can see her point, but, after all, the gang-bang is an agency tradition, a sort of slightly more cutthroat version of the Pillsbury Bake-Off. You and the partner of your choice team up and pit yourselves against the other forty-eight people in the creative department, and let the best work win. In two weeks it's judgment day, the higher-ups are going to put all this work in front of their version of a firing squad, and your campaign had better win and get picked for the new business pitch, because only the winners survive in this business.

I've got my briefing book under my arm—a thick black notebook with PROJECT OMEGA stamped on the cover. Project Omega, aka Koala Cola. Of course, everything is top-secret, as if this were a Polaris submarine on red alert under the polar ice cap instead of an ad agency about to pitch a soft-drink account.

I flip through the pages. "Boilerplate," I say. "There's nothing in here we can use."

A nicotine-stained hand on my shoulder—it's Bruce Berenger, my boss. "That," he says, "is why you are a highly paid officer of this company. Lead into gold? I have confidence. You can do it, Cam." He salutes with his cigar.

"Oh, right, no problem. It's only a seventy-million-dollar account." I hum the theme to *Mission Impossible*. "Dum dum, dum-dum, *dum dum* dum dum . . ."

"Deedledee! Deedle dee!" A match lights under my nose. Juice, my art director partner, is off-key as he and I veer into my office.

His real name is John P. Jusinski, but "Juice" fits him perfectly, because he's an electric current grounded in five feet, nine inches of perfectly pressed all-natural fabrics. Walking into Juice's office, or having him walk into yours, is like encountering a lightning rod. The atmosphere crackles and snaps, and everything is kinetic, and you remember just why you love it so much.

Over the past five years we've teamed up for hundreds of gang-bangs and lived to tell about it. And at least ninety percent of the time, we win.

We're the aces, the A Team, Spartacus in the ring, Grant at Appomattox. Dick Scully, the other creative director here at Missoni & Missoni, has a group as big as ours—twenty-some people—but his group seems stuffed at their desks, frozen in a time warp like Pompeii after the eruption, ashes waiting to be blown away by us in creative shoot-outs. As for our own group, of which I am the creative director— well, if one of them comes up with a million-dollar idea, we're on our feet applauding, but most of the time Juice and I are the ones who come up with the Big Idea, because we click like nobody else. "We're a team," he always says. "Joined at the hip; separated at birth." And he's right. We're partners in more than crime—we're partners in mission: to boldly go where advertising has never gone before.

I'm copy, he's art. Of course, Juice can't even draw a straight line, but he's a great conceptualist, so it doesn't matter.

When you put art directors and writers together, it's like a blind date. Sometimes it takes, sometimes it doesn't.

Did we ever take.

"So," says Juice. "What do you want to do? Brainstorm? Black out? Do drugs?" This is a joke. To do drugs in an ad agency is to slit your own throat, because you blow your mind, and that's all you have to work with.

"Let's go to the movies."

We do this a lot. If it isn't the movies, it's the Art Institute, or the park, or the zoo, or the bookstore. We get out of the office and into the real world. We talk. Away from the phones and the memos and the office, the ideas just happen, babies we find under cabbage leaves.

I check the paper. "*The Scream* is playing at the Water Tower in twenty minutes."

"Who's in that?"

"Jed Durant. The hot new kid."

"Get your coat."

On the way out, I run the gauntlet, sticking my head into offices along the west wall whenever I see somebody inside.

"Any questions? Everything okay? Will we see roughs by Friday?"

But it's like giving a kid a new package of crayons. I know they'll be preoccupied for at least the next few hours.

"Cam, can I see you for a minute?"

I freeze like I do every time Brenda Parker talks to me. She has a nice-enough face, and there's no doubt she's a pleasant person, but she frightens me. Brenda is in her mid-forties, and she's been with the agency for maybe twenty-two years—she was one of Enrico Missoni's original hirees. But her career clock is ticking. She's frankly past her prime; she's outworn her welcome and nobody's told her. In meetings, everyone's polite to Brenda, but we never use her ideas. Sometimes they're actually pretty good, but there's always some kid who's hipper, quicker, sharper. I've been told that Brenda used to be a golden girl. If that's true, now she's just a paled-out Xerox copy of herself, still hanging in there, but uncomfortably close to the cliff. She scares me because I don't want to end up like her. I don't want somebody younger and hotter feeling sorry for me, breathing behind my back: "She used to be good."

Brenda and I go over her copy for the bicycle-coupon ad. Her work is consistent: tight, effective, professional. But when I look at her, I see something in her eyes—resignation. She knows what she is, that she'll never be Mary Wells Lawrence, but she'll take what she's got and do what she can with it. Everybody knows she'll be placated with coupon ads as long as she gets to stay, like the wallflower who's satisfied to dance with the nerd because it's enough to be asked to the dance.

"Nice work, Brenda," I say. "You gonna jump in on Omega? Maybe team up with Clark?"

"I've got some ideas already," she says, trained enthusiasm in her voice.

"Wait a second," I tell Juice. "Let's leave a note for the Mole."

The Mole is a writer nobody ever sees, because he never seems to come to work till after five o'clock, and then only wearing sunglasses. I leave his copy briefing on his desk every night, and in the morning his work is on my desk. I drop the brief onto his desk and close the door on his surrogate, a life-size, full-color Mole-o-rama cutout, complete with wraparound reflector sunglasses and sport coat, sitting in his chair, with a note pushpinned to the forehead: "Back at 5."

"Did you forward your phone?" says Edie at reception in her den-mother voice. "I can't be responsible if you don't forward your phone, you know. You creatives never forward your phones, and when you don't get your messages, all I hear is 'Edie, why don't I get my messages?' I'm only one person, you know . . ."

The elevator doors put her out of her misery.

"Do you think they have Koala Cola here?" asks Juice as we wait in the popcorn line at the movie.

"Are you kidding? They got Pepsi, Coke, Diet Pepsi, Diet Coke, Dr. Pepper—the last thing they need is another cola."

"Yeah, I guess they're all pretty much the same."

"Sure. It's all done with mirrors." Juice dumps half a shaker of salt on his popcorn.

"That's the point. We have to make this product unique. Right now it blends in with the woodwork."

"We could always go the dancing-koala-bear approach," says Juice as we look for seats.

"Cute. Too cute."

"God, that name of theirs is really limiting. What else are you gonna do with a product that's named Koala and has a bear on the can?"

"True. Everybody who's working on this, everybody who's pitching this, is going to come in with some variation on that bear."

The credits come up and a face comes on the screen that's making half the girls in his audience gasp and moan and giggle and do all those things that young girls do when a young guy is so charismatic they can't stand it. Why are all these girls in this movie in the middle of an afternoon, anyway? Are they cutting classes? To see this movie?

"So what do you think?" says Juice.

I have to admit, this kid on the screen has the beauty and presence of innocence gone wrong—a fallen angel. He starts to sing, the girls start to scream, and I get an idea.

"I think," I say, "that the koala bear just went into hibernation."

Juice nods imperceptibly, but I know he gets it. We both stare at the screen. I'll cancel my dinner with the investment banker, Juice will cancel whatever he was up to, and we'll go back to the agency when the movie is over.

The Big Idea is there, and we're going to nail it.

Chapter Two

Abbott's the name,
Crotch is the game.

The meeting is running two hours late as I'm looking at these words embossed on a brass plaque on
the product manager's desk, and I'm restless for two
reasons now. First, we're supposed to present our
ideas for the Omega pitch today to top management,
and I know Juice is probably going crazy wondering
where I am. Second, I'm aware that it's gauche to
stare at the client, or at his desk, but my eyes keep
whipping back like the plaque was at the center of a
centrifugal-force field. How often do you see the
word "crotch" embossed in brass?

Bill Abbott taps a Bic felt-tip pen on the plaque in
a manner suggesting he might be an art critic noting
the finer points of the *Mona Lisa*. "Fifteen years in
fem hyge," he says proudly, launching into his
feminine-hygiene track record: five years on tam-
pons, three years on pads, two especially heroic
stints on minipads.

"I wore one for a week," Bill announces.

"What?" The four other men in the group—Denny
the Client, who is Bill's assistant, and the Suits:

Lance Kendra, the agency account-team supervisor, and his assistant—freeze in their pinstripes.

"A minipad. I wore one for a week," Bill repeats.

"Oh."

The other men examine their shoes.

"I wanted to really understand the product. I had my whole group wear one. Men *and* women."

Bill Abbott is the brand manager of our newest account, Bridal Bouquet Feminine Deodorant Spray.

Bridal Bouquet is the second-smallest and least glamorous of the six accounts in my creative group at Missoni & Missoni, but the basic principles and techniques for every piece of business boil down to one three-letter word: *sell*. Richard and Anson presented this same storyboard last week, and Bill Abbott bounced them out on their ear. Now it's my turn to try to sell the idea, so I'm standing in front of a series of huge cardboard storyboards studded with colorful marker drawings and clip art of tastefully confident Eighties Women that represent the solution to Bill Abbott's problem. Or, as we say in advertising, our *opportunity*. Bridal Bouquet is a dog of an account. The brand is barely breathing. I'm here to perform CPR on Bridal Bouquet to resuscitate a comatose product.

"Bill—with your background I'm sure you'll agree—this spot will show women how Bridal Bouquet helps them feel better about themselves."

Bill walks slowly back and forth, scrutinizing the storyboard frame by frame. Finally he speaks: "Where's the man?"

Denny furrows his brow.

"Uh . . . there is no man, Bill. That's the point. Women today want to be . . . self-reliant. Independent. Free." This is going to be a very long meeting.

"Bullshit. We're talking *odor* here."

A very, very long meeting.

"Odor," Bill repeats. "You gotta convince a girl that it's important to use Bridal Bouquet. How do you convince her?"

I look around the conference table. The Suits sit there like Mount Rushmore. It is precisely this characteristic that is responsible for the fact that they are called "Suits." In all fondness, of course.

Bill scans the office where we all stand or sit in our places—me in front of the storyboards, the Suits behind their shield of the overhead projector, and Denny the Client across the table, nodding enthusiastically as Bill speaks.

"She's gotta be *embarrassed*. Put her in a social situation. What will her date think? What will the guys at the water cooler think? It's all the guy, what *he* thinks."

Denny translates. "What Bill is saying is, the key is the *guy*. That's it. That's the big idea."

I interrupt. "Maybe it's what *she* thinks that's important, Bill." I use the word "maybe" purely as a concession to agency-client professional respect. "She's an Eighties Woman."

Bill sits down at his desk, picks up a copy of the script for the commercial, tosses it back on the desk, and stares at me. "What do you know about women?"

Driving back from the meeting, I'm upset—and not because I'm late. Abbott, the bastard, has touched a nerve.

I double-check in the rearview mirror in case a full moon did something weird and things changed in the last twelve hours. Thick, unplucked eyebrows, weird eyes—one blue, one green, eye shadow blurred but still there, freckles, wavy marmalade-colored hair.

Settled: I'm still a woman. *I just had my period, Bill. That proves it.*

But it hurts. I've spent at least the past ten years showing I can get the account, materialize the Big Idea from thin air, fire up the team, get the scores. Along the way, my marriage became a casualty. I'm a victim of emotional vivisection.

My career, however, is flourishing.

So should I congratulate myself or kill myself? I mull it over as I adjust the bass on the car speakers, tapping my fingernails on the burled-wood dash of the Jaguar. Why the hell should I care about the opinion of a man who wears a minipad?

I hit the windshield wipers. There's just enough snow to bring traffic to a standstill—in other words, two flakes. I call my secretary from the car phone.

"Sally, I'm stuck on the expressway."

"They moved up the Omega meeting. It started an hour ago."

Bad news. Juice and I not only have to sell our idea, which is hard enough in itself, we have to convince agency management to do something they hate—spend money. We have to get them to see that we can't win an account like Koala on a buck and a wing. We have to shoot a finished commercial. No—more than a commercial. An extravaganza. We have to take the bit and run for the finish line. We can do it, and we can win. This is it—my chance to go to Heaven, so named because the eightieth floor is where the president, the chairman, the CEO, the head of research, the head of media, and the chief creative officer all have stratospheric offices, and nosebleed-figure salaries; with Enrico Missoni, our founder, retiring last month, everybody will move up a notch, and my boss will become president. At which point *his* job as chief creative officer opens up, and I want it.

I know that I want it too much. It shouldn't matter if I get promoted or not, but it seems like the fair and natural conclusion of all I've worked for, the only just reward for all the fourteen-hour days and order-in-pizza nights, the holidays on location shoots and business trips, the fact that I'm alone, divorced, and I've made this the thing in my life that counts.

"Tell Juice I'm on my way, will you?"

I punch my home number and call myself for messages. There's my voice: "Hi, I'm not in right now, but that's the funny thing about fashion." I've got to change this message.

"Hi, Cam," says Barry the commodities broker. "I thought we could go to the opera tonight. Call me."

Barry is someone I've been seeing for about three months. He talks a lot about pork bellies, but that's okay. We go to dinner, movies, concerts, ballets. Somehow I feel like it's obscene to be dating when you're over thirty-five, so I never consider that I'm dating somebody. I just "see" him. I'm thinking that this thing with Barry is never going to go anywhere in the long run. He's just too anal. He calls it a mind for detail, but I think that's underrating a man who vacuums his cat with the upholstery attachment.

I check out the iridescent green numerals set into the dashboard. Two-thirty—another lunchless two-thirty. I grab a granola bar, one of the ten or twelve I always carry in my painter's bag for emergencies. Okay, I don't eat right. Believe me, I know the four basic food groups, but that's just too many for me to keep track of right now.

Traffic inches along, going noplace fast. If there's one thing I hate, it's wasting time, which is why I like to do two things at once—say, driving and dictating. I rummage through the painter's satchel on the seat beside me and locate my microcassette recorder. It's important to utilize found time like this.

"Ms. Beatrice Smart, President, Smartco . . . Get the address, Sally. Dear Beatrice. Our lunch discussion was very helpful, and based on your input, we are moving ahead with ideas for new label designs. Thanks for the suggestions, Best."

"Mr. Phil Donahue. Donahue Show. Dear Phil, it was a pleasure being part of the panel last week on your show about women in advertising. The discussion of the industry's use of subliminal imagery was lively, but I stand by my opinion. Thanks for the forum. Sincerely."

"To: Bruce Berenger. From: myself. Re: Staff. Bruce. Can we meet ASAP to reevaluate staffing. My group is working full steam on six accounts that bill almost a hundred million, including Fluffy Bakery, Trendar Hair Care, Stratoglider Bikes, and Smartco, which has four brands. We now have twelve people—five teams, plus Juice and me. That averages out to one-point-five people per account or brand, not counting new business. On the plus side, the group won six international awards last year, and billing is up. On the downside, we're experiencing some burnout. I have a near-term plan that could trim budgets long-term. Can we discuss."

By the time I get to Michigan Avenue, I've finished all my correspondence, so I turn into the garage of the Missoni building with a clear conscience.

Two banks of elevators and seventy floors up, voices yell after me from the coffee room, the audiovisual room, the cubbyholes, the woodwork, as I run down the hall at a trot.

"Cam, they're waiting for you!"

"Cam, you missed the one-o'clock briefing."

"Cam, we're over budget already, and Hector forgot to put in color correction."

Nobody actually makes eye contact. The troops are all focused in on their own drawing boards or cassette recorders or VCR's. Music blares.

I yell over my shoulder as I walk.

"I know I missed the briefing. Did you take notes?"

"No, I can't screen the cassette. Get Juice. An art director should see it. If he likes it, okay."

"Over budget? Maeve, Maeve, Maeve. Get the client to sign the estimate."

Into my office, which is the requisite Corporate Orange. I have no real decor, but then the position of the office is more important than the furniture. I have a very large corner, more like a wedge. A giant high-tech chrome grid surrounds three sides of the room, with a hurricane of notes and memos clipped at the intersection of every wire, plus a spare storyboard strewn here and there, and a few of my more major award statuettes used as bookends. The fourth wall is empty except for a storyboard rail, on which we balance boards of commercials in progress while bashing them senseless with constructive critiques. Sometimes, just for fun, we use real darts. It's assumed nobody takes anything personally in this business. Sort of like living in Dodge City must have been in the days of Matt Dillon. There was a gunfight in the streets every day, and posses of hangmen ran wild, but nobody took it personally. That was just the way it was in the Old West. Maybe that's why so many of us refer to ourselves as "hired guns." This attitude boils down to a total absence of loyalty, but it also means we don't take it personally. Let's clear up one thing: I wasn't born the hard-assed bitch that this implies. None of us were. And none of us are. We're just people who ended up here. I mean, how many grade-schoolers announce, "I'm going to write jingles when I grow up?" No, most of us creatives just sort of floated in with the tide, unlike our counterparts in media, account management, and research, who usually march in armed with MBA's and a decade's worth of objectives.

Not us.

I myself grew up in training to be a corporate wife, or, if I was dedicated, fashionable, and successful, a socialite and charity-fund-raiser, like my own mother. College was supposed to be a place to meet the right people, not take the right courses. Graduate school was the aberration. I had no plans after graduate school except to get married, which I did. I have never read Machiavelli or *The One Minute Manager*.

I landed in the business ten years ago by accident, after I wrote a series of stories about a duck called Fluffy who loved soft sheets and I sent it to the ad agency that did the fabric-softener commercials.

They called me. I went in and talked and talked about Fluffy the duck, and I left the creative director's office with a job as a junior copywriter. Fluffy the duck was my first big success—and he's still a hero in the fabric-softener business.

I loved advertising from day one.

It was like going to school and getting a gold star. On the other hand, of course, you could also get a machete in the back, but for a long time I was too far down the totem pole to be a target. I just loved it.

More than I ever loved being a housewife, or being a wife period.

My intercom line buzzes.

"They're in the Gallery," says Sally.

You don't want to barge in the front door and interrupt the flow of the meeting, so I detour through the projection room at the back, where Zero, our audiovisual director, is manning the video machines and slide projectors. There's a two-way mirror and a sound system between the Gallery and the projection booth, so I can eavesdrop on the meeting for a few minutes before I go in.

The Gallery is so named because it houses the legendary Missoni & Missoni contemporary art collection. It's an extra high-ceilinged octagon-shaped room with no windows, showcasing monolithic canvases by Kenneth Noland, Julian Schnabel, Susan Rothenberg, Jennifer Bartlett, Jackson Pollock, and other high priests of modern art. There's a twenty-four-hour security guard just for this room, which is probably worth more than the entire building.

"How's it going?" I whisper.

Zero's leaning back with his cowboy boots up on a projector case, whittling a canoe from a piece of balsawood. His fine yellow hair is sticking straight up like a baby chicken's, and he's wearing a Monopoly piece in his right ear.

"Slow," says Zero. We have a clear view of the Gallery, but they can't see us—kind of like watching a lineup. "Six teams have presented so far. There's the bodies." There must be fifty storyboards lined up on the four walls. Almost every frame has a drawing of a koala bear. Tony Belini, from Scully's group, is standing in front of the room, holding a stuffed koala, singing and hopping up and down. Scully is tapping his foot. Mercifully, the microphone is turned off, so we can't hear Tony, who's tone-deaf.

Bruce motions to Zero, and he kills the lights and projects a chart on the screen.

"And you can shove those numbers too," Bruce says to the head of research as I slip in at the end of the horseshoe-shaped table, "because we're talking the beverage category here, and it's an image-driven category, and those numbers are the emperor's new clothes. If we don't get input that makes more sense than that, we can't come up with work that makes more sense than this." He flips a storyboard onto the floor. "Shit in, shit out."

I look across the table at Juice, who smirks just enough so I know he recognizes grandstanding when he sees it.

The Doc, who is standing at the edge of the screen with a pointer, sighs, adjusts his glasses, and signals Zero to turn up the lights. He's in research; he's used to this.

"All I'm saying, Bruce, is that the category is saturated. People are waiting for a new soft drink like they're waiting for another grain of sand on the beach. That's why the company's in trouble. They're a commodity product."

Everybody blinks as the lights go up, and Bruce notices I'm sitting there. "Cam, I'm glad you could join us." His tone indicates I have deigned to return from a six-week cruise on the Love Boat.

"Bridal Bouquet ran late."

"Well, this is new business. It takes priority." He points to a chart with his thumb. "I think we need to review this for Cam."

"I'm familiar with the background, Bruce."

"In brief, please," says Bruce, disregarding me, and I can hear everybody in the room sigh: *God, am I going to have to sit through this again?*

Charlie Ness, the account supervisor and King of the Suits, walks to the front of the room to the flip chart. On the cover is a huge can of Koala Cola, complete with koala-bear logo.

"This," he says, "is our opportunity."

He flips a page.

"The Union Bottling Company and their parent, Trans-Corp, are looking for a new agency to put Koala on the map. Right now their share is less than point-five. They're looking for a seven share, and they're willing to invest seventy million to get it."

"Who's pitching?" asks Denise Samuels from media, who is, at thirty-two, prematurely gray.

"Six agencies. Everybody from Thompson to Riney. Chiat bowed out—conflicts. But we have an edge." Charlie smiles. "Harold plays golf with Fred Simmons from Union Bottling, who's head of the agency selection committee."

Everybody laughs, and Bruce pretends he's lining up a putt. "Birdie," he says.

I flip through the deck, as we call the phone-book-size briefing document, and for the next three hours a blur of charts, slides, and exhibits is trotted out. We taste the product. We taste the competition. Hours go by, but who can tell? There's no daylight in the room. Finally Bruce says, "Cam, Juice, how do you see the creative?"

I may have been late, but I'm prepared. With a nod to Zero I stand up, and the music from the cassette Juice and I have had the music house working on for the past two weeks booms through the speakers. It's an unusual sound, hard, driving, but fresh, matching the energy of the images spinning out of the video monitors—a montage of America's heroes past and present. Roy Rogers, Marilyn Monroe, Howdy Doody, JFK, George Washington, Amelia Earhart, Annie Oakley, the astronauts, the Beatles. Then current teen heroes—Michael Jackson, Michael J. Fox, Madonna.

"These people are relevant," I say, stopping the tape. "Koala bears are not." I take the stuffed koala bear and toss it into the wastebasket. "Besides, there's no appetite appeal to a bear. Who wants fur in their drink? I think we have to make this product creatively relevant and appealing across the board."

"Concept-wise, I'm starting to see it," says Harold, the president-soon-to-be-chairman. Harold has a huge advantage in this business—the knack of thinking like the average American. If he gets it, the public will get it. This talent has made Harold rich.

"Execution would be a bitch," says Bruce, throwing up his hands. "It's too broad to appeal to everybody."

"That's just it, Bruce," I say, and I'm really on a roll now—I can feel the idea, I can almost touch it. "We need a big idea. A huge idea. Koala is too small. An Australian identity is limiting."

"What about Crocodile Dundee and the Australian beers?"

"That was yesterday. And they're minor segments of the total market."

I point to the closest screen and Zero rolls the video again.

"Let's stop dancing on the head of this pin," I say. "What if they repositioned the product? What if they renamed it? What if they tapped a whole new market? A bigger market? A mass market?" I'm moving now, pacing the room, stopping in front of Harold, putting my palms on the table, leaning down. "What if?" I say, staring straight at him, challenging.

The room is silent. There's a lot at stake, and nobody likes to go on the line.

"Juice, let's show them what we mean."

Juice never moves too fast. He kind of slides in slow motion to the front of the room, carrying the storyboards under his arm, and spreads them on the railing, backward. It's never good to show your hand too soon.

"Who is the number-one teen influence today? Who's bigger than Michael Jackson and Michael J. Fox combined?"

Juice turns the first board around and a huge picture of a boy-man with smudged half-moon eyes stares at the room. "Jed Durant," says Juice. "His single 'Angel of Mercy' is platinum. His movie *The Scream* is this season's sleeper. Cam and I went to see it. It was packed. Nobody's bigger with the ten-to twenty-year-olds."

"Of course, we don't want to lose the older market while we woo the teens," I say, flipping around the adjacent storyboard. "Who's somebody straight out of American legend for the adult generation? Cowboy Bob. Everybody's childhood hero." Zero flashes the slide of Cowboy Bob, complete with blazing six-shooters.

"Cowboy Bob!" says Harold. "I think I've seen every Cowboy Bob show they ever put on TV. Twice. I watched the reruns after I grew up."

"Jed Durant meets Cowboy Bob," says Juice. "Picture it." He goes through the action on the storyboard, motion by motion, acting it out until you can almost see the pictures come to life.

20

"Hold on," says Charlie. "I don't get it. What's this got to do with Koala or Australia? Every agency that's pitching is going to be on that bandwagon."

Juice and I smile at each other. We love it when meetings go our way. We roll in it, in fact.

"That's just it, Charlie," I say. "We zig while they zag. We don't play their game. We reposition this from a specialty soft drink to the mass market. And we rename the product."

Juice flips over the last storyboard, where one word is printed: *Zing!* Then Zero plays our music track again, this time with the words of our jingle layered onto the instrumentals, and we hear the name Zing! building, building, building until it fills the room and echoes in our ears. When it's over, the room is silent.

I work the room now, making eye contact, pitching, enthusing, using my hands, questioning, teasing, going solo, then in a duet with Juice, then solo again, using everything I've been taught and everything I instinctively know, because this is it, my baby, the Big Idea. Selling it means, at the least, a half-million-dollar test spot for our reels, and, at the most, landing the account. Right now, I don't think about my life, or what time it is, or the fact that the cleaners will be closed when I get home, or I haven't called back Barry the commodities broker, or the fact that I can't get over my ex-husband who's married to somebody else—I'm just reading their eyes and their body language and I'm dancing and parrying, courting them, and I feel the adrenaline surging until my heart is beating a tap rhythm against the silk of my blouse, and right now, at this minute, in this room, this idea, this commercial, is everything to me.

I move in for the kill.

"Why not go for it? Present a finished spot. These guys on the selection committee are used to thinking in terms of Coke and Pepsi and what they do on the air. A storyboard won't have any impact at all. It's just a piece of paper. They need to see it, hear it, feel it."

"Finished commercial?" says Charlie. "What kind of budget would we be talking?"

"Seven-hundred-thousand-plus. Possibly a million."

"That's suicide." Charlie is envisioning his bonus flying out the window. Or maybe all our jobs.

"It's suicide *not* to do it. We can't win without it. You know that in your heart."

Bruce sits there saying nothing, taking temperatures. I can't read him yet. He's never seen this work before, so there's no telling how he'll react. It's not safe, mainstream stuff. Maybe he doesn't want to be the one who blew a multimillion-dollar account —not when they're warming up the presidential suite for him.

"We can get Trans-Corp to reimburse us after we get the account."

"If we get the account," says Charlie.

"O ye of little faith! I believe in you, Charlie. You can sell this."

For about three minutes, which seem like my entire life span, nobody says anything.

Finally, a slow smile from Harold. A nod from Charlie. Bruce looks only semiconvinced. We have to push him over the edge.

"Bruce," I say. "Juice and I and the group want to thank you for all your input on this. You really got us off the ground."

Bruce authoritatively snaps the eraser off his pencil. "Assuming the name tests well," he says, "let's do it."

We have a commercial to shoot, a campaign to pitch, and I'm balancing my little toe on the stairway to Heaven.

How did it get so late?

I push open the heavy wrought-iron grillwork of the front door. That's the thing about landmark brownstones—no doormen and no elevators.

Unfortunately, my apartment is on the top floor, and there's no avoiding the stairs, which, when I am weighted down as I am today with a fifteen-pound canvas bag, an over-the-arm briefcase, and a four-foot-square, thirty-pound zippered portfolio case, is a climb that resembles dragging a dead caribou up the north face of Mount Everest.

The Bird cheeps in the kitchen. Poor Bird. Sometimes I don't think he gets enough attention. I haven't even gotten around to naming him yet, and I've had him three years. He drums on the bars with his beak.

This is the smallest apartment I've ever lived in, and I like it the best. It has a skylight and a working fireplace, for one, and I can sit by the fire, put my feet up on the fifties ottoman, and listen to the hoofbeats of the horses and carriages as they saunter by below—it's that quiet. When I was married, Timothy and I had a huge duplex with a greenhouse on the roof. Timmy was a starving artist, and for the first few years I didn't work, but he had a trust fund so it was easy to live beyond our means. Since I didn't have an income, I felt guilty about having a maid, and I remember it took three days to clean the apartment, more if I oiled the paneling or polished the parquet that week. I can't say I miss it. I've got my bedroom with the brass four-poster, my study with the pine armoire, my Lalique vases, my Amish quilts, and my computer. The kitchen is an obviously unsuccessful attempt to shove as many appliances as possible into a closet. I hate to go in there, but I consider that a blessing in disguise. Maybe tonight I'll have Stouffer's Lean Cuisine.

The Bird cheeps again. Louder. He can get pretty obnoxious, but he's in a cage; he's not going anywhere. I'll get to him later.

I drop my painter's satchel in the hall as I walk toward the bathroom, but there's something wrong with this picture: Somebody has already drawn a bubble bath.

It is my ex-husband, Timothy, and he is in it.

"Hi."

He's out of our marriage, but not out of my life. Every time I see him, something aches, but it's like putting butter on a burn—soothing to the touch, but only for the moment. Later, you still get blistered.

Someday I'll have to stop giving Timothy my keys.

He still can't deal with our divorce, even though it's been six years, longer if you count the separation before the actual divorce, and he is currently married to someone else. Clearly I can't accept reality myself, especially in the Timothy time warp. I also can't accept failure, particularly the emotional kind. I refuse to let it happen, even if semi-failure hurts more.

"Hi, Timothy. Where's Lydia?" Lydia is his wife, his former gallery assistant, whom he married a week after our divorce.

He shrugs and wriggles his toes, which are propped

up on the rim of the claw-foot tub. The water laps his chin. "Oh, she's somewhere."

"Installing a new bathtub, is she?"

"What's new in the ad world?"

"Nothing."

"You look tired, Cynthia."

"I am tired. I was going to take a bath."

"Good. Get in." He clears a field in the bubbles.

"Timothy, Timothy, Timothy." My guard is down, and so I make my big mistake and sit on the edge of the tub. With lightning speed the Creature from the Tub Lagoon reaches up, loops an arm around my waist, and I tumble ass-first into the water.

"Oh, my God! What are you doing?" I'm slipping and sliding across Timmy as I try to scramble out without touching any major body part. *Jesus, he did it again!* He always did it: "Smell this whipped cream, I think it's rancid." I'd lean over the plate and—*smash!*—nosedive into the whipped cream. Or Timothy'd sprinkle salt on a pat of butter. "Did you ever feel the heat butter gives off when you put salt on it?" he'd say, and I'd move my hand over the butter and—*wham!*—he'd slam it down. I always fell for it, just like I'd fallen into the tub.

Timothy hands me a bar of soap, laughing.

I rear up, dripping. "What the hell is the matter with you?" Only a genius with a knowledge of witchcraft could answer that question.

He smiles, and of course it's the one thing that makes me want to get back in the tub with him, in spite of everything, with his dimple under his two-day beard and his eyebrow cocked in a Jack Nicholson sort of way.

"Can't take you anywhere," he says.

"This is not cute, Timothy. This is expensive.

This is a three-thousand-dollar outfit." God, am I angry.

"It looks like shit."

"Of course it looks like shit. It's soaking wet. I'll send you the bill. I'll send Lydia the bill."

He grabs my skirt and yanks it down by the elastic, pulling my underpants along with it. " 'Do not dry-clean,' " he reads off the label. "You're okay." He sits there smirking, and I stand there naked from the waist down, except for my tennis shoes and socks, which feel like lead weights. *What does Timothy want?* I wonder as I involuntarily sink first to my knees, then into the bubbles. *Why is he here?* He didn't want to be married to me, but now he doesn't seem to accept the divorce either. Actually, I understand. Somehow there have been more than a few occasions in the six years since our divorce that through some quirk I've ended up naked beside this man. It always starts out to be an accident, but the end is always the same. Suddenly he's kissing me and, for God's sake, I'm kissing back.

I'm a big bubble, floating into him, bursting onto him. My breasts push against wet wool, the water laps and slaps around us. I can feel my hips bruising, my knees banging into the porcelain, and I gasp; *who gave this body a mind of its own?*

He reaches up and touches the inside of my thigh, and I feel the familiar warmth as his hand slides up across my stomach and presses hard. His fingers are under my soggy sweater, touching my nipples just the way they remember. Part of me wants to let go, to forget for a few minutes, like I have before. *It's like drinking too much—not worth it the next morning.*

But I sink back, back, back, onto the cushion of foam. The shower curtain swirls around us, misted in steam, and I am drowning in kisses, sinking, sinking, going down for the third time, going under. My face slides into the fragrant water and slips down his body, and I'm gulping, gasping, blowing bubbles off my eyelashes. Timothy wraps my wet hair around his hand and pulls me closer; we are water babies together. I'm not naked, but I feel like I am, stripped to the skin, wrapping my legs like seaweed in and around, back and forth. I can't stop myself. I'm in a cocoon of amniotic fluid, unborn, feeling nothing, just floating with the dream, drugged on sandal-wood and steam. The mirror frosts over with my breath and his, until the passion is over and I lie still, floating, and he soaps my belly as if it were a baby's, washing me behind my ears with tiny licks of his tongue, like a cat, and he's whispering, "Mine, mine, mine."

Words to clear the air like a squeegee on glass.

"You're married, Timmy," I hiss, clambering out of the tub. "Married not to me."

"I thought we were friends."

I can still remember the time he vanished on New Year's Day and returning smelling like Chanel Number 5, and I do not wear perfume. I remember holding his shirt to my face before dropping it into the laundry, then changing my mind and ditching it in the incinerator. "Smelling things that don't exist," Timmy had reassured me, "is the first sign of olfactory dysfunction. You could have a brain tumor. Maybe you should see a specialist." I did. A divorce specialist.

I yank the sweater over my head; it splats onto the bathroom floor like a wet sheepdog.

"Why don't you leave. Now."

"I've been thinking," Timothy says. "If John

27

Lennon hadn't been killed, we probably wouldn't have broken up."

"I don't want to hear about John Lennon. He has no relevance in this bathroom." I grab a towel and wrap it around my midriff. My breasts are still exposed, but so what. Timothy has seen them before.

I yank off my shoes and throw them at him because now I'm really angry, but, let's face it, a soggy tennis shoe does limited damage. I can't look at Timothy, who ignores the footwear and leans back, his arms behind his head, grinning the quick smile he knew would hit me like a punch in the gut. Here it comes. One-two—*uuuh*! That hideous, nauseating feeling that gnaws away when the man you once loved is inches away and you know you still love him but you know you just, just can't love him anymore, or even touch him, or it will kill you.

I was never secure about Timothy. A foundation forged from wallpaper, paint and furniture refinishing, arrays of hot and cold hors d'oeuvres, and watermelon-rind pickles is, after all, perishable at best. To put it bluntly, in the four years we lived together before the separation, I figured out how to be pretty goddamn wonderful at being a wife, but I was absolutely lousy at the relationship. I had a master's degree in English, but, believe me, I could have outwifed anybody you pitted me against. Armed with a box of Bisquick, I could have made mincemeat out of Harriet Nelson, Mrs. Paul, Mrs. Olsen, even Betty Crocker. Give me a tile floor that needed to be grouted and I'd take on Bob Vila. The marriage was about on that level—playing house. Of course there were no children in the playhouse. Having a baby meant you were really grown-up, there was no turning back. "Do you think we should have a child?" I'd ask Timothy.

"I am a child," he'd say.

At least he was honest.

Of course, eventually I had to find something constructive to do, but my master's degree in English had prepared me for nothing except theorizing about thematic links between Dostoyevski and Camus. I had no idea at all of how to get a job.

So I fooled around at the kitchen table, scribbling short stories of cowardly dragons and pansies whose faces came to life and pink clouds that talked to little girls, but what did it amount to? I didn't put on a suit, pick up a briefcase, and go anywhere to do it. I didn't get paid for it. It certainly didn't deserve to be called Work. Now, a turnip chrysanthemum—*that* was Work. Garnishes involved finesse and a certain sense of architecture. You had to choose exactly the perfect turnip, according to symmetry and shade, and then you had to know just how to hold it in one hand and slash incisions on angle to create the petals, and how to float it in ice water to open it up just enough to resemble a flower. I was especially proud of the time I made one hundred radish roses and shaved-carrot swans as a virtuoso garnish. The gravy was Franco-American, the casserole was Tuna Helper, but so what? Everything looked like a page out of *Good Housekeeping*—that was the important thing.

Focusing on household details diverted me from concentrating on Timothy. I didn't want to look too closely anyhow. Who wouldn't prefer to close her eyes and dive into an afternoon of peach-peeling as opposed to noticing that your husband just left to "go camping" in his tuxedo shoes, a sure sign that either the pup tent rated four stars in Michelin or he had bigger plans than you suspected? Wasn't it better to keep the sewing machine on a constant state of alert than to wonder why the man you married never seemed to want to admit it? The telephone was listed in my maiden name. So was the apartment. Timothy had another apartment, in fact—his studio. He slept there several nights a week. It was as if I had bumped into this man accidentally, not married him.

Timothy in the bubble bath brings it all back—the Romance. Timothy waking me up at five A.M. on the anniversary of nothing, and looking up in the half-light, I see him standing there, totally naked and completely, gorgeously rumpled, carrying our only sterling-silver tray on which rested two of our four Baccarat crystal wedding-gift glasses, filled with orange juice he had just squeezed himself for the celebration. Or how, spending an Indian-summer afternoon in the park, we'd lie on beach towels, with the cat tethered on a leash under a shade tree, and, as it got dark, we'd sit on a bench and make love under the towels, because we couldn't wait to get home. Or how much I really loved him, which was incalculable, and which I had done since I was in graduate school and he pulled up beside me on his Harley.

"So. Cynthia," he had said, which was enough.

Timothy was the only person in the world who ever called me by my real name. He still is.

"Cynthia."

In one word, Timothy had related to me as a woman. A *woman*, not a child, not an anagram. Cam is not even a nickname. It's an anagram. Cynthia Ann McKenna. CAM. A list of initials. I've always been one-syllable Cam.

But to Timothy I was *Cynthia. Cynthia* was hyacinths and tuberoses; *Cam* was dandelions and mums. *Cynthia* was sachets and Nottingham lace, not no-wax floors, like *Cam*. Timothy became the gauzy filter through which I became Cynthia, and that was that.

A man like Timothy can be very addictive to an anagram.

But even if I'd been able to read the tarot cards and look into the future, I still would have married Timothy. God. It's true.

I'm a smart person. I knew what I was getting into. In a way, I asked for it, marrying Timothy. He always acted the same, before, during, and after the marriage; he was always into this game of emotional push-pull, love-hate.

I've thought a lot about this. It wasn't his looks, which weren't particularly unusual, although he had a slightly musky quality about him. Brown hair, fair skin, a mustache, and, actually, I hate mustaches. He did have incredible eyes, which were a startling ice blue, like a Steamboat Springs sky after a hard freeze, and double rows of lashes, which, when he looked down, made shadows on his cheeks. The thing was actually his voice, which was low, wonderful and soothing, even when he was angry or telling me that he was six hours late because . . . Oh, well. It didn't matter so much what he said as how he said it. Like my name.

"*Cynthia.*"

I wonder if Lydia knows her husband is taking a bubble bath here. Probably. I'm sure he convinced her that it's her fault because she doesn't keep their bathtub clean enough. Timothy always had a knack for making anything seem like anyone else's fault. Actually, "knack" is the wrong word. "Genius" is more like it. With proper documentation, he could probably go in the *Guinness Book of World Records* for "Making Women Feel Guilty."

They say that after a divorce you go through the five stages of grief, not unlike when somebody dies. But for me the adjustment wasn't so great. Timothy had never been home all that much to begin with—I guess he and Lydia were cataloging his slides—and our separation dragged on forever—so it wasn't that I was lonely. I wasn't angry either, although I should have been. Whatever those five stages of grief were, I leapfrogged over them to something worse—I felt like a failure. When your husband dies, you don't feel like less of a person because his heart stops, but when your husband leaves, you feel worthless because you couldn't keep his heart in your hand.

But did I cry myself to sleep? Did I go on a Godiva chocolate binge? Did I pound plastic till my name wore off the cards? Well—yes, a little. But one thing saved me. My work. My job became my knight in shining armor, my awards and my lovers.

Take this Clio, Timothy, and shove it!

Except I still took his calls, including the one on his honeymoon when he claimed he had made a mistake. And I saw him, late at night, or at lunchtime, at his studio. And I did more than see him— one thing leads to another.

Which is why we are here, in this tub.

Timothy picks up a box of Mr. Bubble and starts reading the instructions aloud. " 'Important: To get the most bubbles, turn water on full force. To increase water pressure, place thumb under faucet.' "

"Timmy, come on. I'm exhausted. Go home."

"Get in." He grins, flipping a cascade of bubbles onto my breasts.

I lean over and pull the plug.

"Good-bye, Timothy."

I wrap my towel more tightly around myself, drip my way into my bedroom, close the door, and lock it. When I come out, he will be gone, or maybe sucked down the drain, melted like the Wicked Witch of the West.

Fat chance.

Why am I letting him do this to me? Why can't I let go?

Tonight my brain is fried. I've had it with the Midwest, with men in minipads, with ex-husbands in my bubble bath.

I want things to be different.

I want meaning—capital *M*, please. Sure, I want a job with a "Sr. V.P." in front of it. But I want more. I've read about cashing in, burning out, trading up, scaling back, slowing down, but there doesn't seem to be a category for what I'm after. "Having it all" comes as close as any term, but I'm thirty-eight, I know it's impossible. It's the Grimms' Fairy Tale of the eighties. And if you did have it all, you wouldn't have time for it. Still, I want a man who comes home to me at night and massages my feet and loves me. I want a child that makes the Gerber baby look like Godzilla. I want real life—if there is such a thing. Is that asking too much? Does it make me boring? Self-centered? So what? If I'm not going to be at my own center, who else is?

Under the big window in my bedroom is a window seat where, on nights like tonight when the heat seems to have strangled off in the basement, I can sit and look down at the street. The traffic lights are broken, and they blink back at me: *red, red, red*.

I was raised to be a cautious person. I was never

allowed to remove the lima beans from the mixed vegetables for fear of disturbing the symmetry. I still never cross the street without looking in both directions. I always ask them to hold the red peppers when I order Szechuan food. I've never pierced my ears, or even had a traffic ticket. Old habits die hard.

But the fact is, inside I'm dying to storm a Lamborghini through a red light, be caught without my license, close the officer's hand in my power window, and be arrested for resisting arrest. I would like to bring my lovebird on the David Letterman show and do a Stupid Pet Trick (the bird pretends to be a dental hygienist and examines my teeth). I'd like to wear purple contact lenses and put rhinestones on my eyelids. I could see myself as performance artist, creating the complete Grimms' Fairy Tales in pasta salad. I could get a tattoo in bold-face type. I'd like to bounce on a trampoline, parasail behind a glider.

I shut the bedroom door and lock it from the inside. *Amazing.* After all those years of applying individual false eyelashes with tweezers, struggling into garter belts, and pulling petals off daisies to see if he loves me or loves me not, I'm locking him out like the Boston Strangler at the peephole.

I fall asleep to the sound of water running in the bathtub and a dream of sneaking in and shaving off Timothy's eyebrows.

Chapter Three

"Please, Sally. Please. I'm begging you."

"I don't know. He looks vicious." With a manicured nail, my loyal secretary pushes back the cover
of the bird cage. The Bird lunges for her, his red
lovebird beak crashing into the bars.

"He's not very tame."

"Sal, he's just frightened. He's not the white-collar
type. He'll calm down as soon as you get him to the
vet's. I promise."

She sighs and rolls her eyes as if to say: *Yes, I have
the patience of Job, I type your last-minute memos at a
hundred and twenty words a minute, I get you extra
stamps, but I am not that stupid bird's surrogate mother.
No way.*

"Sally, I'd take him to the vet myself, but they
called an eight-thirty meeting this morning. The vet
wasn't open. Now I have to finish up here and go
straight to the airport. You've got to help me out."

"Okay. But it's gonna cost you."

"Anything."

She gives me her hard-bargain look. "My niece
graduates from college this spring. She wants an
internship."

"What!"

"Okay, an interview."

"Consider it done."

"Deal." She swings the cage under her desk and seeds fly everywhere. "God, I hope he doesn't get out. I hate birdshit."

"It's okay. It's biodegradable."

Juice ambles up. "What you need is a Chinese Potbelly."

"What's that, a stove?"

"A miniature pig. One-tenth the standard size. God, what an animal!"

Sally is nonplussed. "Pigshit is bigger than birdshit."

"What time is our flight again?" I ask.

"Noon. You have two hours."

Juice and I are leaving today for L.A. to shoot the Zing! commercial. It's been a frantic two weeks, what with lining up the celebrity talent, finalizing the storyboard, and getting a director at the last minute. But the group mobilized as if we were plotting the Normandy invasion, and we did it.

"Now all we have to do is do it," says Juice.

Juice and I have been at three agencies together. I probably know him better than I ever knew Timothy. I know that he was a lonely kid, a late-blooming runt of the litter who took refuge in his crayons, colored papers, and paints. The kind of kid who carried a compass in his pocket in high school and turned in papers that nobody understood.

"Do you know what it's like to be the only kid in your class who doesn't have a date for the senior prom?" he asked me once.

"Yeah. I didn't have one either."

We formed an instant conspiracy, two outsiders who overcompensated to be noticed.

We're stars. And we're friends.

Juice saw me through my divorce, and I've seen him through his five-year separation and twenty-two girlfriends. Nobody appreciates us like we do, but we've had the good sense to keep things on the commiseration level.

"Got time for a quickie?" says Juice, pulling me into his office.

"Sure. What is it?"

"The Tropical Growers Association. Image campaign." He throws me an orange.

"What if we open the spot with a sunrise," I say, lobbing the orange back to him.

"Sunset," Juice says, tossing it back. He misses and it bounces on the couch.

"Sunset. And the sun will turn into a huge egg."

"Fried egg, as in breakfast."

"Fried egg. And the egg will turn into . . ."

"A planet!"

"Saturn!"

"Which will turn on its axis to become . . ."

"An orange!"

"That's it!" Juice pulls three oranges out of his pockets and starts juggling them.

"And our line will be: *Sunrise oranges. Out of this world.*"

"Perfect."

"No. Not perfect."

"We can do better. You're right."

"Claymation."

"The Raisin Board already did that."

"Cole Porter."

"Maybe."

"Reggae."

"Caribbean."

"Sunrise oranges. Taste the tropics."

"We take a couple at the kitchen table . . ." says Juice.

"And suddenly the table's not in the kitchen anymore," I say.

"It's on a beach in Jamaica," Juice says, and he grabs a handful of markers and starts scribbling and we're off.

Technically speaking, I am the head of the group, the one with the title and the office, but that's only technical. Creatively, we're equal; I listen to Juice, he listens to me, and we respect each other. It's a partnership of perfect symmetry. I have to admit, however, that when I got the promotion to vice-president, I was worried about how Juice would take it. But it was no problem. He just smiled and shrugged and said, "Cam, I'm your biggest fan. Besides, you can deal with all that bullshit. You're good at it. And I know what I'm good at. It evens out."

So, we get along.

Suddenly there's a huge crash in the hall outside my office, followed by bloodcurdling profanities.

"I guess you better look."

A swivel chair hurtles by the door as Juice cracks it open.

"Jesus, Tony and Adam."

He closes the door as the inflatable tyrannosaurus bounces off it. If Tony and Adam aren't fighting about what an idea should be, they're fighting about who really had the idea. Once Tony broke Adam's jaw in a dispute about which of them actually named a microwave pancake product that made it to test market, and Adam had to drink liquids through a straw for two months. Juice and I thought they were pretty pathetic.

Unlike us.

So now I'm watching Juice wave a tissue layout that vaguely resembles a three-year-old's uncoordinated sketch of a can of pop. He's wearing blue jeans and an immaculately pressed and pleated tuxedo shirt, collar open and sleeves rolled. He flips a shock of hair off his pale forehead. From across the room, I spot the pig in the ad. Juice loves pigs. His office is a study in pig-o-belia: pig cartoons, books on pigs, clay pigs, wood-carved pigs, and a portrait in oils of a porker in a business suit. But he may be going overboard here. "Juice, Juice, Juice," I say, looking at the layout.

"Intelligence," he says. "As far as the animal kingdom goes, it's the ape, the porpoise, and the pig. Besides, it's my trademark. Let them kill it later. Right now, I want to wallow in the concept for a while."

"You're sick."

The door slams behind him.

A perfunctory tap and I have company again. It's the Doc, from research—two PhD's and an MBA. "Congratulations, Cam." He grins, and I smile back and shoot him the thumbs-up.

"You guys broke the bank on the Zing! concept test," the Doc says. "Stratospheric scores from the mall intercept. Talk about clutter breakthrough—consumers loved that kid." He adjusts his glasses.

"Great!" Recall is our rainbow's end. We have to test every commercial nearly to death, and only if people remember something about it will it survive to go on the air. So we resort to tactics like celebrities, breaking bottles, exploding cans, charging bulls, and nursery jingles. You know how you always wanted to throw a brick through the TV screen when you heard them yammer, "Ring around the collar"? Excuse me, but—admit it—you remember it.

"Good luck. But I'm glad I don't have to shoot this thing." The Doc makes an Ed McMahon-type salaam, I dip in an answering curtsy, and he moves on to spread the word down the hall, like a prophet.

I check the time. Maybe Bruce will be back from lunch. I don't wear a normal watch. It's a sterling-silver stopwatch, and it hangs from a chain around my neck. On the back, "Clio, 1988," is engraved. The Clios are the Oscars of advertising. Every writer has a stopwatch of some sort, to time copy.

Suddenly three of my four phone lines start screaming simultaneously. I pick up on interoffice. "Hi, Arnie. What's up?"

"The Bakery client wants an intro spot for their new cakes." He sounds concerned, but that's okay. That's why I hired him. Arnie has the capability of always sounding concerned, a priceless trait. He's not as talented as Juice, but people like his attitude, which almost carries more weight.

"Good," I say, riffling through my Filofax to check Barry's number. I still haven't returned his call. "I know you'll handle it."

"I don't know, Cam. This is touchy. Remember the Ident-a-Cake assignment? The Bakery transfers a person's photograph onto a sheet cake and airbrushes a portrait on the frosting?"

"Yeah. Weren't we going to just plug an announcer into the old Ident-a-Cake jingle?"

"That was okay for birthdays and anniversaries. But now they're expanding. Funerals."

"Cakes for the dead?" I skim one of the thirty memos in my In box while I talk.

"Yeah. The customer brings in a photo of the

deceased and they memorialize the guy in frosting. Mmmm-mmm, good."

"Wait. Didn't the ancient Egyptians do that?" Arnie and I chuckle grimly. It's not the weirdest thing we've heard in this business, not by a long shot. "I guess the jingle is out, then."

"Right. Especially since they show the deceased *in* the coffin."

"I know you'll think of a . . . sensitive solution," I reassure Arnie. "Why don't you give Brenda a shot at this?"

Silence. Nobody ever wants to work with Brenda.

"You'll work it out."

I punch line three, and it occurs to me that I shouldn't be picking up my own phone—this might be Timothy. Maybe a miracle has happened and he's calling to say he's sorry he messed up my tub and my life, and can't we just be friends and care about each other and he'll never fuck with my mind or my body again.

I hang up fast, as cigar smoke heralds Bruce's imminent descent from Heaven.

VISUAL	AUDIO
1. A LONG HALLWAY, FILLED WITH WATER.	1. SFX (over): *"THEME FROM JAWS"* DA DUH, DA DUH, DA DUH . . .
2. FROM A DISTANCE, A HUGE SHARK APPEARS, A CIGAR CLAMPED BETWEEN HIS RAZOR-LIKE TEETH. HE SWIMS TO . . .	DUN DUN, DUN DUN . . .
3. AN OFFICE DOOR.	3. SFX: MUSIC SWELLS.

4. CLOSEUP OF THE	4. MCKENNA.
DOOR REVEALS THE	
NAMEPLATE . . .	

Let's set the record straight. I admire a lot of things about Bruce. Nobody presents like him, nobody can outschmooze him, and I'm not denying he's smart. But the truth is, Bruce and I have an adversarial relationship. Bruce has a major case of ambivalence about me. He probably would have trumped up a case and fired me long ago, but I keep winning awards at international festivals, getting my picture in magazines.

If you've ever read any books or articles on managerial women, you know what you're supposed to do to fit into the corporate structure. Basically it boils down to:

1. Grow up having passed over Barbie and Ken in favor of team sports.

2. Emulate Dad, unless Mom is Elizabeth Dole.

3. Get an MBA.

4. Dress for success.

Having done none of these things, I've had a lot to overcome. Whatever the reason, I've never fitted neatly into the business hierarchy. My fallback plan has been to do good work and let it pull me through. This worked fine until Bruce. Maybe Bruce and I would get along better if I'd been a shortstop or a fullback or something.

Brucie is the kind of person who commands space, and he takes over my office as he comes in puffing, but he's not your prototype adman. No, he looks more like a particularly wide-eyed office boy, which has certain advantages, in this business. He is highly Not Slick, meaning he does not blow-dry his hair, his wardrobe is boring with the exception of his one fashion statement, his suspenders, and he has an open, friendly face and a grin that borders on hayseed.

Huckleberry Snake.

"So, Cam. You're off on a boondoggle." He clamps the cigar between his teeth and mimes a perfect putt.

"This is a new campaign, Brucie."

"You bet it is, Cam. Now, I know you'll do your usual great work on this—"

"Thank you."

"You have my confidence, you know that. Whatever. You got it. There's just one more thing. Very minor, but worth sharing."

"What's that?"

"You're way behind on your time sheets."

"Sally is supposed to be taking care of that."

"You're in, you're out, you're here, you're there—how the hell is a secretary supposed to keep track of that?" He hitches up his suspenders. "But I'm not here to criticize, I'm here to help." He tosses a pile of yellow time sheets on my desk. "It's always dangerous to overdelegate. Here. From now on, why don't you do your own time sheets?" He waves his cigar over the sheets like a wand. "Code Oh-oh-one stands for personal time. But I guess you know that already. Heh-heh."

I buzz the mail room. "Steve, can somebody please Fed Ex my two suitcases and one portfolio case to my hotel in L.A.?"

I never bring luggage on a plane, since everything

I've ever checked has always gone to the Bermuda Triangle. So I always Fed Ex my suitcases straight from the office and carry on just my purse, my lap-top computer, and my pound-and-a-half printer in a shoulder bag.

Steve disappears with my suitcases as, in a puff of smoke, Brucie inches closer to my desk.

"Bruce, we agreed that we wanted this shoot handled on the senior level. You approved the expense request." I cough pointedly, fanning away the noxious fumes, and turn on my Polinex air purifier with my foot.

"Jesus Christ, Cam. You're never here. And now you're leaving the department for two weeks?" He's smiling, but he grinds his cigar out as if he were crushing the life out of a baby bird. He knows I have to handle this shoot myself. He's just giving me a hard time. But why? Something is definitely up.

"You have to learn to delegate—I'm only trying to help you out, you know."

"I thought you said overdelegating was dangerous." I check out Bruce's socks: black with orange flecks.

"And another thing," says Bruce. "I was going over your production estimate . . ."

Sally appears tentatively in the doorway, waving my plane tickets.

A ring of cigar smoke floats to the ceiling as Bruce leans over my desk and we go over the scripts and boards one more time. I point to each storyboard frame, describe the action of the scene it represents, and read the copy that's typed beneath it on a label.

"Great," Bruce says, pacing. "This is great. Just great. The creative process never stops."

I freeze.

Bruce is about to change something now, three minutes before I am leaving for the plane to shoot the first commercial in the pool. How do I know this? Because "the creative process never stops" is a tried-and-true euphemism for "I am about to slash this commercial, which you thought was finished, to ribbons. Pick up the pieces if you can."

Bruce frowns. The duel is about to begin. Whoever gets the credit for this commercial will walk away with the marbles. Bruce wants the credit so he can get promoted. But if he gets promoted and I don't, he'll put somebody right on top of me in his old job. So I need the credit if I'm going to finesse my way to the eightieth floor.

He points to the picture of Jed Durant. "Are you sure we should be using an unknown for this?"

"We are not using an unknown. We're using Jed Durant, who is a very famous singer, and we're not using him alone, we're using him with Cowboy Bob, Mr. Bandanna, a legend in his own time."

"Cowboy Bob—well, that's one thing. But that kid singer. The bottlers are over fifty—they can't relate."

"We bought into this concept, Bruce. Everyone loved it. Remember? Who would you rather use?" I ask this rhetorically, since Durant has already been signed for the test spot, and then I flash on the hidden agenda. Brucie is setting me up, so that in case this pitch fails and we don't get the business, he can later safely say, "Yes, I had doubts about Durant. We should have used Sinatra or the koala bear."

Next, Bruce will be figuring out some way to cover himself in writing so that if this occurs I will be nailed to the wall, like a botanical specimen on a pin.

"It's probably fine." He pats me on the head; maybe he thinks I am a spaniel. "But just in case, for insurance, we should start thinking backup track. Maybe a backup singer. Somebody to dub over Durant. And maybe another version of the song, with the name Koala in it. I'll just get my thoughts together and put them down on paper for you. Of course"—he pauses and smiles boyishly—"this is just a worst-case scenario. I'm sure things will go fine in New York."

"I'm not going to New York. The pre-pro is in L.A."

Two inches of ash fall onto the carpet. "The account team called in. One of the fat-cat East Coast bottlers is available for a prepresentation briefing. If we presell him, he'll lobby for us with the selection committee. Your favorite account exec, Lance, flew out with the guy this morning. You and Juice are meeting them in New York. For dinner. With the bottler. Tonight." He grins charmingly and does a little tap dance, singing off-key, "I-I-I-I-I love New York!"

"I didn't hear from Lance or any of his people." Correct me if I'm wrong, but did Bruce not see me send my suitcases to L.A.? He stood there and watched me send them to one end of the planet, knowing he was about to catapult me off in the opposite direction. When did Bruce start trying to undermine me? Or am I being undermined? *Am I paranoid? Or is he a bastard? It's hard to tell with bosses.* Ever since I became a boss myself, I've tried to give them the benefit of a doubt. Of course, there is one dead giveaway. Bruce didn't hire me; he inherited me from a predecessor who got the ax. *It's never good to work for a boss whose predecessor got the ax.* Especially if you're sitting on a big salary. The new guy is always itching to pack the group with his own loyalists, and your salary could be theirs.

But then again, you can never be sure when it comes to office politics. Sometimes, continuity is what counts. Clients don't usually like disruption. And you never want to believe that the knife is poised at your own particularly stab-sensitive back. At least, I don't. It's not unlike when your husband cheats on you. You always want to believe his version of the story—say, you're coming down with a brain tumor—before you'll face up to the fact that this is no perfect sunset. Besides, Bruce has a way of making the outrageous plausible. It's his gift.

He shrugs. "The time difference—you know." Pause for another puff on the cigar. "Lance called from the airplane. They'll meet you and Juice at a restaurant called Mortimer's on Lexington and Seventy-fifth. Go over the storyboards and final scripts at dinner."

"Let's prioritize, Bruce," I say. "How will I get to the West Coast in time for tomorrow's meetings with the director and the casting people?"

Bruce shrugs, trailing ashes on the carpet. "I told Candace to book you and Juice on the red-eye. You won't miss a thing." He beams. "God, the miracle of modern transportation! You'll be in L.A. in time for your breakfast meeting. If you leave now."

We'll be in L.A. in time to drop dead. The red-eye, the dreaded red-eye, leaves La Guardia at midnight and hoves into L.A. a scant six hours later. Still, I have to go, I *want* to go. I am a lioness, defending my young.

"Maybe I can catch Steve. I gave him my luggage." I reach for my phone.

"Too late, Cam," says Sally. "Fed Ex just made their pickup."

Brucie slaps the surface of my glass table. "I knew I could count on you, Cam. You're a Player."

"Okay, Bruce. I'll call in."

I blast out of my office, motioning to Juice that I'll meet him downstairs, by the first bank of elevators. I dodge to avoid Brenda, and I just keep going—down the Corporate Orange hall, past the entire side of the building where my group lives.

"Cam! Can you approve this rough cut?"

"Cam! The client wants an answer today."

"Cam! Have you seen your picture in *Ad Age*?"

"Cam! Can I bounce this idea off you?"

"Cam! Cam! Cam!"

The creative department is a nursing infant that demands constant feeding and attention. There is no beginning, no middle, and no end. It's like the Food Chain: Create. Criticize. Kill. Recreate. Even the best ads gobble themselves up, sacrificial lambs on the altar of bigger billing.

I keep walking—past the mail room and out the heavy double glass doors to the elevators.

Out. Out. Out.

Charlie Ness bounces ebulliently off one of the eight elevators. "You know that potato-chip spot?" His jacket opens, and I notice that he's wearing Corporate Orange suspenders.

Of course I know the potato-chip spot. I wrote it. Who does he think negotiated the rights to

Mr. Potatohead? I get on the elevator without answering.

Charlie smiles, bouncing in place. The Parakeet of Doom.

"The client hated it," Charlie chirps as I pound on the "Close Door" button.

Chapter Four

I rearrange the silk scarf around my neck, but it's useless. Mortimer's is the kind of restaurant where women eat french fries in Montana and St. Laurent—and I don't mean the big-sky state or some French island in the Caribbean—Jerry Zipkin is a fixture unto himself, ex-kings, queens, Nan Kempner and the Duchess of York drop by, and a terrorist attack at dinnertime would wipe out the entire editorial content of *Women's Wear Daily*. It's also been named the Rudest Restaurant in America by *Money* magazine. I'm surprised anyone would choose this place to meet—The Palm would be a less stylish but more typical choice. It's so dark in Mortimer's, I can barely see Juice on a barstool beside me, much less a storyboard. But sometimes clients surprise you; never underestimate them. Maybe Simmons has been reading *WWD*.

I myself would never have picked this place. I'm happiest at Billy Goat's, a grease pit on lower-level Wacker in the grimy underbelly of downtown Chicago, where the menu is limited to *cheeseburga, cheeseburga, cheeseburga*. I'm sick of radicchio, arugula, and other weeds with PR agents. But the rule is, if the client wants to go to dinner at the rudest restaurant in America, you go to dinner in the rudest restaurant in America.

Since Jerry Zipkin is not with our party, Juice and I have been relegated to a holding pattern at the bar. Through the sepia haze of the room, I can make out several empty tables, but as far as we are concerned, those tables are not empty. Christian Lecroix, the entire cast of the Last Supper, or a paste-up guy from *Spy* magazine might decide to stop by for a crab cake, and what if *we* were sitting at a table, occupying potential celebrity space?

The thought is apparently too horrifying for the maître d' to contemplate. He's blond and very smooth, his suit looks like it costs ten times what even I spend on clothes in a decade, and he's ignoring us.

"If this were my restaurant, people wouldn't have to wait."

"I'm sure they wouldn't, because nobody would show up. The only thing you know about restaurants is how to check your coat."

"Come on, it's obvious. If they took out that bar in the other room, they could fit in more tables."

"Cam, what's with you? You're always trying to repackage the world. Can't you ever just settle down and enjoy the moment? You drive me nuts, you know that? Relax. This is a restaurant. We are meeting clients. We will eat. We will leave. Okay?"

Sometimes Juice can get a bit iconoclastic.

"Excuse me," I say, tapping a waiter on the shoulder. "Where's the ladies' room?"

"Past the kitchen." He gestures to a back hallway.

There's a line. A woman in a paisley smoking jacket. A man in an ascot. Someone who looks like David Hockney, but is not. One of the two doors opens and three girls spill out, giggling. Everyone has perfect skin.

An ax murderer looms into the kitchen doorway. A six-foot-four ax murderer in white, with a bloody cleaver in his hand. Actually, I can see that he is a chef, but that doesn't make me any more comfortable in his vicinity, especially since I get the feeling that he's checking me out, or, to put it more bluntly, he's staring at my ankles, my calves, my knees—his eyes are moving up my legs like a monorail on a track.

I cross my arms, turn on my heel, and leave with as much arrogance as is possible to muster in a bathroom hallway.

The chef smirks as I walk by. "Careful, lady, I got dairy products back here. They might curdle."

I emerge to see Lance pushing his way through the crowd by the front door, followed by a man who has to be Simmons, the senior V.P. of new products for Koala. He is easy to spot because he has bright red hair, but also because the others are deferring to him. Whether this is due to his charming personality or the fact that he controls the biggest budget in the beverage industry is open to debate.

I wave from the bar, and Juice makes his way to the front of the restaurant to guide them back to our bar stools.

"Cam," says Lance. "This is Earl Fender and Fred Simmons. Earl is from Union Bottling, and Fred here is senior vice-president of marketing at Trans-Corp and head of the agency selection committee."

"Fred, Earl," I say, shaking their hands first. "Hi, Lance." My business handshake could be better, but what do you expect? I was raised to greet dance partners at the dinner table, not Lee Iacocca at the conference table. On the other hand, my manners are perfect. I can peel a peach with a knife and fork.

"We should have a table in no time," says Lance. Juice raises an eyebrow at this obvious lie. "Meanwhile, who in this illustrious group wants a drink?"

I order my fourth Perrier and check out the exposed brick walls, the art-nouveau etched-glass fixtures, the mirrors reflecting two enormous bouquets of sunflowers that droop downward, as if disappointed that they wound up here instead of on a Van Gogh canvas. Men and women lean close over scores of candles flickering on tabletops. "Look at these people," Juice says, mercifully changing the subject. "They could probably exist forever on an intravenous puree of smoked salmon and champagne."

"Now, Cam," Simmons says. "The reason I wanted to have this little howdy-do is because Bruce tells me you have the information Earl here wants."

"What Fred really means," says Lance, "is that you should share your thoughts with Earl."

I look at Lance. He has an incredibly sincere Midwestern expression on his face. His hair is long for an account guy, over his collar, and he has the look of a kid in grown-up's clothes. You have to wonder what's in his head. You never know, because he just sort of paraphrases what other people say.

"What's that?"

"Just a few minor details. Now, Lance showed me the storyboard, and the spot's very good, very fine work indeed," he says. "Earl and I think that the screening committee may have just a . . . concern about that boy."

"The talent?"

"The talent." Lance nods.

"Goddamn bubble-gum zitface," mumbles Earl.

I jump in. "Earl, believe me. He's the hottest thing in the music industry. He has three platinum albums. The kids love him."

Earl taps his teeth. "Never heard of him," he says.

I feel relieved. I know how to handle this; it happens all the time. "Well, we can show you his Q score, which is like a popularity rating. He's right up there at the top of the charts."

"Sinatra," interrupts Earl. "What I'd like to know is, did anybody look into Sinatra?"

"Did anybody look into Sinatra?" says Lance.

I twist on my bar stool. "I think I see a table turning over." I may as well have spotted the rings of Saturn, but at least I've changed the subject.

Sure enough, Simmons charges through the crowd to corner the maître d', trailed by Lance. Earl peels off in the other direction.

"They can't change anything at this point," says Juice. "They're just flexing their muscles."

While I formulate our strategy, I check out the scene: a woman with graceful hands is gesturing at a nearby table, and I notice the flash of a gemstone diamond—or is it a Kenneth J. Lane diamond? Each table seems to have a dozen wineglasses in varying degrees of emptiness.

A Euro-vampire with black patent-leatheresque hair and the whitest skin I've ever seen materializes at my elbow and hands me an embossed business card. It has no phone number, just the legend "Zurich/San Francisco."

It's weird how New Yorkers will come up to you and just start talking. "Do I know you?" I ask.

"Would that you did." The Euro-vampire has an elocution-school accent. I wonder if he's ever been exposed to a ray of daylight in his life. "Perhaps you might have dissuaded me from sacrificing my life to my ambition."

"Which is what?"

"I was trained to be the fifth Mr. Doris Duke."

"Are things working out?"

"By the age of twenty-one I could see it wasn't going to happen. So I've taken up canasta. I've decided it's the only thing of real social value." He peers over my head and scans the crowd. Doris Duke is not in it.

I'm calculating the odds of making the red-eye when Juice suddenly elbows me in the ribs. "Claus von Bulow," he notes as a tall man with a pink silk paisley pocket handkerchief glides through the crowd like a ghost walking on air.

Mary McFadden, in a black satin hoop skirt, sweeps by them both. Is that Jackie behind her?

"Perhaps I could buy you a drink," offers the Euro-vampire. He stares at me. "You look very familiar." He blinks. "Yes. Oprah. I saw you on the Oprah Winfrey show last week. Did I not?"

They must have rerun the advertising show I was on six months ago. "Yes. Probably."

"Oprah is my heroine! The passion! The truth! My God, the time she cried about her childhood . . ."

The maître d', having broken Simmons' death lock, swoops by. "Armando," exudes Zurich/San Francisco, stopping him in mid-swoop. "Don't you recognize my dear friend—"

"Cam."

"My dear friend Cam from the Oprah show?" His voice drops to a level of high confidentiality. "She *must* be seated at One-B." He nods toward the window table just to the left of the door being vacated by Bill Blass' party and melts off into the crowd, his hand on the maître d's shoulder.

"The Oprah show is the Platinum Card of the Nineties," says Juice, chomping on ice cubes and ignoring Zurich/San Francisco. I notice the whites of his eyes are showing underneath the irises. He's very good at looking puppylike, especially at this time of night with no food in him. A blond in a micro-mini, whom I recognize from the ladies'-room trio, crosses her legs and casts him a sympathetic glance. This is the secret to Juice's seemingly inexplicable success with women: despondency.

I've been working with Juice since I was a junior copywriter and he was a junior art director—over six years. He's been separated from his wife the entire time, so he's managed to span the best of both worlds: married, but free to date. His estranged wife is a travel agent, and about twice a year they jet off together to Tahiti. The rest of the time, he's quasi-single, and a magnet for women. He has a vulnerability that makes them want to take him home and feed him Cream of Wheat. It's a highly cultivated and deceptive facade.

"This is why we have no life," he says, readjusting the strap of his Italian leather shoulder bag. Juice is the only man I know who can get away with carrying a purse. He unzips the front pocket, pulls out a package of Newports, lights one, and seeps out the smoke in a protracted sigh. "This is why I can't get a decent relationship going. I can't even get a decent divorce going." He frowns in the direction of Simmons.

"Clients?" I ask.

"Precisely. We gotta take care of the clients before we take care of ourselves. Who wants to be out with clients every night when you could be . . . bowling? Who in their right mind would live like this?"

I can't imagine Juice bowling; he's much too conceptual. "You would."

So would I. There's no denying I picked this over normal life. At times like this, I like to remind myself that I consciously chose client dinners and fourteen-hour days over a husband and family. If I were married to Timothy right now, I'd be phoning home to get a toneless ring, and he'd be out getting engaged to another woman. Then again, maybe there are other options. Maybe everything isn't so black-and-white. I remind myself that my new plan of attack is to be open to change. Ever since women became the men we wanted to marry, it's been impossible to do anything but waffle in your personal life. I fall back on the Scarlett O'Hara Theory of Personal Development: *I'll think about it tomorrow.*

A flying wedge pushes through, chattering in French, the maître d' and Simmons in their wake. We thread a path through the tables and I wedge myself into a bentwood chair at the former Kissinger table. Necks crane to see what world-renowned celebrities have netted the coveted Table One-B. Zurich/San Francisco leans over a man in a tuxedo and baseball cap and a woman in a veiled hat and elbow-length black satin gloves.

"Would that I could join you," he says. "But I have an early meeting with my trust officer."

"We understand," says Juice.

Simmons raises his glass. "A toast." I lift my Diet Coke.

I turn to Earl. "I'm willing to go out on a limb here," I say. "I'm willing to hope that this campaign with Jed Durant will give Zing! a ten share within the first six months. That's how much I believe in it. Of course, nobody has a crystal ball, but, after all, Earl, think of the strength of our marketing position. We have the first soft-drink product that spans the demographics of the teens and the eighteen to thirty-fives. And, take my word for this, Jed Durant is news. Especially the way we're going to use him—teamed up with the golden greats. Cowboy Bob. Howdy Doody. Marilyn Monroe . . ."

"Marilyn Monroe is dead."

Juice jumps in. "In body only, Earl!"

"What Juice is trying to say . . ." says Lance.

"Earl. Fred. Let's regroup here for a minute," I say, whipping the miniature color Xerox copies of the storyboards out of my Chanel shoulder bag. "Let me show you how this is going to work." Now I'm on familiar ground—presenting storyboards. I must have presented three thousand storyboards in my career.

I point to the first hand-drawn frame. Earl squints, and I push the candle closer. "Now. In the first frame, we see a bubbling mist. Primeval. Mysterious. Then in the second frame, the Zing! can bursts through the mist."

Juice cuts in. "Very dramatic," he says. "The camera moves in on the logo to a double exposure, which wipes the scene to reveal an Old West ghost town."

I pick up. "Suddenly, hundreds of kids come into the street, from behind trees, inside buildings. Everyone is carrying a Coke or a Pepsi."

"Then," says Juice, "Jed Durant appears, up here, dancing, very cool."

"Drinking Zing!"

"From up in the sky, Cowboy Bob descends, on a cloud, on horseback."

"The two heroes face each other down. It's a showdown. Cowboy Bob draws, and . . ."

"Durant catches the bullet in his hand, flips it over his shoulder, and offers Cowboy Bob a can of Zing!"

"Then. Everybody in the town drops their Coke and Pepsi and grabs a can of Zing!"

". . . and we hear the music. 'Zing!'s got class! Zing!'s got sassafras! Put some Zing! into your walk, make it how you talk. When you got Zing! You got everything. Zing!' "

"Ouch!" The storyboard gets too close to the candle, and it catches on fire. Juice dumps the flaming remains into his water glass.

"Well, isn't it fabulous? You're going to blow the competition off the map!"

Lance clears his throat. "Well, Cam. Earl has a question."

Earl nods.

"Cam," Simmons interrupts, "Earl here has reason to believe that this Durant kid doesn't drink soft drinks. Period."

I scan my menu. "Hmmm. That doesn't seem likely. He has to sign an affidavit. But we'll look into it."

"He doesn't," says Earl. "It's a known fact. Documented."

"Documented?" Juice and I look at each other.

"I read it in the *Enquirer*," Earl says, stressing the first syllable. "You're going to look like a bunch of guys who jumped on the caboose after the train left it behind. If you get my drift."

I grimace inwardly. The thing is, he could have

a point; you never know about stars. There was the famous incident when a glamorous female star was the spokesperson for a hamburger chain, and then it turned out she was a vegetarian.

"We'll look into it, Earl," I say. "But I can assure you that Durant will drink the product in this campaign. Or somewhere in his life. Anyhow, it's the law. Truth in advertising."

"That's right," says Juice. "Remember that famous case when that soup commercial got pulled off the air for putting marbles in the bottom of the vegetable soup, so it would look like there were more vegetables?"

A look of horror crosses Lance's face.

"Well . . ." Juice is getting excited now, because he's discussing litigation. "That was before our time, but they've been vigilantes ever since. You can't fool the consumer. We wouldn't even try, believe me."

"Fine," says Earl. "And the committee will want to see his Adam's apple moving. None of those fakey-fake drinks."

"No fake drinks," Lance reemphasizes.

"Order me the rack of lamb," I say, pushing my chair back. "Medium rare." I'm thinking I'd better get to a phone and have this checked out before I get to L.A.

"That's what I'll have." Earl nods. "Rack of lamb, well-done."

I walk out of the dining room through the passageway to the pay phone, passing the kitchen, where somebody is singing a medley of Bing Crosby Christmas songs.

I reach Daria, the producer, in L.A.

"I don't know," she says. "He's a kid. He has to drink soft drinks. Besides—truth in advertising."

"Do we have it in writing?"

"I don't think so."

"Great. Call his manager tonight. Now."

"His manager is his mother."

"Well, call her now." I'm beginning to get a not-good feeling about this, but for the moment my hands are tied. I go back to the table.

Juice leans over. "No sweat," he says. Juice was there when the barn we'd propped for a hayride shoot burned to the ground. He was there when we Krazy-glued Dumbo ears on the Indian elephants and they stampeded down Wall Street. This is a cakewalk.

Simmons and Fender are engrossed in a side conversation. I can't make out much, their tone is confidential, just "goddamn amateurs," "pull the account," and "two months." I freeze. Then I hear the words "Ellery and Queen." *Jackpot!* That's all I need to hear to know that their current agency of record, Ellery & Queen, is in trouble. If we play our cards right, we could win more than Koala. Spirit could be plucked like a ripe peach.

Juice and I look at the sunflowers, but we both heard it.

Juice picks at some melted candle wax. "You should move the brand regardless of anything," he says, then smiles to take the edge off it. "Your problem is, the Japanese took over Ellery and Queen, and they're calling the shots now. What do they know about American soft drinks? They're foreigners. It's a documented fact. Only one in fifty Tokyo residents drinks soft drinks."

Juice just made this up for impact, as he frequently does with statistics. Anybody who believes a statistic from Juice deserves what he gets.

"What!" says Fender, shocked at the interruption. "Where did you get that?"

"Yankelovich." Another bold-faced lie. Juice has never cracked a research report in his life.

"Juice is right," I say anyway. The conversation is going our way.

I notice Lance is frowning. He may know more about research than previously suspected.

Suddenly the maître d' taps me on the shoulder. I am being paged.

Daria's voice is panicky. "The kid doesn't drink soft drinks. The mother's secretary confirmed it. Jesus Christ. She assumed we'd use a double for the drink shots or cut away to a table shot."

"Don't panic, Daria," I say. "I'll take care of it. Meanwhile, do not say anything to anyone. Nothing!"

"No, don't worry. I won't."

"Let's not second-guess this."

"No. Let's not." Her voice is quavering. I take a deep breath. "Arrange a meeting with the mother tomorrow."

"Right."

"And don't panic."

Back to the table.

The waiter sets our main course down. I missed the appetizers, what with being on the phone, but the lamb looks pretty good. I reach for my fork.

"No, no, no, no, no!" says Earl.

He points at his plate. "This lamb is fucking *bloody*. It's fucking on the *hoof*. Baa!" He imitates a lamb bleating. "Didn't I say well-done? Waiter!"

Lance's hand shoots into the air.

The waiter saunters over.

"Please take this back. I'd like it well-done."

The waiter disappears into the kitchen for a nanosecond, and then he's back with the plate, like a boomerang. "The chef says this is perfect."

Earl freezes in his place. What with his thousand-acre ranch and radio station and bottling empire, he is not a man who is used to being countermanded. *Who needs this? There are enough problems at this table.*

"Earl, here, take mine," says Simmons, picking up his plate.

"Back in a flash," I say, leaping up.

The waiter escorts me and the plate back to the kitchen.

The heat hits me first. *God!* It must be a million degrees in here! I suddenly feel like I'm wearing a shower curtain. My scalp starts to sweat. There's three huge open pots of boiling water on two six-burner stainless-steel stoves, several ovens with things going in and out, a broiler, a grill, and probably a flamethrower.

"It's hot in here," I mutter, gripping my Chanel purse as I duck beneath . . . Is it a scale or a meat hook?

"About a hundred and twenty," says the giant ax-murderer chef, who looks about medium-well-done himself at close range. His white apron is smeared with blood—probably lamb-chop blood, but who can be sure?—his hair is tied back in a ponytail, his shoes look like they could crush the state of Oregon. Six-four, over seven feet if you count the hat, two-hundred-twenty-plus pounds, a white rag tied around his neck. I was right to leave the hallway. If I saw this guy coming down the street, I would cross to the other side as fast as my Maud Frizons would carry me.

"Could we discuss the lamb my table sent back? There's a problem."

63

"What's the problem?"

At least he's not staring at my chest. "It's too rare."

"What're you, English? Listen, honey," he says, dodging through five other people in whites. "This is the best rack in the city. What are we talkin' about here—people or animals?" I find myself zigzagging across the tile floor so I can hear him above the sounds of knives chopping and pans clattering. He pulls a tray of tomato halves out of one of the ovens.

"The man out there is my future."

Earl Fender appears on cue in the doorway. "I'll just have a hamburger," he announces.

I can tell he's furious.

"I told your fiancée here, we don't have hamburgers," says the chef. "They have hamburgers in England?" he asks me.

"I'm not from England. I'm from Chicago." Now *I'm* getting angry. "And that man is not my fiancé, he is my business associate."

Suddenly he smiles. I can see he has a chipped front tooth. "Chicago? I'm from Chicago myself."

Juice materializes. "Earl, you should see who's out here. Elizabeth Taylor." Earl vanishes. Mission accomplished.

An open pan of hot oil bursts into flame on a burner. The chef picks it up nonchalantly and holds it off to the side. "Go, Bears," he says. "How about that Mike Singletary?"

A hand reaches past me for a piece of fresh mint as a waiter announces that somebody in the Streisand party has ordered quail eggs in pastry shells. And this guy is complaining about a lamb chop?

"How does one make *quail eggs*?" I ask. Maybe he'll get my drift.

He doesn't.

"Very carefully. Two minutes twenty seconds exactly and then they're soft-boiled. You tap one end and you start peeling. Dunk them in cold water. Then you put them in the little pastry boats that underneath have the duxelle sauce. On top goes the hollandaise. A real pain in the ass."

"Good for Easter."

"Piece of cake. You don't need dye. The eggs are speckled."

You have to smile. How many guys have a sense of humor about quail eggs?

The frying-pan fire having died down, he grabs the rack of lamb off the plate with a pair of tongs, lobs it into the pan, and sears the hell out of it. Then he removes it like you would pluck chewing gum from your shoe sole and drops it back onto the plate, where it lands with a meaty thud.

" 'Cause you're from Chicago," he says, heading toward a man who is cutting bread into razor-thin slices. Waiters are rushing in and out with plates and orders, trying to avoid me.

The chef grabs a knife that looks like a machete. "Okay, gotta cruise. Catch ya later. Let me know the next time you're in town. Ask for Jamie, honey. But call in advance. They'll take good care of you."

Honey. Being a published feminist, I hate being called *honey* by anyone, especially a strange man with a frying pan. But there's something about the way he says the word that makes me kind of like it. He has a whiskey voice, the kind of voice that is made to call women "honey." He doesn't seem so scary anymore. He seems sexy, in a weird culinary way. I'm suddenly flustered, and my purse falls onto the floor. Everything spills out and clatters under and around the stainless-steel island. The chef looks at me with, I swear to God, pity, but he laughs. Somebody carrying a roast on a platter steps over the debris, and all I can think of is how well the quilted leather will blot up the grease on the floor.

The chef kneels down in his white pants and apron and starts handing me things, calling them out like a surgical nurse. "Filofax. Comb. Videotape. Walkman. Map. Plane ticket. Aspirin. Tape measure. Light meter. Lipstick. Business card. Script. Pen. Pen. Pen. Pen. Pen. Pen. Notebook. You a writer? Polaroid. Keys. Tampax. Platinum Card." He looks at the card. "Cynthia Ann McKenna. Pretty name. Suits you. You look like a Cynthia. A hya-Cynthia."

I grab the card out of his hand and stuff it into my purse. "Thanks, but they call me Cam. I'll get out of your way."

"You're not in my way, honey. You're just a very attractive obstacle."

We're kneeling next to each other at this point, and since we're both on our knees, he doesn't tower over me now, and I see his eyes, which are huge, pale green, with gold in them, like an autumn pond. He has long curly lashes. Incongruous eyes, and they stop me, because they are so direct. He's not so much looking at me as into me.

An older man in an impeccably tailored tweed sport coat strides in, stops dead, and stares over the top of his glasses as if he owns the place.

"He owns the place," says the chef.

The owner glares at us, particularly me, and I'm not surprised, since I'm crawling around on his kitchen floor on all fours. "*Puh-leese,*" he drawls, probably in the same voice he uses for throwing out tourists in Bermuda shorts, and now I'm feeling like a real jerk, groveling by the broiler with my purse and my Platinum Card, so I leap to my feet. Crash! I smash my head on a colander.

"Kitchen groupie," says the chef, deadpan, handing me my unwaxed mint dental floss and about four dollars in loose coins.

"Jamie's not entertaining in the kitchen. Please leave," says the owner. His tones are glacial.

I brush some potato peelings off my knees, force the zipper of my purse shut. *What a mess!* I need a few seconds to pull myself together, but I'm trapped between the kitchen and the dining room by the . . . *phone!* That's it. I'll vamp for a few minutes, take deep breaths, call my answering machine at home. Friendly voices will have left messages. Maybe Daria will have reached the mother.

It turns out there's only one message, from Laurie, my former college roommate, who's a sportswear buyer at Marshall Field. I used to talk to Laurie all the time—we'd have lunch, drinks, go to movies. But now we don't have much time to meet in person anymore. She's off on buying trips to Italy or I'm on a shoot—we never seem to be on the same schedule. If we talk it's usually on pay phones, or office phones, or late at night when we're too wound up to sleep.

"Call me at home," says Laurie's voice. "I ran into Timothy. He says you're getting back together."

Chapter Five

Three thousand miles up in the air, halfway between New York and Los Angeles, I am reorganiz-
ing my Filofax. It's amazing how one little green
crocodile binder can give a kind of looseleaf order to
the universe. I've color-coded the sections: orange
ruled pages are for business, pink with no rules is
personal, green is household, beige is addresses and
phone numbers, purple is restaurants. I've tabbed
separate sections for New York, L.A., London, and
Paris. I only get to Paris about once every two years,
but then, that could change. In the back, there are
little white envelopes for my expense receipts and
five plastic sleeves full of critical business cards. I
have fold-out maps of Chicago, New York, Paris,
and L.A., and a tube map of London. I have a
micro-thin Filofax calculator and the Filofax ruler
that clips into the binder rings. And a sheaf of Filofax
storyboard paper in case I get an inspiration for a TV
commercial. Nothing can replace this little notebook,
which cost me five hundred dollars, loaded, and is
worth every penny, and I know why: even when my
life is in turmoil, it gives me a sense of control.

I've got three hours to kill, and I've already seen

the movie and read all six of my magazines. Juice is useless; he was asleep before the wheels left the ground. I pull out a fistful of wrinkled yellow time sheets. All the clients and their code numbers are printed on the back, and there's a grid of the days of the week on the front, so the agency will know how to bill out your time, or see if an account is profitable. I stare at the codes and the grid. None of it makes sense. There is absolutely no way I can reconstruct the last twenty-four hours, much less three months of back time sheets. This makes me angry. *What am I supposed to be? A creative person or some goddamn green-eyeshader with a calculator?* I stuff the time sheets into the pouch of the seat in front of me, next to the barf bag.

Now what?

The plane is packed, so I can't activate my usual strategy of staking out three adjoining empty seats. The Oriental kid across the aisle is playing an endless game of Pac-Man: *Beep! Boop! Beep! Boop!* First class is not an option; it's against M&M policy.

Maybe I'll call Laurie and see where she ran into Timothy.

I wedge my way through the seats and up the aisle to the air phone. Why is it that the only time I can talk to my friends is when I'm in transit—on the car phone, the air phone, in a phone booth at an airport gate?

"Laurie?"

"Cam. Where are you?"

"Thirty thousand feet in the air."

"East coast?"

"West. En route. So what's this about Timothy?"

"I ran into him at Sandburg Supermarket. He said

you were getting back together. He wasn't wearing his wedding ring."

"That fucking maniac."

"I know his game, Cam. He's always been like this. He's threatened by your success, that's his problem. Everybody knows that." Laurie sighs sympathetically, but I wonder if she really understands. She married a nuclear engineer with two PhD's who is threatened only by the Russians.

"And now he's spreading lies to my friends. You didn't believe him?"

"Are you as crazy as he is? I shouldn't have even left that message. You're getting upset." A suspicious pause. "You didn't, uh, see him before you left, did you? You didn't give him any ideas?"

"Uh, Laurie, we've hit some turbulence here. The seat-belt sign is flashing."

"Did you?" Her voice rises. Laurie was there, all those years ago, when I met Timothy on the steps of Deering Library in the dead of winter. She took one look at his black leather jacket and she warned me he was not my type. She's been repeating herself on this subject for more years than I care to recall, so I push the button and kill the connection. Back in my seat, I spritz my face with Evian from a miniature pink-and-white can and pick up my Filofax to zip it back into my carry-on. Something falls out and into my lap. It's The Picture. Proust had his madeleines. I have The Picture.

It's a black-and-white snapshot from those days when black-and-white pictures were tiny; there I am, a bald baby sitting in a little plastic pool in the backyard of our Miami Beach house. I recognize the foliage, that big green jungly stuff that bordered the yard, and the scrubby armored grass that felt like broken glass when you walked on it barefoot. The picture is cracked, the edges are frayed, and I suppose I'm fraying them more as I run my fingers over and over it. I look at The Picture, and I want to talk to Theo, my grandmother. I could call her on the air phone, but I'm sure she and Russell are at a party or out to dinner; they don't stay home much. Theo is not your typical home-cooking-type grandmother.

My grandmother, Theodosia, is an incredible woman. She looks ageless, but not by trying to look like Linda Evans. She could wear a tablecloth to a ball and be the best-dressed woman there, because she has an aura about her: intelligence, grace, and curiosity. She's the kind of person who's always interested in every trivial detail of your day, who never seems bored, who is endlessly emotionally available. When I talk to Theo, I feel like I am resting my head on a down pillow. She is there for me, especially when my mother is off cruising the Aegean or wherever her open-ended itinerary and current escort are taking her.

Needless to say, I have had the Timothy Conversation with Theo more times than I care to count. It goes like this:

"I hate his guts, Theo. I mean it. He's marrying her (calling me, bouncing that check, putting the flowers in the catbox, ignoring me) just to spite me, I know it. But that's okay. Really. I'm over it. It's history."

"Oh, I don't know about that."

"History."

"It doesn't have to be over, Cam. You can just move it to a different place."

"Like where? Siberia?"

"Cam, this is no different from when you had that blanket and you sucked your thumb on it. It was filthy, you dragged it everywhere. You were ruining your bite. And you wouldn't stop sucking on it or sleeping with it. You wouldn't let anybody throw it away. So we just told you we'd keep it for you, put it in a new place for a few nights. And you could get it out anytime. And soon . . . well, you cried for a few nights, but soon you'd forgotten about it."

"I was five years old! Besides, you can't have a relationship with a blanket."

"You can try."

"Okay, so I admit I had—have—a problem with Timothy."

Then there's my father. I never knew him, which is another problem, but only when I'm feeling sorry for myself. I do know he was South American. My mother met him at Hialeah racetrack, during the Flight of the Flamingos—between races, when they paddle canoes onto the little lake inside the track, stir up the flamingos, and get them airborne for about two minutes to prove they're not lawn ornaments. It must have affected my parents profoundly. They eloped. They moved to his home in Argentina, and my mother immediately got herself on Eva Peron's blacklist by refusing to attend a party at the Pink Palace because she knew they kept prisoners under the dance floor. Evita's retaliation involved confiscating my mother's passport, leaving her in a sort of loose state of shopping-spree arrest until an international incident involving America occurred, causing the abrupt return of her passport. My parents fled the country. They got as far as Miami Beach, where I was born.

All my mother will say is she never understood

the Latin mentality. When the marriage was over, none of us ever saw my father again. He vanished into the depths of Brazil, like Mengele, and my mother fled to the society pages. But last month, after I was on the Oprah Winfrey show, I got a letter from his sister, who reached me through the show: my father had died thirty years ago in an accidental gas explosion. She enclosed a black-and-white picture of me, the baby in the plastic pool. It had been in his pocket when he died. I tucked The Picture in the front of my Filofax, and every once in a while I take it out or it falls out and I look at it. I just look at it, like I'm doing now.

Apparently Timothy is a dead ringer for my father, which I had no way of knowing.

Timothy didn't look Argentinian to me, but then neither do I, but this explains why my mother hated him on sight. According to my therapist at the time, it also explains my irrational, sicko-masochistic love for Timothy.

This is one of those Freudian theories that I will believe when I see the certified photographic side-by-side comparison, as we say in advertising. Personally, I believe I just happened to be a typical sheltered, chauffeured twenty-three-year-old who had a perfectly normal attraction to a long-haired, leather-jacketed artist on a Harley. Believe me, it could happen to anybody. Millions of girls fell in love with James Dean and Elvis Presley, and these men certainly did not in every single case look like their fathers.

It's simple. I have tried every possible relationship with Timothy—dating, engaged, married, separated, divorced, speaking, not speaking, amorous, murderous. I have tried everything except not having a relationship, because the common link here is some sort of sick attraction. He's not good for me, and I can't get over him, and I must not want to or I would get rid of him. I figured this out for myself, without the help of a psychiatrist or a how-to book for women who love to love creeps, but it doesn't solve anything.

So here I am, thirty thousand feet in the air, looking at my baby picture which belonged to the dead father I never knew, thinking about a jerk I used to be married to that I can't get over. I'd be better off reading the diagram of emergency exits in the seat pocket in front of me. I *will* read the diagram of emergency exits. I stuff The Picture back into my Filofax and snap the strap around the crocodile cover.

Chapter Six

I wake up with a start. *Where am I?*

A ringing phone and bright blue chroma-key sky. Fat blocks of primary colors climb up the side of a hotel—gaudy squares of red, blue, white, and yellow. *Garish:* I must be in L.A., where the term was invented, poolside at the Mondrian Hotel. I push myself up on an elbow and squint at the pool, a pale blue L about waist-deep. There is a weird multicolor snaky sculpture, a few medium-size potted trees, and bright orange hibiscus in square wood planters. Power lunches are occurring on the patio one step below, people in suits huddled under gray umbrellas clinking silverware against bowls of cobb salad and glasses of iced tea. Beyond the pool is the city, stretched flat underneath its smoggy blanket. This is where Juice and I have chosen to recover from jet lag and this morning's breakfast meeting, for which we were catatonic. If this were my hotel, the first thing I'd do is provide jet-lag packages for every room—vitamins, gallons of Evian, free massages.

The tan from my last L.A. trip three weeks ago has faded to drab khaki, and is that cellulite on my inner thighs, or has someone applied orange peels while I was sleeping? Lumpy thighs are never good, but on the Coast they're about as welcome as nuclear waste.

The Coast has its own rules and regulations. Your skirt must be six inches shorter and three inches tighter, your hair four shades blonder than normal. Otherwise, head straight to Melrose Avenue and make yourself over. If your skin lacks the proper glow, hit the tanning parlor. Your cheekbones aren't sculptured? Get implants. On the other hand, if you are a man, and you are straight, it does not matter if you look like the Phantom of the Opera without his mask; you will be a social success.

"What do you think Bruce plans to do with this account?"

"Nothing in this business is rational." Juice shrugs and sucks the lemon from his iced tea. "You want rationality, be a loan officer."

Juice is right. People who earn their living deciding which way the bears will dance around the cereal box are not in the business of being rational. "I think that if our Zing! campaign comes off, we can call the shots."

Juice snorts. "What's going to happen is what always happens. We work sixteen hours a day for a month, we get into the finals, we work sixteen hours a day for another month, we make the pitch, we're great, we get the business, and Bruce will take the credit and get his six-figure bonus, and we'll get zip."

"Not if we play our cards right."

"What do you mean?"

I take a sip of iced tea. "Harold." Where the chairman clicks in is when policy must be decided, or a major change or campaign is approved, or new business is looming on the horizon.

"Spirit would be a real plum piece of business. Especially if we brought in the lead, not Bruce."

"One step at a time. Besides, every account is the same, don't kid yourself." Juice grimaces. Then he gets more serious. "Don't get into it with Bruce, Cam. You can't win."

Maybe not, but I'm thinking *leverage*. Maybe I can leverage this spot into something. Bruce has been a thorn in my side, a ceiling over my head, ever since he joined the company. If this commercial is a success, and it cracks the door to the Spirit account, I'll finally be free of him. Even if he's my boss on paper, I'll be untouchable. And he'll be vulnerable. Of course, he knows this. I don't say this to Juice, though. It would sound too paranoid, and I really don't think these scenarios out. They just are there. Facts, not politics.

"Come on," I say instead. "A major soft-drink account is just not in the same league as, say, Bridal Bouquet. You know that. If there's a chance to do good work at all, it's on accounts like Zing! They've got the budgets, and they'll spend them on creative. Look at Pepsi. They spent seven million, got Michael Jackson, and you may not like his moonwalk, but somebody got a shot at some hot work. Why shouldn't it be us?"

"You're starting to talk like *them*."

"But don't you want to hit a home run on a really major national brand? God, think of what we could do with it." I'm getting on a creative high now, my adrenaline has me actually sitting up in the lounge chair. I've forgotten about my jet lag. My work is still the gold star. That's why I'm addicted to it, and why I can't let it go.

"Look," says Juice, shaking the shock of hair off his forehead. "All we have to do is breathe smog for a few days and go home. You worry too much about bullshit, you know? You're turning into a copy slut from hell. That's your problem. Aside from your ex-husband, but let's not get personal." He flicks a fingerful of crushed ice at me. "Don't take Bruce on, Cam. Not unless you're carrying a very small revolver in your purse."

What is it about people you work with that gives everybody the automatic right to be psychologically intimate? You'll tell the woman you have coffee with things you wouldn't tell your own mother, much less your shrink. Your marriage is breaking up? Your secretary is the first to know. You suspect your husband is a bigamist? Don't mention it to him: tell the director of finance. You have hemorrhoids? Post a sign in the ladies' room. Juice and I tell each other everything. Is this good or bad? We spend more time with each other than with our husbands, wives, shrinks, best friends, and certainly than our mothers. "Don't kid yourself," Juice told me. "*We're* your family. You only sleep at home. It's us you *live* with." He was right, too. I've eaten more meals, traveled more miles, spent more late nights, split more croissants, laughed more, sworn more, done just about more of anything with Juice than I ever did with Timothy. The office is the family of the Eighties.

I've never set foot inside Juice's apartment, but I know him as if I lived with him. I know his entire wardrobe, item by item. The faded denim shirt that he wears with the red suspenders. The pants in every shade of beige, cream, and white, all impeccably pressed and crisply creased. The overcoats—vintage, current, and evening wear. The Armani tuxedo. I know the dent on his left index finger from the last-minute presentation he was slicing together from the clip art files. I know the nooks and crannies of his face, the shadows under his eyes when he's been up too late, the little patch near his collar that he always forgets to shave. I know when his shoes need to be resoled. When he's coming down with a cold. When he's off the grapefruit diet and onto bee pollen on yogurt. I know his triglyceride level, his IQ, the results of his AIDS test.

I never knew Timothy's triglyceride level.

Poolside, Juice is wearing white handkerchief-linen pants, a blue workshirt, sneakers hand-painted with winged pink and purple pigs, pink socks, and mirrored L.A. Eyeworks sunglasses on leashes. He applies several layers of number-thirty sunblock to whatever skin is exposed, sitting under the only tree that offers any shade, peeling an apple with a Swiss Army knife.

I should listen to Juice. He's right. I'm here. I'm not in the office. I don't have to play guerrilla today. I don't have to go home and wonder who will turn up in my bathtub. All I have to do is what I love to do—create. I decide to relax. Take a deep breath. So what if I clog my lungs with carcinogens? The ocean is at least within striking distance; the sun is shining. I am poolside at the Mondrian in Los Angeles. Things could be worse.

"You're not going to believe this location," Juice says happily, flipping a map onto my lap. "Absolutely desolate."

A man in a bathing suit walks by carrying a guitar

case. A teenage girl with red hair giggles into his ear, but I can hear her: "I'm supposed to be a star fucker."

Juice yawns, stretches, and unfurls a map. "An hour and a half. That's how long it should take to get there. I got the Polaroids." He reaches into his canvas bag and hands me a deck of pictures that show rocks and dirt from every conceivable angle.

"There's not a whole lot of . . . nature value here."

"Right. That's the point. It's a clean canvas. We can make this place look like anywhere! No buildings, no palm trees, no streets. We're starting from scratch."

"How much?" I am aware that Juice would raze and recreate the entire planet if he could, for aeshetic reasons. The average commercial that our agency shoots runs about two hundred and fifty thousand dollars, including music and postproduction costs. This shoot is budgeted higher—almost a million, including the celebrity-talent six-figure fees, the location construction, the choreography and extras.

I lean over the side of my chair and squint at the budget, a computer printout which is lying on the rock-pebble surface of the pool deck. "Do we really need two cranes?"

"We want to cover that shot from two angles."

"The helicopter?"

"It's a new product introduction, for God's sake!"

"What about the condor?"

"Daria has the trainer lined up—the guy who trained the rats for the movie *Willard*. You talk about budget. That's what's going to put us over budget. The trainer has us over the barrel. Condors are an endangered species or something. There's only one or two trainers who work with them."

The ghost-town dance sequence ends with a valiant swoop of a condor across the sky. I guess I'd better start thinking about what it takes to make a condor swoop on cue.

"What about the talent?" We never say "actors" or "actresses." Always "the talent."

"Callbacks start day after tomorrow. Durant and Cowboy Bob are on ice."

This is the crux of the plot of the commercial we are out here to shoot: teen heartthrob meets classic legend of the Old West, the famous Cowboy Bob. The original guy, from the fifties TV series.

"Has anybody checked out Cowboy Bob?" I ask. It's always good to check out living legends ahead of time. I remember being sent to Majorca to shoot a certain living legend for a tea commercial. The Legend had degenerated and could not drink the tea without rattling and chattering the cup, spilling the tea and sopping the wardrobe on take after take. The footage was unusable and the shoot was a write-off.

"Cowboy Bob never appears in public without his bandanna. Even with his street clothes. That's all I know. He lives the role."

I open my pre-pro notebook with all the shoot details under different-colored tabs, plus the hotels and phone numbers where everyone is staying. Juice, Daria, and I are at the Mondrian. The account group is at the Beverly Wilshire, which is a more gray-flannel hotel. Altogether, we have a contingent of about twelve people out here for three weeks. Longer, if we don't get good weather.

The wind ruffs my hair—palm trees are actually rustling on cue. It feels good just to be someplace else, to know you're not easy to reach, you can lose yourself in your work, maybe even order fresh raspberries from room service at three A.M. if you want, and someone else will make your bed. Believe it or not, I used to hate business travel. I still remember my first business trip, which was also to Los Angeles. I had no idea how to rent a car. I got lost on the freeway and ended up in Santa Monica. The only exit I recognized was the Slauson cutoff, because I remembered it from Johnny's monologue on the *Tonight* show. It was pouring rain and there was a landslide behind my hotel. Since I knew nobody in L.A., I went home to the hotel every night, called Timothy, and ordered a cheeseburger. I couldn't wait to leave.

And now I can never wait to come back. Is this because I now have a Platinum Card and have pinpointed the location of Rodeo Drive? Because they know me at the hotel and bring complimentary baskets of fruit and wine to my room? Because I know how to reserve a room with a whirlpool tub? Because I have friends here now, and I go to Morton's or the Ivy and then on to the Improv after dinner, instead of back to my room? Because I've got California cuisine down pat and can order a duck pizza from Spago with the best of them? Because I love to put down the top of my rented Rabbit convertible, drive up to the top of Mulholland and zigzag my way back down, breathing the fragrances of honeysuckle and velvet? Say what you will about L.A., it has a feeling of promise about it, a sense of beginnings, a fertility. Sometimes I drive out to the Santa Monica pier and walk out on the wooden planks to the end, buy a cotton candy, watch the sun go down, and I feel like I'm standing at the edge of the earth, and if I take two more steps, I'll be in kitsch heaven.

This is not the real world, but sometimes that's the exact last place you want to be.

The pool girl approaches, carrying two fresh iced teas and a telephone. It's for Juice.

"Hello," he says. "Yeah. Yeah. I'm in a meeting, okay? Preproduction business. Yeah. Yeah. In hell she will. I'll get back to you. Call me later." He hangs up. The receiver bounces onto the concrete. "My lawyer."

"Your tax lawyer, your contract lawyer, or your divorce lawyer?" Juice believes in the lawyers' full-employment act.

The wind whips the empty Sweet'n Low packets off the tray and into the pool, and they skim across the surface like crumpled pink petals. "The tax implications of this divorce thing are ridiculous. It's going to cost me a fortune. I don't know why I'm getting divorced. I don't know why I got married to begin with. Ever since I started dating, life has been one big blank check. Women! You can lead 'em to water, but you can't make them get on the bus."

We've been through this before. This litany of complaints is, as we both know, nothing but camouflage. Juice does not hate women; he loves them. Too much.

"Don't look at me like that," Juice says.

"Like what?"

"You know. That goddamn feminist glint in your eye. Somebody's gonna come up one day and punch it off your face. Like me."

"Far be it from me to cast stones." Juice was there when I broke down and cried because Timothy sent a process server to the office when he sued me for divorce. We were working late on the razor-blade account, and if we'd had any product in the office, I might have considered using it—not on my wrists, for God's sake, but on Timothy's throat. He'd always hated my job, especially once he realized that more than taking dictation was involved, and things really got out of hand when I started making more money than his paintings brought in. We separated then, and it was all downhill from there.

Anyhow, I'm not about to get into an argument with Juice. It's never good to argue with these people when you are on location: your partner, the director, or the client.

God, my neck hurts when I try to turn my head. Maybe I'll go to bed early tonight. Or, better still, maybe I'll get a massage. I've tapped into a fabulous masseuse who's on twenty-four-hour beeper and comes to the hotel room at any hour, carrying an assortment of aroma-therapeutic oils, creams, and essences, a sheepskin-covered massage table, and, as an extra added benefit, she knows all the gossip of the Rich and Famous, especially the plastic-surgery circuit. From Wendy I learned what famous boxing-movie star had his lips pumped with collagen, that a certain male sex symbol was in a master-slave relationship with a European director, who was also male, and that a certain physical-fitness icon had her rear end liposuctioned. A session with Wendy is worth a year's subscription to the *National Enquirer* and *Spy* combined.

I check my stopwatch. Almost eleven. I pull on a Music Animals sweatshirt and tap Juice on the shoulder. "Casting at noon?"

Juice nods. "I'm really up for this," he says. "You know, with any luck, we might actually do something good."

This is the hook. There's always the next spot, the

next shoot. There's always the chance that this one will be magic and it will all be worthwhile. You could create the next Pepsi extravaganza. You could do music with the next Barry Manilow. You could cast the next Bruce Willis. Anything can happen.

"Anything can happen," I say. "Meet you in the lobby."

Chapter Seven

The casting director is an Amazon: six feet tall, with two-inch-long persimmon-lacquered nails, skin-tight acid-wash jeans, a gold-and-white warm-up vest, straw cowboy hat, lavender glasses, and a white long-sleeved T-shirt that's scooped out in front to show cleavage enhanced with a push-up bra. Her antelope suede cowboy boots have three-inch heels, so she's towering over me as she taps the glass table with her index finger. Three diamond-studded gold bracelets jangle on her bony, tanned wrist. "Okay. We're not casting at the bottom of the barrel here, but we're not casting from the cream," she says.

We've been looking at casting tapes for three hours. Juice and I glance at each other and reach silent agreement: the casting stinks.

I hear a gnawing sound, and out of the corner of my eye I notice the production-company mascot, Cream Puff, who is an albino short-haired dog of some nondescript type, chowing down on a rawhide chew toy.

The casting director whips out an eight-by-ten black-and-white glossy and lays it on the table. "What about this girl? The scene calls for her to take a drink. I know she'll be a good drinker. She was a superb eater for us on a muffin commercial."

Juice stands up. "Look, Carolyn. I hate to get into more casting, but let's drop the age down a few years. We said sixteen and we're getting twenty-year-olds here."

"Twenty-year-olds can play sixteen."

"In your dreams. Let's specify . . . thirteen-year-olds. Okay? Thirteen. Let's see what we get."

At the table against the far wall, Lester Herio, our director, is rummaging through a huge pile of cassette cases. "What's all this shit," he screams, sweeping the entire pile into a trashcan. Lester is brilliant, but temperamental. "I can't even see my 1900 Exposition poster."

Everyone in the room tenses up. Cream Puff looks ready to spring, so I walk over and pet his head. His eyes and nose are pink. I pick up the rawhide chew toy and tease him with it. He chomps it between his jaws, and I wiggle it back and forth playfully. "Wanna fight, boy?" I say. "Grrr—wanna fight?"

"Jesus Christ!" Juice yells at me. "Will you let the dog alone!"

Under pressure, Juice tends to overreact.

The production-company producer, a mild-mannered, budget-conscious guy who wears a weird hairpiece combed sideways from ear to ear over an otherwise bald head, cringes. "Cam, I think it's best to let Cream Puff alone. He's very gentle—a pussycat—but he can be skittish with strangers. Now, Lester—we get a fifteen-dollar credit on each of those cassettes. That's an expensive way to clean up."

I'm getting hungry, but I know we should go over the storyboards once more with the director. I want to get all possible controversy ironed out now, so we're organized and together.

I motion to our agency producer, who is the liaison between us and the production company. "Daria, do you think we can wind this up? Maybe Lester can sit down with us for five minutes to go over the boards?"

Daria shakes her head. "We don't have Lester."

"What do you mean, we don't have him? He's right over there, across the room. I can see him."

"We only had him till seven. Now he's working on his feature." She looks admiringly at Lester, who is apparently too famous to disturb. Lester is one of those commercial directors who are on the cusp of fame in feature films. Like Tony Scott in *Top Gun*, Adrian Lyne in *Flashdance*, he will imminently be joining the elite fraternity of commercial directors who have crossed over into features, fame, and fortune.

"I need to talk to the director," I say. "We haven't worked out this dance sequence yet."

Lester overhears me. He's a tall, thin Englishman with dark hair and eyebrows that meet on the bridge of his nose. He waves his hand airily. "Cam, my precious, we cannot do a thing at this moment. The choreographer will be flying in tomorrow. At that point, we will map the whole thing out with the precision of the Normandy invasion." He whips his head in the opposite direction. "Who has the bloody keys to my car?" he yells.

"Juice," I whisper between gritted teeth. "Are you worried?"

"Nah. You?"

"Nah."

We look at each other. I wonder who's more worried, and about what.

The director, trailed by his producer, his A.D., the casting lady, and Cream Puff, exit.

"I guess I'll go to Tower Records," Juice says. "Want to come?"

We serpentine our way down the canyon. It's dark by now, and I can see millions of colored lights below, like a Neapolitan Christmas tree gone punk.

"God!" Juice explodes. "When did directors start taking pit bulls to pre-pro meetings!"

"What pit bulls?"

"That dog. The one with the fangs. You're lucky you still have your hand. If it weren't for me, you probably wouldn't. So. Now you owe me your hand. Okay?"

I petted a pit bull. I check my fingers to see if they're still there. "Oh, my God."

Juice is ranting. " . . . socially irresponsible! What if that thing had attacked you? Or worse! Attacked me!"

The car zigzags its way back to Sunset and we fly past all the gargantuan billboards that scream stars' names five thousand times bigger than life, past the Comedy Store, past North Beach Leather with all the skintight stuff in the window, past the funky lingerie place to the bottom of the steep hill where Spago is on one side and Tower Records and Book Soup are on the other. We idle in an uphill position; the parking lot at Tower is always full, even when it's the middle of the night.

"So what are you going to do tonight? Want to go to Dan Tana's and O.D. on some garlic bread?"

This is actually possible. Dan Tana's serves garlic bread with whole cloves of garlic slathered on each slice. Usually I'd go for it—who doesn't love the feeling of garlic burning the roof of your mouth? But tonight I just can't get psyched up. "Maybe I'll meet you there later," I say.

Juice nods. The restaurant scene on a shoot is no big thing, there's too much work. Then he narrows his eyes. "Isn't that David Byrne?" His eyes open wide again, he's blinking in disbelief. "David *fucking* Byrne."

Juice has few idols, but David Byrne is one. We've discussed it a lot. Juice considers himself an artist, which he is. He can conceptualize, dish up images and ideas, with the best of them. His design for round hot dogs, for instance, was brilliant and turned the entire product category around. But, let's face it, hot-dog conceptualization, shooting commercials, and the repertoire of things we do is not in a class with the Talking Heads. Say what you will about David Byrne's tailor, we're jealous. Maybe advertising is creative, but is it creative enough? Would Chagall have drawn storyboards for a living? Would Proust have written a Hyundai commercial? How would Einstein have explained the Excedrin headache? We torture ourselves with questions like these.

David Byrne gets into a red Porsche and we watch the Porsche until it disappears in the traffic on Sunset.

Within fifteen minutes I am back in my hotel room. Actually, it's a one-bedroom suite, the requisite hotel layout for a woman in business, as you discover the first time you conduct a meeting sitting on the edge of your bed. This particular suite at the Mondrian is what you would call neutral: gray low-nap industrial carpet, gray flannel couches in the living room, stainless-steel bar-refrigerator, charcoal gray Formica pedestal table, on top of which I have set up my computer. The gray bedspread has been turned down and there are two foil-wrapped candies on the crisp white pillows on each side of the king-size bed. I immediately eat the candy. The red light on the bedside phone is blinking, so I call for my messages as I wonder if I can get room service to bring up an entire box of these mints.

Sixteen messages. Three calls from my secretary, one from Bruce, three from Arnie, four from the production company, two from the front desk about packages, which I know are casting tapes to be reviewed on the VCR in my room, one from the real-estate woman who always tries to sell me the Donna Mills House or the Jane Wyman/Ronald Reagan House or the Carole Lombard House when I come through town. Maybe I should check out a few houses and apartments and get a feel for the prices. One call from Ramona—she'll see me in Santa Barbara on Saturday—one from my mother. That's it. It's too late to call the office, so I hang up and flip through the turquoise section of my Filofax for Wendy's beeper number.

I hang up and order smoked salmon and raspberries from room service and run a bath in the whirlpool tub. Wendy arrives three minutes after the smoked salmon and raspberries. I greet her with a big California hug, and I peel a piece of salmon off the plate and offer it to her pet chow, a fixture who goes everywhere with her. Californians are big on animals.

"I don't know if Doggie should eat that." She frowns. "I had him on the interro machine the other day and they said he should be on a vegetarian diet."

"What's an interro machine?"

"Oh, you should try it. It measures your electro-magnetic energy fields so you know where the imbalances are." She unfolds the padded massage table and sets it up at the foot of the bed. "It tells you what your body likes."

"And I thought I knew."

I can always count on Wendy to turn me on to the latest West Coastisms. It was Wendy who got me out of dress-for-success and into iridescent minis from Maxfield Blue and strapless T-shirts from Fred Segal. Wendy steered me toward sixties furniture when it was vintage only in attics and junk sales. Without Wendy I would never have discovered that zinc stops your hair from breaking, ice water keeps your breasts firm, and the power of amethyst crystals. I like to think that if Gidget had been born into the New Age, she would have turned into Wendy.

Wendy tosses a sheepskin throw on the massage table and covers it with a towel as I hang my T-shirt and black denim jeans on the bathroom door, looping my turquoise-and-silver concha belt over the doorknob.

Wendy has shoulder-length red-blond hair and a fresh-faced look that's emphasized by her loose white cotton shirt with rolled-up sleeves and her sneakers. Three crystals dangle from gold chains around her neck. With her huge, innocent brown eyes she looks about twenty years old, but I know she's closer to thirty.

It always surprises me that Wendy used to be a hooker. When I first met her, she was giving massages on a free-lance basis, but her real job was under the auspices of an L.A. madam. I never learned the details; she was just "the madam." Then sex became unsafe, and Wendy switched into massage and aroma-therapy full-time. She was very open about telling me all this, and I thought it was fascinating. Summarizing my life and my friends, most of the people and situations I know are one step to the right of *Leave It to Beaver*. I'd grown up in the suburbs, gone to a white-bread high school, a Big Ten university. My first and only act of rebellion was marrying Timothy.

"So how's business?" I ask as she pours almond oil onto her hands.

"Gosh, it's really busy. The Arabs are incredible. They're so demanding." She starts on my shoulders. "Look at you, you're so tense. All knots." She pushes with her thumbs, and I can smell the almond oil and feel the warmth of her hands. "Sweetie, I can see right now we're going to have to give a lot of attention to your fourth chakra."

"What's a chakra?"

"Sanskrit. That's the energy center where your love is located. Emotions, relationships, self-love, they're all here." She traces a pattern on my middle. "We'll just unlock this chakra and put a rose-quartz crystal on your heart."

"What'll that do?"

"Heal it. The body is a wonderful receiver. Here, hold this."

She presses a crystal into my hand. I can't imagine it will do anything, but I hold on to it anyway.

Wendy pours on more almond oil. "You know, Cam, I can feel you are very conflicted."

"Well, who isn't?"

"The path of healing is in acceptance. You have to learn to listen to your heart. Maybe if we unblock the fourth chakra . . ."

My eyes are closed, but I can feel Wendy frowning. "Get hold of a black tourmaline," she intones. "It deflects negativity."

"I'm through being negative. What do you know about Jed Durant?"

"His mother manages him. She lives with that broken-plate artist. He hangs out with the girl who plays the teenage bitch on *Falcon's Lair*. The one who used to go out with Michael J. Fox. Why, are you seeing him?"

"Wendy, give me a break. The kid's a baby. I'm working with him."

Wendy tugs on my fingers. "They say he's the illegitimate son of one of the Beatles."

"No kidding! Which one?"

"Does it matter?"

"No. But it would explain his . . . I don't know. He has something, that's for sure." I try to recall Paul's eyes or John's nose in his features, but I can't.

"Myra Durant was a major groupie. Actually, Jed could be anybody's son. She was never married. The madam told me all about her. She's very shrewd."

"Did she work for the madam?"

"Not directly. But sometimes the madam made . . . introductions for certain people. A certain TV evangelist, for example . . ."

"But the Beatles?"

"Sweetie, you just never know. That was so long ago, nobody remembers."

I doubt it. In this town, everybody remembers everything. "So how did Jed Durant become such a big star?"

Wendy rubs my scalp. "Well, he does have a good voice. And of course, that *presence*. And Myra Durant knows the record scene inside out. The real power is with the big record producers, and, shall we say, she knows how to get her way with them. But, sweetie . . ."

"What?"

"You never heard any of this from me."

"Right."

Twenty minutes later, Wendy and I are sitting side-by-side on the massage table, and I'm keeping Wendy on the edge of her seat as I describe the time I threw the engagement ring into the hearse, all the classics, right up to the time I actually accepted his collect call on his honeymoon during his next marriage.

Wendy stares at me. "You listened to that garbage-head?"

"Wendy," I say, "the good news is, I've started a new life. I really don't love him anymore. In fact, I despise him."

"That's great. Lie back down." She uncaps a new bottle and I smell strawberries. I can tell from the tone of her voice that I have been less than convincing.

"I mean it. Timothy is gone for good. Banished from my life! I mean it! Out! Exorcised! History! I am never speaking to him again. And you know what?"

"What?" Wendy pummels my back.

"It feels great. You know, I never actually made a decision about this before. I mean, I made a decision, but it was passive aggression. I never did anything about it. I never acted on it."

"Not making a decision is making a decision. You should focus your mind on your sixth chakra." She touches the center of my forehead. "Here."

"I finally realize I *want* things to change. *I* want to change. I'm not going to settle. You'll see."

"Oh, sweetie, don't talk about it. I can feel you tensing up when you think about him. He's no good for you."

Doggie starts growling at her tone of voice.

"Doggie, be a good boy. He senses everything."

Wendy turns my head to the left, then to the right, then she massages my temples. "Let's change the subject. What do you think about Cher? Doesn't she look great? Do you think she had elbow chips put in her cheekbones."

"Elbow chips?"

"They take little chips of cartilage from your elbow and implant them in your cheeks to give you bone structure. I don't know what it does to your tennis serve."

Suddenly Doggie barks and leaps to his feet.

"Are you expecting someone, sweetie?"

"No."

The knock on the door gets more insistent. So does Doggie's barking.

"Cam? You in there?" It's Juice's voice.

I get up, wrap myself in a towel, and stomp to the door, cracking it open. "Okay, Juice. What is it?"

"A goddamn emergency, that's what." He barges in.

"Wendy, this is Juice."

She nods and checks him out. "Your back is in spasm, I can see it from here."

Juice heaves himself onto the L-shaped living-room couch. This is why I got a suite. "My goddamn *mind* is in spasm, that's what," Juice says, throwing a manila folder onto the coffee table and lighting a cigarette.

He finally notices I'm only wearing a towel. "Nice outfit."

"What now?"

"The mother."

"Whose mother?"

"The kid's, the baby heartthrob's mother."

"Myra Durant? Listen to this, Juice. Jed Durant may be the illegitimate son of Myra Durant and one of the Beatles."

"I thought he was the baby on the Snowstorm Detergent box." Juice tells us how it turned out that the mother on the box was a former porn star, and Myra Durant sued for damages to her son's image, assuming you buy into the proposition that a six-month-old can have an image to damage. Of course, she won. Myra Durant has a will of tungsten steel; she never loses. And she's smart: the publicity catapulted her son into the limelight, where he's been ever since. For his sixteenth birthday Myra bought the rights to some long-dormant Buddy Holly songs, rearranged them herself to a new-wave beat, and gave them to Jed, who recorded them and went platinum. The rest is history.

I tighten the towel. "So what's with Myra?"

"Now she's threatening to pull the kid. She says nobody showed her the storyboards."

"What!"

"Lance was supposed to send them out three weeks ago."

Juice shrugs. "Well, you know Lance. This woman is saying Jed Durant will touch the product, but he won't drink it on camera. Surprise."

"Jesus. Daria was supposed to clear this up with the agent."

"The mother is the agent."

"Great. Just perfect."

I sit on the couch next to Juice. Wendy wanders over and perches on the edge of the coffee table, nibbling grapes from the complimentary fruit basket. In spite of the drama of the scene, we don't really mind problems at all; we sort of welcome them. Problems let us prove what we already want to believe—that we're stars. Other people, the Lances of the world, may fuck up, but not us. We're the A Team. On the other hand, I know damn well that Brucie would love it if I fucked this up, or, at least, if he could pin it on me. The idea is to come back with your shield, not on it. "So where is he?" I ask.

"Nah, Daria's been calling her all day. She refuses to talk."

We sit silent for a minute. Then I say, "Wendy, do you know the name of a twenty-four-hour florist?"

"In L.A.?"

"You're right. That's crazy."

"Wait a minute," she says. "I do have a client who's a florist. He owns an orchid greenhouse in Venice."

I throw myself at Wendy's mercy. "Wendy, please, please, please do me a huge favor. Please. Please call this guy for me and beg him, bribe him, whatever, to open up and make an emergency arrangement."

"What's the emergency?"

"It's a career emergency."

Wendy shrugs.

"A karmic emergency, okay? Think of it in those terms."

"Sweetie, I think you are taking all this a bit too seriously. This happened to an actress friend of mine. She just got so wrapped up in auditions, there was so much pressure, that she turned into one of the characters, you know?" Wendy fluffs her hair while she's dialing the phone. "Vincent, sweetie," she purrs into the receiver. "It's Wendy, with an emergency. Remember the time you couldn't straighten up after yoga? And I saved you? Well, now you've just got to save my friend, sweetie. She's just like my sister, and she needs you." She hands me the phone.

"Vincent," I plead, "you don't know me, but if I don't get the most spectacular arrangement on earth into the hands of a particular person in the next sixty minutes, my life is over. Believe me. Yes! This is life or death! Yes! I love dendroviums. Cymbidiums, fine! Phaleonopsis, wonderful! Moss. Moss! Okay, great! Make it like a . . . a rain forest!" I tell Vincent the budget is three hundred dollars, if he gets the arrangement into the hands of Myra Durant within one hour, with a card that reads, "You are a star," signed, "Cam McKenna and your friends at Missoni & Missoni." I tell Vincent to deliver the flowers personally and to say that Ms. McKenna is waiting at the Mondrian to hear whether or not Ms. Durant liked the flowers.

I look at my watch. "If she hasn't called here by ten-thirty, we're going to have to blast a jeweler out of bed."

By now Wendy has Juice on the table. "Just take off your shirt and hold this green tourmaline," she says. "We can ease that tension in fifteen minutes."

I wave my hand. "Go ahead, I have a headache anyhow." I rub my hair. It feels oily.

"Watch that blood sugar, sweetie," Wendy calls out. Juice lies down, but refuses to take off his shirt.

One hour later, the phone rings, and I hear the businesslike voice of Myra Durant. "Ms. McKenna, these flowers are ridiculous, but the Durant Organization understands the sentiment of cooperation. Jed will be at the shoot, and he will drink your product, provided he does not have to share any close-ups with any has-been actors who shall go unnamed. In the spirit of give-and-take."

"You have my assurance on that," I say, flashing Juice and Wendy the okay sign.

"I want it in writing," says Ms. Durant.

"Tomorrow—"

"Not tomorrow. Tonight."

"How—"

"I am meeting some friends after dinner. Please meet me with the papers."

I scribble the address with one hand and plug in the computer with the other. Thank God for the computer. I hang up and type a letter of agreement, then print it out on my portable printer.

Juice struggles up from the table. "I'll drive," he says, and I throw on a black leather miniskirt, white T-shirt, rhinestone clips, and a pair of Keds, and we're off. I blow a kiss to Wendy. "Thanks. I owe you a big one."

"It all evens out," she says. "I'll let myself out."

Snaking our way up a narrow canyon road, it's a lucky thing Juice is driving; I would have surely gotten lost or crashed into a ravine, not because I have no sense of direction, but because peering into the half-hidden windows of the houses balanced on the hillside takes your eyes off the road. I love these houses, even the future earthquake casualties on stilts. "What do you think it would be like to live in one of these?" I ask Juice.

He sounds shocked. "What! You wouldn't really want to do that!"

"Why not?"

"Because they're in California. And everybody in California is crazy."

"But they're crazy in such nice weather." I grip the armrest as the car downshifts and careens around a hairpin turn.

"You know what's wrong with you? You've never spent any real time out here. How long have you spent out here?" Juice doesn't wait for an answer. "Well, I lived here once for six months—I was shooting a package, millions of dollars, all fucked up—and I can tell you what it's like. It was all fucked up."

"Mm hm." I'm not really listening. I'm thinking that maybe I could live out here. Maybe I really could.

The car slows down. "This must be it," says Juice. About twenty of the most expensive cars in the world are lined up bumper to bumper on a precarious shoulder of the road—Maseratis, Ferraris, Mercedes, BMW's, a couple of vintage Corvettes, a Morgan—you name it. We slip into the end of the line and hike up to the door. Juice is unimpressed. "Where's the valet parking?"

A houseman in a white coat ushers us through a Mediterranean-style, heavily stuccoed hallway with an overabundance of arches and pale, hand-painted friezes. There are no curtains on the arched windows, just borders of painted draperies. The place looks like a playroom where grown-ups have been allowed to finger-paint on the walls, very California naive. A Warhol triptych of Jed Durant hangs across from the front door. We pass through one of the massive archways, which is embedded with bits of colored glass, into a huge turquoise-and-coral kitchen with a Mexican tile floor and several buffets set on counters. I notice a Biedermeier credenza on the far wall. The houseman gestures toward an exotic-looking woman with waist-length black hair. She is beautiful and looks about my age, in her skintight white shirred Ungaro dress. "Ms. Durant," the houseman whispers to me. I turn to Juice. He's cool. That's one thing about him—nothing seems to astonish the guy.

I, on the other hand, am not cool. In fact, I feel a rivulet of sweat starting at the nape of my neck. I hate that about myself; when I get nervous, I sweat. I wish I could lacquer my sweat glands shut.

The houseman taps Ms. Durant, and she spins around, her hair whipping like fringe on a jacket. This woman does not fit the stereotype of the stage mother. Or of a mother, period. She puts her hand on the arm of a stocky white-haired man and propels him in our direction.

I unfreeze my feet. "Ms. Durant," I say. "I have the agreement right here. I'm so sorry to disturb—"

"We're so glad you could stop by," she says, smiling, and her teeth could star in a Pepsodent commercial. "This is Lawrence Tucker."

The heavyset man extends a spongy hand, which Juice and I shake in turn.

"He is Jed's publicist, and this lovely home is his."

"Very Carl Larsson," says Juice. Lawrence shrugs modestly, but you can tell he is proud that Juice made the connection to the esoteric whose use of color and design changed Swedish decorating.

"I just moved in," says Lawrence. "This is the former Bela Lugosi House. He lived here for thirty years—until he died."

"Is it haunted?" I try to make a joke, but Ms. Durant is studying the letter with steely concentration, Lawrence is staring over my head to see if there is somebody better to talk to within striking range, and Juice has spotted a Jennifer Bartlett sculpture through the archway. I notice Michael Caine and his exotic, high-cheekboned wife in the next room, talking to Richard Gere.

"Myra tells me you send nice little nosegays," says a voice at my shoulder, sounding like molasses dragged over sandpaper. I turn, and standing there is the single most anatomically perfect human being I have ever seen, and I realize it is Jed Durant. He does not look like John, Paul, George, or Ringo. He has his mother's black, shiny hair, cut short—shaved, almost—for his current role as a cadet in a military academy, and a bow-shaped upper lip. His eyes are pure turquoise. His teeth are as perfect as his mother's, his skin has the petallike quality of a very young person, that rare, poreless skin that is poised between adolescence and young manhood. I'm sure of one thing: he has never had a pimple in his life. In fact, he's hardly human. It's one of those cases where the pictures do not do a person justice.

Juice has wandered off in search of artistic master-pieces and seems to have Lawrence's ear. Holly-wood people love to show off their knowledge of modern art, or, at least, tell you how their collection is finer than Steve Martin's.

"Darling," murmurs Ms. Durant to her . . . son? They look so much alike, but more like brother and sister than mother and son. "Darling, perhaps Miss McKenna would care for a drink. It's probably been a long drive."

I look at this . . . kid, child, man, creature—whatever—and I'd say I'm possibly attracted to him, but only a lunatic would admit it, so instead I say, "Well, I'll just go over and have a Diet Coke, and then I'll get going."

This person, who looks like something that might have been painted on the ceiling of the Sistine Chapel, looks at me and smiles, like we share a secret, the kind of smile that immediately envelops you in intimacy. We walk toward the bar at the end of the living room, and he says, "I'm really looking forward to the spot. Cowboy Bob has always been one of my heroes. When I was a little kid, I used to wear a holster and watch his reruns, and wish I could draw a gun like him. I tried it once, with my cap gun. My finger got stuck in the trigger."

His unassuming attitude is not what I expect. After all, he is a star—a star with a prima donna mother and an angel's face. So I laugh. "I used to take the caps straight out of the package, unroll them onto a stone, and hit them with a spoon."

"You don't happen to have a cap gun in your purse?"

"No. I'd probably shoot my foot off."

We're just standing there talking, and I forget about the Diet Coke. The houseman hands me a glass of red wine, and I take it.

"Lawrence just got this place," says Jed, rubbing the edge of a wineglass slowly across his lower lip.

"I know. He told us about Bela Lugosi." My foot accidentally brushes Jed's, and I knock my wineglass over. Red wine spills like a bloodstain across the top of the table, which I now see is not just a mere table but a construction made of pale ossified slabs with shells and what looks like prehistoric fossils embedded in them. The wine seeps its way slowly into every nook, cranny, and crevice of the thing, which is soaking it up like a porous paper towel, except for the pools of drops that have made their way to the edge of the table and are splashing onto the pale Aubusson tapestry rug.

VIDEO	AUDIO
1. DAN AYKROYD	1. AYKROYD: Museum-quality rug?
HOLDS UP AUBUSSON RUG.	
2. GUEST DUMPS RED WINE ONTO RUG.	2. Obnoxious spills?
3. AYKROYD STUFFS RUG AND GUEST INTO BLENDER.	3. Combine the two and what do you get?
4. HE PUSHES BUTTON, RUNS RUG THROUGH BLENDER.	4. A mess! You need . . .
5. HE HOLDS UP APPLIANCE RESEMBLING MINIATURE SPACE SHUTTLE. SUPER: When your guests make a mess.	5. New Mess-o-matic!

"Oh, God! Now I've done it!" Jed exclaims loudly as, in an instant, he knocks his own wineglass and spills it onto the tabletop, blotting out my spill with an even bigger stain, and he does this so fast, with subtle bravado, reaching for a napkin with one hand and grabbing his forehead in mock-self-disgust with the other, that nobody notices that I was the one who actually wrecked the table. Well, I'm sure it's wrecked. How do you get red wine out of fossils?

Lawrence materializes, and you can tell from the twitch at the corner of his mouth that he's hysterical about the table, or maybe the rug, but he doesn't dare say anything to Jed, the Star, his livelihood, so he forces a laugh and pats him on the back. "No problem, Jeddie," he booms, encircling his shoulder with his arm, and as they walk away together, Jed breaks off and takes a step back to me.

"You know, I think you were right. You probably would have shot your foot off," he says.

"I . . . We'd better get going. Early meetings."

Jed reaches for my hand, but he doesn't shake it. He pulls me toward him in a move that doesn't seem like he's pulling me at all, more like I'm drawn into his force field, leans close. "See ya," he says.

Are those really the eyes of an eighteen-year-old? And why is he looking at me like that? I'm old enough to be his . . . well, at least his godmother. *You flatter yourself, Cam. The kid's not looking looking at you. He's examining your face to document the fact that it's humanly possible to get wrinkles and pimples at the same time. He's probably going to call Ripley's* Believe It or Not *the minute you walk out the door.*

Juice is waiting for me at the door, with Ms. Durant. "Thank you for the flowers," she says in a gracious voice. She hands me back a signed copy of the agreement. Then she eyes me closely for a fraction of a second.

"In the spirit of compromise, I've made a small amendment. Jed will drink the product on camera, but for no longer than three seconds, and never in a close-up. I'm sure you understand it's important to protect his image from overcommercialization."

"Of course. Naturally."

"How long will you be in town?"

"A week or ten days."

"You'll be working very hard, I'm sure. But perhaps you'll be able to join us for a little diversion after the shoot—say, a polo match? Do you ever get up to Santa Barbara? We have a little ranch in the valley . . ."

"Well, we were thinking of going to the Biltmore for the weekend after the shoot."

"We'll keep in touch."

"Now, please excuse us for intruding on your evening, Ms. Durant," I say. "And please tell Lawrence good night for us." I just want to get the hell out of there before I encounter any more Aubusson rugs.

Juice yawns as we walk toward the car. "I saw the way the kid was giving you the eye. Or maybe you were giving him the eye. And don't give me that innocent look, Miss Rebecca of Sunnybrook Farm." He lights a joint as we head back toward Sunset. "Want to stop by the Improv? There might be some adults there."

I let myself into my room, step over the message slips that have been left under the door, and sit down at the round pedestal table. I flip open the computer again, hook up my modem, and log in to my bulletin-board program to see if any of my computer pen pals left notes. There's one—a chess move from a person who calls himself Hi-Tech: pawn to queen's knight.

I'll have to get back to Hi-Tech.

The phone rings.

"Hello."

"Hi, Cynthia."

"Timothy."

"Yeah."

"What do you want?"

"I just think we should talk."

"Who told you where I was?" I'll kill whoever it was.

"Nobody. I figured it out."

"I'm hanging up now. Good-bye, Timothy."

I hang up. God, am I proud of myself. I can run fifty million dollars' worth of accounts, but I won't give you two cents for my ability to hang up on Timothy. It occurs to me that he has a problem too. I can't get rid of him, but he can't get rid of me either. But tonight I'm in Los Angeles, I'm free. I pick up the phone. "Operator," I say. "Please hold all calls and put a do-not-disturb on this phone."

Just as I hang up, there's a knock at the door. Probably Juice, with a location map.

"Candygram," says a voice with a Spanish accent.

"Juice, you're a laugh riot tonight," I say as I open the door.

It's Timothy.

Chapter Eight

Calories consumed after midnight don't count, do they? So I'm sitting on the bed, cross-legged, wrapped in a sheet, alternating spoonfuls of raspberries with cream with healthful swigs of San Pellegrino. All of which would be forgivable, except for the fact that the raspberries are being spoon-fed to me by my ex-husband, Timothy.

"Cynthia, we were immature. That was our problem. Think of how much we've learned since then."

"For instance, I've learned your wife's name. It's Lydia, in case you've forgotten." Which I'm pretty sure he has, since his hand is rubbing my naked breast. I can still smell the almond oil on my skin.

"Lydia was a rebound thing. I finally realized that." He takes my face between his hands and looks directly into my eyes. "Lydia is over. I moved out. I'm moving here, in fact. To L.A. You want to change things. You say so all the time. We can change together. Move out here with me."

"What are you going to do out here, Timothy?"

"They have ad agencies here. And I have a collage show opening next week."

"The stuff where you superimpose movie-star posters over weather maps?"

"Yeah, but you haven't seen it with the antique compasses. It's got real dimension now. The L.A. *Times* is reviewing the show. I think it's just the beginning. One of the art dealers is lending me her pool house and I'm looking for studio space in West Hollywood."

The female pronoun puts me on the alert. Of course the art dealer is a woman. He's charmed her out of her pool house already, and probably out of her pants.

Timothy brushes my hair behind my ears with his fingers and feeds me a raspberry, which I eat as if I were his pet. "We're flip sides, Cynthia. Isn't that what you always said?"

"That was years ago. We have nothing in common now." I'm licking his fingers as I say this.

"You're a pretty good actress then," he says, indicating the rumpled bed where we have spent the past two hours messing up the sheets.

I want to cut the cord here, I really do. But it's like Pavlov's dog. The register of Timothy's voice, his touch, even the musky way he smells are triggers that turn me into an alien. It gives me insight into crimes of passion. That headmistress that pulled the trigger and pumped a gunful of shells into the diet doctor? I can see it. You become dependent. And even if you hate his guts, some other you deep inside would rather do anything than lose him. So either you kill him or you cave in. Superwoman by day, Superwimp by night. Do they teach Insecurity 101 at Harvard Business School?

The point is moot. Timothy has pulled the sheet over us like a tent, and he's whispering in the dark.

"Remember how we used to dress up the cat in costumes and take his picture with the Polaroid? . . . Remember the time we flew kites at the beach in January?"

"I don't care about remembering, Timmy. That was five years ago." I count on my fingers. It's more. I was never good with numbers. "Can't you see? I want something *now*. We can't reinvent the past. We really can't."

"How do you know? You won't give it a chance. Cynthia." A kiss melts across my throat.

"What?" I wriggle away.

"It's not your body that's lying. It's you. You can't trust yourself."

"It always boils down to that, doesn't it?" I toss the sheet back, get up, and pull the curtains open. Suddenly I am in a terrible mood. "Right. Something is wrong with *me*. *I* have a brain tumor. *I* screwed you up. *I* have a problem."

I flip on the lights in the bathroom and turn on the faucets furiously. If there's one thing I hate, it's being blamed for myself. I grab the Evian spray can from the glass shelf and spritz my hair and fluff it up with a vengeance.

"Did it ever occur to you, Timmy, that you were unfaithful to me with Lydia, and now you've just gone vice versa?" I peer into the mirror and swab under my eyes with baby oil to wipe off the smeared mascara, as if it mattered how I looked.

"You're keeping score?" He comes into the bathroom, wrings out a wet washcloth, and pats the raspberry stains off my lips.

I look at him. He's always done just what he wanted. I've always loved him for it, but I can't be like that; there are too many things stopping me. And bringing him into my life just makes me crazy. What's left is the not wanting to let go. I want to, but I can't. *This is an obsession*, I tell myself. It's sick.

I put down my hairbrush and lay my head on his shoulder. It feels comfortable and familiar, not sick at all. I have spent a lot of time on this shoulder.

I know every contour; every muscle is an old friend; I have memorized the scent and the imprint of this shoulder.

What if things had worked out between us? What if, during this fight or that dinner, I had said or done something differently? Would he have loved me more? Or been less interested in someone else? To change a storyboard, you pull off one frame, draw a new one, and tape it on. It spoils you for real life, where you have to settle for "if only."

"It's four A.M. They're picking me up at six-thirty."

"Let's go for a drive. I have something to tell you."

"Okay." Why did I say that? What could he possibly say that I haven't heard before? A thousand times.

His car is parked in front of the hotel—a white fifty-something Mercedes with red leather seats and a vertical speedometer. I wonder where he got it. As we head up Laurel Canyon, the air is fresh from the rain. We don't talk—just drive. He stops at the lookout point at the top of Mulholland, and we turn off the engine and watch the spangly lollipop lights below, rinsed clean from the rain. Heavy droplets shake from the trees and drumbeat onto the convertible top. *All you need is love*, the Beatles sing over the radio, and I close my eyes. I'm in school again, in jeans, boots, shoulder-length hair, and we're on the Northwestern campus, the big lawn in front of Deering Library. It's one of those early-spring days when the dandelions are still fresh as newly churned butter and the grass is so soft you can comb it with your fingers. The crocuses are up—purple and white, the school colors—and Timothy is picking them and weaving them into bracelets around my wrists and I really do believe that love is all you need.

I wish I could erase the years, like a tape.

Timothy takes my hand and puts it between his legs, but it's not sexual this time, just a warm, familiar place where I once felt safe.

That's all. Really, that's all I feel. I hear a sigh. Is it me?

"What did you have to tell me, Timothy?"

He turns my head with his palm. "Let's not let it go, Cam. Let's try again."

"What are you saying?"

"I want you. I want you back. We should be a family."

I remember the first time we decided to get married. I did the proposing, tickling him until he agreed. I used the same words he is using now: *We should be a family*. It's too much. I start crying. This relationship is like water in my hands—it doesn't travel well; by the time I get where I'm going, it's slipped through my fingers. Timmy strokes my arm and he slips something over my hand—a Victorian amethyst bracelet, studded with seed pearls, intricately worked. "A ring seemed redundant at this point," he says, and he kisses my wrist where the bracelet clasps.

Can it work? Can we go back and piece our lives together? I want to do it. I hate sad endings—I always want to rewrite them. I shiver with the anticipation of it all.

"I'll try," I say. "If you will."

Chapter Nine

It's seven o'clock in the morning on our third
location day, but I already feel like I've been in the
Simi Valley for a month. By all respectable stan-
dards, it's not even breakfast time yet, but already
the doughnut table has been decimated, the coffee
urn drained dry, the chuck-wagon breakfast catered
by Eat Your Heart Out has been pillaged, and I've
made about fifteen calls on my portable phone. Right
now I'm having a music-track crisis.

"What do you mean he's 'in the hospital'? "

"Cam," says the studio assistant at Nuclear Music, the New York music house whose T-shirts say
THE SOUND THAT SELLS, "all I know is that Sam's wife
left a message that he was unreachable in the
hospital."

"Which hospital?"

"I don't know."

"Is he all right?" Okay, okay, I feel sorry for the
guy, but at the same time I'm livid. I'm sure they
know exactly where he is. They're covering for him.
How could Sam leave me in the lurch like this? Sam,
who called in the graham-cracker jingle from the pay
phone in the labor room when his wife had their last

baby, Sam, who won us three Clios in two years for music, Sam, who never lets me down. Especially when there's a problem. Like now.

Ramon, the choreographer, informed us yesterday that the beat was simply not strong in the mix, and he simply could not choreograph with a weak beat. "Yeah, baby," he'd said, oozing across the floor like a panther, "you've gotta have attitude. And this is not it."

I listen to the track for the hundredth time. Of course it's just a temp track, temporary for use on the shoot. But we need the beat to work now for the dance sequence. The answer comes clear: switch from real drums to an electronic sound. This is what I am trying to arrange, but Sam, the head composer from the music house, who personally scored this track, is unreachable, in the hospital, perhaps dying, and nobody else knows what to do.

"Just try to find him, okay?"

"Sure."

"And give him a message."

"Okay."

"In the refrain, change the ba-das to ba-ba-da-ba-da. The ba-ba-bas will increase by about three seconds . . ."

"Two ba-das?"

"Yes, plus a ba. And a half."

"Two ba-das plus a ba and a half?"

"That's it. Like what he did on the scalloped-potato spot. A stronger beat. Switch to synth. He'll know what to do, I'm sure."

"We'll try to reach him."

"And if that fails, please fax me the lead sheet with his notes and I'll find somebody out here."

"Oh, no," says the assistant quickly. "We'll take care of it."

"Thanks."

I hang up. We have to locate this guy. "Daria!"

She trots over, carrying a clipboard and wearing a black satin jacket with GHOSTBUSTERS II embroidered on the back that she got from her boyfriend, who was a lighting guy on the film, and black rubber sunglasses on leashes. Daria is a detail-oriented producer, which is the best kind, but she does go for that West Coast razzle-dazzle.

"Daria, Sam Gold is in the hospital."

"Oh, no! Anything serious?"

"No. But we want to send flowers. Today."

She gets out her pencil. "What hospital?"

"I don't know. We better call all the hospitals in New York and find where he's registered. Or have the P.A. do it for us. Then tell me right away where he is."

"Before I send the flowers?"

"Yes."

"Then what?"

"Then we call him in the hospital and, first, make sure he's alive and it's not serious, which I'm sure it isn't, since he's in contact with the recording studio, and then I get on the line and sort of briefly tell him our problem—very briefly, so as not to tire him out or anything. You never know."

"But if he's in the hospital, he won't be able to get into the studio. I'm not sure how we'll get around that."

"He'll hum the new arrangement over the phone. Okay, where's Ramon?"

"Putting the kids through their steps over there by

those rocks." She squints into the distance. "I told him to be careful."

"They can't get hurt. They're just stand-in rocks. Papier-maché."

We walk about a quarter-mile down an unpaved road, which the crew is in the process of making look even more unpaved. Daria and I compare the site to the storyboard. The object is to achieve the atmosphere of an Old West cowboy town. The location, which at dawn today was scrub valley, is becoming a beehive of activity. A crowd is swarming around the main trailer area, and teamster types lean up against Caterpillars, road graders, and other earth movers, as the crew push camera trunks and lighting equipment by on dollies. A convoy of black stretch limos is pulled off into the grass. Under a shaded tent two dozen teenage dancers are stretching in sweats and warm-up suits.

"By the way," says Daria, "here are some messages that came in for you at the production office."

I go through the pile of six or seven pieces of pink message paper. One is from Bruce. One is from Barry the commodities broker, who I have forgotten exists.

"I'll have to get to them in a few minutes," I say. "Right now, I have to go over the script again for timing."

Daria signals the P.A. to bring a portable phone up to the place under the trees where seven huge RV's are circled, like wagons: one is Jed Durant's dressing room, one is Cowboy Bob's dressing room, one is for the girl extras, another for the boys, one is for the agency, another for the crew, and one is for the wardrobe. A vision emerges from Cowboy Bob's trailer—tall, in his trademark skintight white suit, massive white pearl-handled revolvers in silver-studded holsters on each hip, white fringed suede jacket, white cowboy boots, silver spurs, white ten-gallon hat, and a bright red bandanna. Cowboy Bob looks exactly the same as he did when I used to watch him gallop his palomino to the rescue on Saturday-morning TV.

Juice appears. "He always wears his costume. They say he *is* the character."

"What about the bandanna?"

"Probably wears it in bed." But Juice and I don't laugh at this. We've worked with too many big-name celebrities. For the most part, they haven't gotten where they are by being the guy next door. Most of them have an act, and they've perfected it, on and off camera. They're bigger than life. That's why they're big.

We introduce ourselves to Cowboy Bob. Kind gray eyes flicker above the bandanna, and his face breaks into a crinkly smile. However, he does not shake hands. He salutes. Just like he used to on Saturday-morning TV.

"There," he says, pointing to a huge rock pile. "That's Cowboy Canyon. That's where we shot the opening of the show, where the palomino reared up."

"Did you do your own riding?" asks Juice, and, for once, he seems truly in awe.

"I started as a stuntman," says Cowboy Bob.

The two of them wander off in the direction of the ice chests that hold the soft drinks, and I think I hear Juice asking Cowboy Bob for an autograph.

The sun is burning off the early-morning haze, so I slip on my visor and settle into a canvas chair to time the script once more. There aren't many on-

camera words, since this is a musical commercial—
just the dialogue between Cowboy Bob and the boy,
sort of a space-age *High Noon* kind of thing—but you
can't be even a fraction of a second over. I've got my
hand on my stopwatch when a stretch limo and a
Mustang pull up by the trailers. Myra and Jed Durant get out of the limo, and Lance gets out of the
Mustang.

I see right away how Jed Durant has become a
star. "You know," I hear him say, "I was wondering
if you'd object if we rewrote the opening scene of
my new film so that I'm reaching into a refrigerator
for a can of Zing!"

Myra Durant shakes my hand. She's wearing a
white Valentino pantsuit, which makes me feel like a
construction worker in my safari shorts, socks, and
Keds. A beeper goes off in her green Hermès duffel
and she disappears back into the limo to make calls.

"Everyone, everyone," calls the assistant director
through a megaphone, and then I notice Cream Puff,
leashed to a tree, sleeping.

I catch up with the director, who is giving orders
over a walkie-talkie. "Lester," I say, and I admit I'm
feeling a little uneasy, "is that dog a pit bull?"

Lester waves his hand airily. "Well, his mother
was a pit bull, and his father was a pit bull."

"Don't let him loose, okay?"

Lester is shocked. "Of course not! He's a pure-
bred! Do you think I'd risk him getting hurt with all
this equipment! Now, Cam." He raises his voice,
since twenty or so carpenters have just begun ham-
mering, sawing, and drilling. By lunchtime they will
have constructed our slice of the Old West. "We've
already covered just about everything for today, with

the exception of the dance sequence," says Lester, looking over his shot list.

The toupeed producer thrusts a piece of paper at me.

"What's this."

"Overages for you to approve."

From the sidelines, Lance whirls around when he hears the word "overages."

"Overages? How did we go over budget?"

"Well, as you can see, there's that bulldozer over there, which we had to call in to level the ground because your art director changed the angle of the third shot. There's the helicopter for this afternoon. There's the extra casting and wardrobe. The model-maker for the miniature of the canyon—"

"Talk to Daria, will you?" I say. It's never good to ruin your artistic relationships over budgets.

"Where's Jed?"

"With Cowboy Bob, learning a fast draw."

"Where's the choreographer?"

"With the dancers. We're ready to rehearse the showdown scene."

The cast and crew reconvene at the site of the big dance number. Music blasts over speakers, and the choreographer's assistants demonstrate the steps one last time. Everybody's been practicing in a rehearsal studio for the past three days, so they're already pretty good.

"And-one-and-two-and-three," yells the head assistant, a black man with a platinum-blond buzz cut, and thirty kids spin in unison across the dirt road.

Jed Durant takes his position at the head of the group, facing Cowboy Bob, and suddenly it's Hollywood, and, for about an hour, everything works exactly as it should. The same steps are repeated over and over and over, never as a whole sequence, but always in short stop-and-start spurts, as they will be filmed. And then it starts to rain. To pour, actually, and everyone runs for cover under the tents and in the trailers and cars as lightning streaks across the sky. Lance materializes a golf umbrella and whisks Simmons into the Mustang and away.

"Didn't anybody check with the weather bureau?" I ask Daria as we run for cover. I reach into my painter's satchel and pull out the fold-up poncho which I always take on shoots.

"Yes. They never mentioned rain. There's been a drought for two months. This must be a freak storm."

The freak storm continues for two hours, and all we can do is sit around in the trailer eating bad snacks.

Lester stomps in, dripping, in an Australian outback coat. "Do you want to call a rain day?" he asks.

I look at Juice. We both know that a rain day will cost the production fifty thousand dollars and will put us behind schedule.

"I can't believe a freak storm can last much longer," I say.

"It can't last much longer," agrees Lance.

Thunder rumbles across the valley, and the rain drums relentlessly on the roof of the trailer. Lester frowns. "There's lightning out there," he says. "With all this electronic equipment, we have a safety hazard now."

Juice yawns. Rain makes him sleepy. He ambles to the dressing-room area in the back of the trailer and curls up on the backup wardrobe.

At about three o'clock the freak storm begins to subside, and I actually see a rainbow. Everyone ventures cautiously outside. My sneakers are soggy and make squishing sounds as I step down into the mud.

That's when I see another limo pull up.

Bruce gets out.

What is he doing here?

Bruce never shows up on shoots, and at no point was the possibility of his presence on this one even mentioned. When the chief creative officer appears on location, it's usually a matter of dire emergency. What could be the problem? For about half a second I wonder if he's come to collect my time sheets.

"Aha! Cam!" he calls out. "Just the person I wanted to see." He stops and executes a make-believe golf putt.

"Bruce." I slog toward the limo. I wish Juice was with me.

Bruce waves me over, under the shelter of a tree. "Jesus Christ, Cam," he mutters. "What have you done?"

"What have *I* done?"

"This shoot." He gestures helplessly, as if indicating the explosion of the *Hindenburg*.

"Bruce. It rained. It was a freak storm. Actually, things are going very well. We're all very glad to see you, but you really didn't need to fly in."

"As it happens, I was planning to fly out for a little golf with Simmons. Just to calm him down, mind you."

"He was happy in New York. And he seemed happy an hour ago when he stopped by the set."

"Cam, you are misreading this situation. But be that as it may . . ." Bruce pulls a cigar out of his jacket pocket and clips off the end. "This delay is costing money. Until we get this brand and get it launched, it is a risk. Money I am not convinced was necessary to spend."

"Bruce, there was lightning. It was a safety hazard."

Bruce's eyebrows fuse together in a straight line, and his eyes glitter at me. "Cam, what are you doing here, giving birth to a glass bicycle? I didn't like the idea of this extravaganza to begin with."

"Bruce, we are launching a soft drink."

"I'm aware of what we are launching, but from the beginning this project has been out of control. And this only proves it."

I hope I can restrain myself from doing something stupid. I'm wet, bedraggled, and mad, but hell will freeze over before I'll let myself lose control. Bruce lights his cigar, and the wind carries the smoke into my face. "What, exactly, are your overages?"

"Well, Daria has them itemized."

"I want to see the budget, I want to see your overages, and, Cam, I want you to understand that it's not me, but . . ." He pauses to relight his cigar. "It's not me, you understand. It's just that Harold thinks I should be a presence on this shoot. And, frankly, I agree with him."

Bruce is telling me that he's going to take over the shoot. It's a big shoot, an important shoot to be associated with, and he wants the credit. Me—if there's any blame left to go around, I've been elected to get it.

I stand there speechless. All these months of work, leading to this, the masterpiece of my career, and I see it going down the drain before my eyes. I've always thought women who cried in business were spineless pieces of spaghetti, creatures to be pitied, but now I'm glad it's raining, because I'm sure there are tears on my cheeks. God, I hate this bullshit. But then, that's the point—it's not personal, it's politics, pure and simple. You can't fight politics unless you're political, and I'm not. I don't schmooze, I can't brown-nose. I've always believed that good work, hard work, wins out.

I was wrong.

Bruce whirls around. "Shit!" I hear him mutter, and he trips over something which I realize is Cream Puff, tethered to the other side of the tree.

"Yeaahhhoww! Goddammit! Aaauugggghhh!"

I blink the wetness from my eyes and there's Bruce doubled over, struggling and kicking wildly, and I see Cream Puff attached to his ankle, and there's kicking and screaming and growling and squealing and I'm frozen to the spot.

People come running from every direction. Women shriek. Somebody screams, "Pit bull! Pit bull!" The dog is pelted with rocks, sticks, and mud, poked with umbrellas, but nobody dares get too close.

Lester races up, yelling. "Cream Puff! Down! Down! Off! *Somebody get me a stick!*" He whacks at the dog with a cassette case, but it clings relentlessly to Bruce's leg, flipping into the air, all four paws off the ground, as he kicks and thrashes. Bruce grabs the dog's ears with his hands and desperately yanks at its head, but Cream Puff only moves his jaws up and down Bruce's lower leg as if he were sampling corn on the cob.

"Somebody call the police!" screams Daria.

By now three or four men are trying to pull the dog off Bruce's leg, and Bruce has fallen over into the mud and is writhing on the ground. A gaffer races up and jabs the dog with a microphone boom, but Cream Puff is Jaws incarnate.

"Stand back!" a commanding voice booms out, and

suddenly there's a shot, then a squeal, then silence, and I turn around just in time to see Cowboy Bob twirl his huge pearl-handled pistol once, then snap it back into its silver-studded holster.

"It was only a flesh wound," says Juice.

"You call forty stitches and the prospect of microsurgery a flesh wound?"

"I meant the dog."

I drag a comb through my hair, which is damp and snarly. My hand is shaking, my scalp is numb. I'd like to go back to the hotel, take a shower, pack, and go home, but I can't. I'm still the creative director, this is still my job, I still give a damn.

I'm sitting behind the wheel of the biggest RV, drumming my fingers on the console while Juice massages my shoulders. The ambulance has come and gone, Animal Control has come and gone, and we've gotten word that Bruce was released from the emergency room after they stitched up his leg, that he was rushed straight to the airport in a wheelchair and put on a flight to Chicago, where a neurosurgeon from Michael Reese is standing by.

"He's lucky he was only bitten by the *dog*," says Juice. "You and I could have done real damage."

"Shut up, Juice. I feel like shit."

"Yeah."

I'm not sure if I feel like shit because of what happened to Bruce or because of what happened to me. Bruce's leg will recover, but his feelings about me won't. If he was threatened before, or whatever craziness was in his mind, he'll hate me now. He's on some vendetta. It doesn't make sense, but it doesn't have to. He's the boss.

"Juice, you know Bruce was going to take over the shoot? That's why he came."

"He only thought he was going to take over. He's incapable of taking over. Even the dog sensed it."

I retie my shoelace, which is caked with mud. "Maybe I should just quit." I mean it, too. I really don't think I have the stomach for this business anymore. It's getting harder and harder to take it all in stride. I want the success, I like the work, but it's starting to beat me up. Maybe I'm burning out. Or not eating right. Maybe I'm getting too old. I'm not forty yet, but in this business, forty is old and fifty is almost nonexistent. Maybe I just don't have the stomach for it anymore—is that what I was trying to tell myself in Chicago?

It's time to put things in perspective. When the shoot is over, I'll have to think about what happens next: Timothy, L.A., job. When this job is over, I'll stop and reevaluate.

Juice stares at me incredulously. "Get a grip! This is the business. You know that. It's nothing. It'll blow over as soon as they see the film. Especially if it's good. And we know it will be."

We stare out the trailer window. Daria walks by and glances up at Juice with an interest that seems other than purely professional.

Outside, it's turning into a gorgeous pink-and-yellow sunset, and the rainbow is still there, shimmering over the hills.

"I wish we could get that on film," I say.

"Well," says Juice. "Why not?"

"Let's do it." Suddenly I'm fired up again, an idea is coursing through my bloodstream, and the adrenaline is running, fueling, blotting out the miserableness. Suddenly all I can think of is the film and how wonderful it will look, and how I'm going to turn this situation around.

In an instant we're up and out of the trailer. "Daria," yells Juice over his shoulder, adjusting his baseball cap. "Find Lester! Find Ramon!"

Daria yells back, "Lester is in a state of shock. They've got blankets around him."

"This'll fire him up," I say. I grab a megaphone from the food table and toss it to Juice. "Let's go shoot a rainbow!"

The thing about being on a shoot is, it's like a dream that happens when you're under anesthetic. You forget all the men that ever treated you like shit. You forget your boss—unless, of course, he or she shows up. You forget you are fifteen pounds overweight and three weeks overdue for a haircut. You forget the fact that there's a stack of bills six inches high at home and you forgot to buy stamps. You forget you have a family. Or friends. In fact, you forget everything except the scenes, the cuts, the music, the lyrics, the readings, the performances, the timings, the camera angles, the lighting, the angle of the sun, the length of the day. A commercial is only thirty seconds long, but that's exactly the point—you've got to compress so much into so little, it takes total concentration. You have to distill your awareness to fit.

So here's Bruce, deflected by fate and a pit bull, and I know I have my chance to pull an ace. Like I said, I'm not the political type. I'm not going to get involved in internal maneuvering and CYA memos. I don't have to. My work is good. No, not good— better than good, and from time to time, even great. The fact that Bruce showed up on the set, pulling rank—well, true, it upsets me, but I'm not going to let it kill me. The only thing that could really kill me is a bad commercial.

Juice and I are going to pull this one through with flying colors. Like we always do.

I locate Lester in his Land Rover. He's huddled up in a blanket, listening to classical music. I tap on the window.

"Lester? Can I come in?"

The door unlocks.

"Yo-Yo Ma," says Lester as I climb into the passenger seat.

"Of course."

We listen to the music in silence for a minute. A minute is about all we have. We're losing the sun.

"Lester," I say gently, "did you see *The Wizard of Oz*?"

"Ah, yes, Judy Garland."

"A classic, don't you think?"

"A classic. Certainly."

"Well, Lester, look up. Look at the sky. There's a rainbow up there, just like in *The Wizard of Oz*."

"Well! So there is." He stirs beneath the blankets.

"You know, Lester, we have the chance to shoot that rainbow, to use it."

"Where?"

"The dance sequence. Can't you just see it under a rainbow?"

"No. There was no rainbow in the storyboard I agreed to shoot."

Now I'm getting frustrated. "Lester, it's beautiful. It's gorgeous. It'll be your masterpiece."

"Cam, my darling. This is not and never will be a masterpiece, it is just and will always be only a fucking thirty-second commercial, can't you see that?

I have lost my dog, and I am not shooting any fucking rainbow."

"I see your point. You're upset. But this is a once-in-a-lifetime creative opportunity."

Lester closes his eyes.

"Can't we just try it? I think it could work."

Lester doesn't answer. I can't tell if he's thinking about his feature, his dog, or his Yo-Yo Ma tape. I decide to try another tactic. The light is fading fast, so I jump out of the car. "Wait here," I say. Unnecessarily, since Lester is displaying all the mobility of a paperweight.

When I look up, the rainbow is gone.

"Juice, the rainbow is gone."

"Yeah. I can see that."

Luckily, this is commercial, not real life. It doesn't matter if the rainbow is actually here or not, just as it won't matter that Marilyn Monroe is dead.

We can strip the rainbow in later, in opticals, as a special effect.

In fact, it'll probably look better that way.

The last thing we feel like doing after this shoot is laughing, which is exactly why Juice decides we should go to the Comedy Store. Besides, it's just across Sunset from our hotel.

"The word is, Robin Williams is going to try out some new material," says Juice as he leads the way to the front of the line. "Lester's people arranged guest passes."

"Before or after the dog?"

I'm feeling pretty glum. What I'd really like to do is see Timothy, but he left a message that he had a business meeting tonight. Which is why I'm surprised when I do see Timothy—ahead of us in the crowd, his arm around a woman in a white leather jacket, his face close to hers, blowing her bangs off her forehead.

Timothy always did have a very personal way of doing business.

I want to gag. I want to throw up. I want to stuff the amethyst bracelet down his lying, cheating, fuck-around throat, but I can't, I'm not wearing it.

Should I confront the bastard? What's the point? I feel like Charlie Brown after he's made his hundredth run at the football that always gets yanked out from under him. Well, at least I can count on this: love always lets me down. Actually, I should thank Timothy. He probably just saved me ten years of my life, not to mention my career. *God! What if I had quit today!* I am propelled by fury.

I walk up to him, stand there and stare until he looks my way. He blinks cautiously, his face impassive.

"This is Patricia. She owns the Malibu Gallery," he says.

"Hello, Patricia," I say. "Timothy and I used to be . . . like family."

Sunset Boulevard is a neon blur, and I spin on my heel and run into the crowd, the street, the night, anywhere the pain is a little farther away.

Chapter Ten

"Maybe we should get an agent." Juice is ten feet ahead of me, walking as fast as he can past the Santa Barbara Biltmore. Ever since he's gotten into race-walking, it's been hell keeping up with him.

"What?" I'm panting. A weekend in Santa Barbara is just what we need. We deserve it. We've earned it. We tell ourselves it's worth whatever it costs, and look the other way when they pound the plastic. But everything in California is always so . . . *physical*. Swimming, tennis, hiking—you never know what you'll get yourself into. Last time I was here, I ended up hunting wild boar on horseback.

"A packaging agent. Those guys who put together all the writers, directors, stars, and producers. For a cut, of course. Maybe we can get them to branch out into advertising." We speed past a multimillion-dollar oceanfront mansion.

"Or we could get into movies. A commercial is a thirty-second screenplay. All we have to do is expand on that."

I walk faster and catch up. I've never thought about writing screenplays.

"I know we could do it," says Juice. "We're from

the Midwest. The Midwest is very big out here. Johnny Carson is from the Midwest."

We serpentine past a botanical garden where a wedding is in progress. Through the trees I catch a glimpse of lavender dresses.

"Well, I'd get something to think about."

"The problem with you is, you think too much. Just do it. You have to open up. Go for it!"

We slow down and stop for a minute and I look out over the ocean, where the waves are lolling like cabochon aquamarine floats. The sky is a perfect crystal. Overhead, a man in a parasail glides by.

"Maybe you should get married," says Juice emphatically as he starts walking again. "That's the only way you'll get over that asshole."

"He didn't get over me when he got married."

"Yes he did. He got over you when he married you. You're the only one who doesn't see it. It's an obsession, and it's making you sick. Crazy. You're a human yo-yo. You're hyper. You've changed."

"Me?"

"No. The man in the moon. Eldridge Cleaver. Who the hell are we talking about? You know, you used to be a really nice person."

"I'm not nice anymore?"

"No. Look at you. You're cutthroat. You'd knife your own grandmother to get your own commercial shot."

"Oh, and you're Little Red Riding Hood."

"In a cape." He puts his sunglasses back on. "Seriously, Cam. You should back off a little. You'll live longer. Or at least I will."

"It hasn't been so bad, has it? You've done all right." I'm a little testy now. I don't like being told to back off; it's usually my cue to go for the throat.

"Yeah," says Juice, and he flips his sweater over his shoulder. "All right."

We jump over the curb and up onto the wide green lawn of the Santa Barbara Biltmore for one of our favorite West Coast rituals—guacamole. Dropping into the white wrought-iron chairs, we start in on the salsa.

"Juice, the fact is, it does bother me. You still paint, but I'm not sure I can even write anything but commercials anymore. I don't know what I'm doing now. We're kidding ourselves. We don't really create. We just . . . hype."

"Don't downgrade what you've done, Cam. Why do women always do that? Think about it. You're a vice-president of a major advertising company. You've won every award in your field."

"So have you."

"Yeah," he says, and I can't tell where he's looking because of the sunglasses. "But they're really your awards. You're the creative director. I'm just the wrist who puts it on paper."

"That's absurd. It doesn't even merit discussion."

"Well, Oprah never called *me*."

We stop to order the food.

"We have become our résumés," I say, and we both laugh, mostly because it's true.

"Timothy is moving to L.A."

This is the first time I've spoken his name since our twenty-four-hour reengagement. The amethyst seed-pearl bracelet is stuffed into my suitcase with my dirty socks. I'd like to stuff him in there with them, but what did I really expect? I've decided to blot him out of my life—pretend that he's dead. He died in a car crash, it was tragic. He fell off a cliff. Someone pushed him.

"He's probably wired to some chick already."

"An art dealer, I believe."

"Well, that explains everything," says Juice, licking the salt off his margarita.

I stand up and shade my eyes. Across the street, at the beach, two puppies are playing in the surf. I wish I were them.

"You know," I say, "the story of Timothy and me could be a movie."

"You're right," says Juice. "A horror movie. The guy who plays Michael in *Halloween* could play Timothy." He shrugs. "It would sell. More guacamole? Some nachos, maybe?"

"No, thanks. I think I'd like to walk on the beach. Slowly."

He waves me off. "Go ahead. I hate sand."

The tide is out, and the beach is wide as I zigzag along the sand. No shells. I'm always surprised there are never any shells in California. You sort of expect them.

I poke in the sand with a stick and uncover a half-buried dead seagull. The wind picks up, and I pass houses backed up to a tumble of broken-rock seawalls. I'm wondering if they'll fall into the ocean when the big earthquake comes when I see Jed Durant walking down the beach toward me. I wonder if Juice can see this. I'll never convince him it was a coincidence.

"Cam!" He says this as if he'd been looking for me for hours. "There's a comet tonight." He unfolds the newspaper he's carrying under his arm. "Sitwell's Comet. Comes into our solar system once every fifty years. This is the best place to watch it from. At three A.M., it says here."

"I'll probably be asleep."

"The world would still be flat if Galileo had thought like that."

"Well, good luck. Just don't overdo it, serenading the comet. We're going to need your voice in New York next week."

He rolls up the newspaper like a telescope and trains it on me. "You know, it was total madness on that set, what with the dog and all. I wanted to tell you I was really impressed at how you handled it."

God. If only he knew the truth. "Thanks."

We start walking together. People recognize Jed and stare at us, but nobody stops us. "You were terrific," I say. "The dance sequence is so hot. You should do more dancing in your movies."

He reaches out and grabs me, ballroom-style, and we tango across the sand, finishing off the move with a dip so low my hair brushes the seaweed that's washed up on the beach.

"I could show you some lifts," he offers.

"That's okay."

"Some Dirty Dancing?"

"Really, that's okay."

"Your nose is running. You must be cold."

"No. I don't think so."

"Yes, you are. You're cold." He takes off his sweatshirt and slides it over my shoulders. A group of teenage girls point at us, and Jed gives them his heartthrob smile.

"What's it like?" I say.

He knows exactly what I mean. "It's my job. Those girls? They're my boss. They pay the bills." He waves at them.

"Don't you ever feel you want a private life, where you're not recognized?"

"Well, once I went to Tahiti and nobody knew me."

"How'd it feel?"

"Terrible."

We both laugh. At least he's honest.

"You know," he says, more softly now, "that boss of yours is an asshole."

He notices more than I realized.

"It's lucky he had to leave so . . . suddenly. I would have refused to work if he'd been hanging around all day. I can't stand guys with attitude."

"He's not so bad."

"Sure he is. Look, you're such a nice person. You went to so much trouble for Myra. Thanks."

We're not walking anymore and he's looking at me and, this is insane, but I feel like I'm being hustled by a teenager. Or maybe that's what he wants me to feel, his form of flattery.

"You're at the Biltmore?"

"Yes. Now, just how did you know that?"

He grins. "Myra knows all. Hey, can you name any constellations?"

"The Big Dipper."

"Good. You pass. Comet-watching starts at three A.M. I'll pick you up."

That's how, at three-thirty A.M., I am on the Montecito beach with binoculars, looking for a comet with a teenage heartthrob.

A faint speck appears on the horizon. "What's that?"

"An airplane."

"Oh." The sky is completely murky and foggy.

Jed lights a joint. I pass. I hate smoke of any sort.

We walk back to the car, and he hops onto the hood. "You look good in my sweatshirt."

That's the last thing I can remember him saying

before we end up kissing. First off, let me say, I have never had a romantic relationship with any man I worked with, much less with the *talent*, much less with teenage talent. Second, let me say that this is probably the least rational thing I have ever done in my life, second only to the time when I was three years old and stuck a hairpin into the electric socket to see if anything was in there. I suppose I could analyze why I'm alone on a beach comet-watching with Teen Angel, trot out my vulnerabilities and securities or lack of them, but let's say the atmosphere is more conducive to inspection than introspection.

I'm surprised at how thin he is. So slight, and barely muscled. His face is smooth and unweathered, his eyelids lush and fluttery against my cheek. He's soft, like a fresh, ripe peach, not really like a man at all. He doesn't have the musky scent, the coarseness, the roughness of the hands and lips.

But he does know how to kiss.

He exhales into the nape of my neck, and I'm responding.

We melt slowly to the sand and it's all over. His hands are inside my clothes and mine are inside his, and we don't even take our clothes off, not even our jackets. We burn right through them and make love there, dressed, in the open, on the beach, under a comet that threw a party and forgot to come.

Sunday: Somewhere in the pell-mell dash of hooves, helmets, and mallets is Jed Durant, but I'm not sure where. I'm not even sure which team he's on. All I know for sure is he's a three-goal polo player, because Myra Durant has just told me so. We're sitting on the bumper of Jed's silver Lamborghini LM002, a kind of six-figure racing jeep, watching the practice match. Behind us, Jed's bodyguard is taping the action on a video camera.

"Zoom in on his hands, Chris," says Myra Durant, focusing her binoculars.

"If he's going to ride better, he has to use the knees, not the hands." She watches intently. "We always do a replay after the game. It's educational. Then we compare with videos of the high goal players. I tell Jed, 'Always copy the best.' So we watch tapes of, say, the Argentina matches and he memorizes their techniques. That's when you realize just how much horsemanship you still have to learn."

She hands me the binoculars. "I decided Jed needed more exercise than he was getting at the discos," she says. "If you're going to control a thousand-pound horse going forty miles an hour, you can't drink and do drugs and stay out all night. Besides, it's a game that teaches you how to relate to people."

The Santa Barbara Polo Grounds are about fifteen minutes from the Biltmore, and when Myra called this morning, I have to admit I was a little queasy about the whole situation, but somehow Friday night's comet episode seems like a movie I saw several weeks ago—I can't remember the details, just that it was good. I wonder if Myra knows what's going on. Probably. As Jed says, Myra knows all.

"Great belly shot!" says Myra as Jed scores a goal, and we both clap and cheer. One thing I'll say for Myra, she doesn't seem to have a star complex—she's cheering for her kid like any mom, but of course, she's not just any mom.

"Fast game," I say. "What if he gets hurt?"

"Then he gets hurt. Neither of us is afraid of a little risk." She laughs. "When you think of it, our lives have always been a risk." She toys with her three-foot braid. "When I got pregnant, people couldn't believe I actually had the baby. You didn't do that then. Especially not at seventeen. My parents never spoke to me again."

"Pretty ironic."

"Let's visit the ponies."

We walk over to the stable area, where some horses are lined up in stalls, others being walked by grooms. Myra expertly checks the bandaged leg of one of her ponies. She's dressed entirely in white, but somehow she seems to repel dirt.

"You know, Myra," I say, right off the top of my head, because I have an idea right now, this minute, "wouldn't it be interesting if Zing! became a corporate polo sponsor? Jed could play on a celebrity team, and we could propose a TV special around it. The Zing! Polo Invitational."

"Interesting concept," she says, tapping her leg with a riding crop.

"It would let his fans see a new dimension of his personality. Plus it would showcase the commercials."

"*Very* interesting." Myra takes my arm, and we walk to a shady area. "I like the way you think," she says, "and so does my son."

I try not to squirm.

"How would this idea proceed?"

"I'd work up a presentation on it, run it past my management at the agency, then bounce it off the client. Of course, it would be very helpful if we could say we had your enthusiasm behind it." I'm loving this idea. It's a major promotional event, the kind sponsors love. Plus it's upscale, a good image for the brand. Plus it isn't golf! Brucie won't be the automatic expert, like he is with football, baseball, hockey, basketball, and every other sport. I'm positive he's never been on a horse in his life, except maybe to ride a merry-go-round with his kids. This is sounding better by the minute.

"We could bring in the best players in the world," I say, leaping aside to avoid a hoof on my foot. "Brazil, Chile, England, maybe even Prince Charles. Bring together first-rate people in a world-class performance. Stress excellence, vitality. Why not? There's precedent—Cadillac backed the hundred-thousand-dollar World Cup." I read this in a polo magazine Myra showed me.

Myra leads me behind the stables, where the Durants' Winnebago is parked. Inside is a pine-paneled, air-conditioned room with wine-colored paisley couches and chairs, old paisley shawls draped here and there, bookshelves, and brass bowls of fresh fruit. She pulls several books from the shelves and heaps them on the table. "We'll send you these," she says, "so you can read up. Polo is the world's oldest team sport, you know."

"Sure," I say. "Marco Polo." And she laughs. I really like Myra. She's fun and supportive, and you can work with her.

"Just one thing," she says as she hands me a cold bottle of Evian. "I've found, and perhaps you have too, that ideas like these can be, shall we say, less welcome, when they come from a woman."

I nod.

"I proposed the entire baby idea to the soap people when Jed was six months old, and they took his picture and tried to run it on all their packages with just a thank-you-very-much. I had to sue to get fair compensation."

"God."

"Well, we won the suit. And that money financed my son's career. But, if it would help, Jed and I will write you a letter thanking you for your suggestion. I'd hate it if certain people conveniently forgot where it came from. For your sake."

The woman is shrewd. "Thanks. I'm sure it'll work out."

Jed bounds into the trailer in a blue short-sleeved polo shirt with number four on it and tight white pants tucked into mahogany leather boots, carrying a bridle and helmet under his arm. He smiles and he seems disarmingly young, but his eyes have an edge today, a passion for courting danger that comes through and forces you to recognize the intense competitive spirit that has made him a star personality. After what went on between us, any other kid would be blushing and ducking, especially with his mother there.

Not this one. He comes close enough that I can smell the sweat, the heat; he knows it's sexy.

"So," he says. "You like horses?"

"I can ride. A little. I used to hunt."

He drops his bridle onto the table and forages in the refrigerator.

"Hunt? This is a piece of cake compared to steeplechasing. You can really crash and burn on those fences."

Myra smooths back the hair that has fallen over his eyes, and he smiles at her touch.

"Jeddie, you're going to love this. Cam is working up an idea for sponsoring an international polo tournament."

He drinks an entire bottle of water in one swig. "There's a lot of things that could happen with that," he says when he puts it down.

"Could Chris maybe tape a few minutes of you talking to the video camera, telling the soft-drink people how much you like the game, and how you'd look forward to a tournament sponsorship?"

I'm thinking of the presentation. A videotape would practically clinch the sale. If Jed could mention Simmons by name, it wouldn't hurt either.

"I'll go tell Chris," says Myra, and her braid bounces on her back as she goes out.

We're alone in the trailer.

"Hi," says Jed very, very softly.

"Hi."

"It's hard to look at you sitting in that dress."

"Why?"

"You know why."

I stand up, smoothing my skirt. "Isn't there going to be a lunch right about now? Something under those yellow-and-white awnings?"

"Yes." He picks up the bridle from the table, tosses the reins around my waist, and pulls me toward him. He drops his head to my shoulder.

"One thing about polo," he says, his voice so low I barely can hear it. "If you take it easy and stay rational, you have the advantage." He touches my collarbone.

I can feel him breathing onto my cheek, and the velveteen smoothness of his skin, and what I feel is anything but rational.

"Absolutely," I say.

VISUAL	AUDIO
1. OUT-OF-FOCUS, SLOW LONG SHOT OF COUPLE RUNNING TOWARD EACH OTHER ALONG THE EDGE OF THE GRAND CANYON.	MUSIC (Under): Theme song from *Chariots of Fire*.

VISUAL	AUDIO
2. THE WOMAN COMES INTO FOCUS. SHE HAS LONG WHITE DRESS AND MY FACE. SHE THROWS HER ARMS OUT TO MAN.	MUSIC swells. Voice-over: The perfect couple?
3. MAN COMES INTO FOCUS. HE IS JED DURANT. THEY FALL INTO EACH OTHER'S ARMS AND OVER THE EDGE OF THE CLIFF.	VOICE-OVER (cont'd): Why risk perfect love on a less-than-perfect choice?
ACTION FREEZES AND CUT TO AN 800 NUMBER.	Call Computer Companions. Operators are standing by.

Chapter Eleven

"Rainbow to go, coming right up. Pick a color, any color—pink, blue, purple, or yellow? Chartreuse, cerise, tangerine, or mauve? How about blue, green, silver, or peach?" David, the technician from the animation house, flips some switches and the colors toggle back and forth, like in a kaleidoscope.

Juice and I are back in New York, and for the past five hours we've been in an animation studio, which resembles a Gemini capsule, staring at a piece of electronic wizardry called the Paint Box, which has nothing whatsoever to do with paints. David is painting our rainbow into the scene with an electronic stylus, and then adjusting the exact shades on a board of toggles, dials, and switches. It's sort of a grown-up version of an Etch-a-Sketch. Thanks to the miracle of modern technology, we can add rainbows wherever and whenever we want.

The dailies are in, and they're spectacular. The product looks heroic, the footage is beautiful, the showdown scene is incredible. Lester pulled through for us, in spite of his depression, although he did launch an ASPCA investigation against the agency for cruelty to animals. We are countering with a PR blitz about the condor, which, as an endangered species, got the VIP treatment from the agency. I personally overcame my fear of helicopters and rode with the pilot and the trainer, and I want to say for the record that things turned out a lot better than the famous condor shoot for an automobile which shall go unnamed. The condor was supposed to swoop low over the car. The pilot took off with the handler and the director as the car streaked across the desert below. The condor had a forty-foot wing-span, so they taped the wings to its body. When the director yelled, "Cue the condor!" they pushed it out of the helicopter, whereupon it crashed to the earth like a stone, the crew having forgotten to untape its wings. *Our* condor swooped right on cue.

Of course, the film is in preliminary pieces now. We only have a rough edit, but the skeleton of the commercial is emerging. Our storyboard is coming to life in front of us.

Juice tosses a copy of *Ad Age* into my lap. "Check out that headline," he says. " 'Trans-Corp Agency Shift Rumored for $75 Million Spirit Account.' It doesn't surprise me. Those pencilheads deserve to lose it."

"Hm, we may have that shot sooner than we thought."

"Maybe that's why Bruce was so uptight."

"Don't make excuses for him. He was an animal." We're squinting at four monitors while we talk. "What do you think—the red too hot?"

"Yeah. David, tone it down. But it makes sense. A show of force in front of the client. Don't take it personally."

"Oh, I don't. But I'm really getting sick of these antics. David, watch the cyan."

"He got his just deserts."

"Yeah, and as usual, he's turning the tide in his favor. How much is he suing the production company for? Five hundred thousand? Plus he'll get workmen's comp."

"Look at it this way. They didn't put the dog to sleep, and Lester is countersuing,"

"It wasn't even the dog's fault. Bruce kicked it."

"Tripped on it."

"Whatever."

I move over to a light and skim through the *Ad Age* article and my blood curdles. "Listen to this, Juice. The Koala account isn't the only thing that's up for grabs. They're saying the Spirit account is going to be thrown into the review. The speculation is that Trans-Corp, the parent company, has decided to consolidate the agencies and give all the business to one shop. A grand slam! I wonder why Bruce didn't tell us this. He and Harold must have known."

We're silent for a minute. The thought that a million dollars' worth of work on Zing! might have been a total washout is sobering. Not to succeed is one thing. Not to have a chance to fail is worse. On the other hand, an agency review puts the free-for-all for Spirit out in the open, and if the Zing! campaign turns out as well as we think it will, we'll have the edge coming out of the gate. For a change, I wish I were back in the office, because that's where you hear all the scuttlebutt.

Up on the monitors, Jed Durant is strutting across the screen. "What do you think of Jed Durant?" says Juice, and I jump out of my seat.

"Why?"

"Relax, will you? You're a nervous wreck."

I'm wondering if Juice can sense anything here—

he's usually pretty intuitive. "Jed Durant is a very talented guy," I say. "As a dancer and singer."

Juice peers at the video monitor. "I'm glad that's how you feel," he says, "considering." He hands me a folded tabloid, and I open it and see my picture staring back at me from the front of a supermarket sleaze rag. Oh, my God! It's a picture of Jed and me coming out of the ice-cream place in Westwood. The caption says, "Heartthrob Jed Durant Linked to Mystery Woman."

"So how does it feel to be a mystery?" says Juice. A little too smugly, I'd say.

I crumple the paper up and throw it in the trash. "This is pure sleaze," I say. "Me, a mystery woman. A mystery anything. That's a laugh. Well, what can you expect, coming from a journalistic vehicle that reports Elvis is alive and Martian test-tube births?"

"Yeah," says Juice, squinting at the screen. "Is this getting too red?"

"Yes."

"Out robbing the cradle when I wasn't looking," says Juice. "I can't say I'm totally surprised, though. I did see you together. There was definitely something there—puppy love, maybe?"

"Oh, give me a break! The kid is a baby! An infant! I was just buying him an ice-cream cone. That's what you do with kids."

"That's it?"

"Well, I did meet him at a polo match. His mother was there. It was business entertaining. For God's sake, Juice! Men play golf with clients and business associates all the time. Why shouldn't I be able to eat ice cream and go to a polo match?"

"Horsies, ice-cream cones. Next thing we know

you'll be throwing him a birthday party with pin the tail on the donkey. Or maybe spin the bottle."

Should I tell Juice the truth? We usually tell each other everything, but lately, things have been so nuts that we haven't really had a chance to really get into anything. In a way, I feel like talking, but what would I say? No matter how I phrased it, he'd never understand that it was just a diversion, something fun and not sordid, just a lollipop. Of course, Juice knows me too well. Which means he's probably figured it all out on his own already anyhow, and he's a man, so it goes without saying that he's applied the double standard. Should I take a chance and try to explain things to him? I decided it's too risky. It's never good to spill your guts. "Listen, Juice," I say. "Relax. Really. It's under control. Listen, I sent Simmons a framed glossy of his picture with Cowboy Bob, plus a copy of the Ten Commandments of the Old West."

"He'll love it."

"Yeah, he's our friend." It's amazing how when a client's happy, all the problems in the world disappear. Simmons sent out a letter after New York, commending our attitude. A good sign.

"Okay, guys," I say. "You've got it under control. I have to split. The music session starts in fifteen minutes."

In the cab downtown, I pull out my miniature makeup kit for a touch-up. I use the two-hundred-dollar set of silver-handled sable brushes I always carry in my satchel so it looks natural, the way I was taught by Morgan Fairchild's makeup artist. The blusher brings out my cheekbones, but no way does it make me look fifteen years younger.

What I had almost told Juice was the fact that I

have seen Jed Durant socially exactly four times—that first time in Santa Barbara, then after the dailies in L.A., after his concert at the Hollywood Bowl, and at Helena's, where he ditched his girlfriend the soap star and his bodyguard and we went off to the Westwood ice-cream place, where somebody snapped a flash picture, but it was just a kid with an Instamatic. Now a *rich* kid with an Instamatic.

Until now, I'd been kind of proud of myself. I'm putting Timothy behind me and I'm finally doing it—shaking up my life, making a change. Okay, so it is not a change that is in the unquestionably best of taste, but in the global scheme of things, we are not talking about a capital offense—he's single, I'm single. If he weren't on the cover of *Teen Beat*, I could almost see it. He's a very nice person. A *young* person, true—but nice. A step in the right direction.

I get to the recording session just as the musicians are filing in. Sam, the jingle composer, is there in charge, sprung from his stint in the hospital.

"Sam, I'm sorry we had to bother you while you were sick. I hope it wasn't serious."

"Ulcers," he says. "I gotta watch what I eat. Thanks for the flowers." He combs his fingers through his beard and I notice he's wearing a camp shirt that has MUSIC ANIMALS and a howling wolf embroidered on the pocket.

"But, hey, no problem. We just went back into the studio, tweaked this and thwacked that, and it sounds great. Listen, do you want Durant to sing to picture?"

"Do we have a monitor out there?" I tap on the soundproof glass wall that separates the technical booth from the studio, which is huge, red-carpeted, dominated by a grand piano, banks of mammoth ceiling-mounted speakers for playback, a small fleet of music stands and folding chairs, a couple dozen microphones, and a drum kit.

"I'll call for a monitor," says Sam, picking up the intercom phone. "We'll have it when he gets here."

We don't expect Jed until after the music tracks have been laid down and roughly mixed. At the shoot, we worked with a temporary track, but now this is the real thing, and we've booked some of the best studio musicians in New York. For the most part, they back up the big rock and recording stars, or play in classical orchestras. Except for the drummer, everybody brings their own instruments. A young woman drags in a huge harp case on rollers, followed by a flock of men carrying violin cases, a drummer with a rolled-up case of drumsticks, and several people with trumpets, tubas, and electric guitars. There's a little small talk, but not much. Studio time is a thousand dollars an hour, and nobody wants to waste it.

Sam greets his players and goes into the studio to pass out Xerox copies of the sheet music, while the engineer plays the temporary track for everybody. Meanwhile, he's still setting up the mixing board, which makes the Paint Box look like a Tinker Toy. God knows how many tracks, sweetenings, and mults we're dealing with here. Everything is computerized, so sound levels can be measured and matched to the slightest fraction of a decibel.

My feet are killing me, and I pull off my new Susan Bennis Warren Edwards shoes. These shoes cost me the equivalent of a week's vacation in Capri, but in New York you have to look put together. My entire L.A. wardrobe does not apply here, which is why I had to divert through Chicago on my way from L.A. to pack another suitcase. Even though the leaves have barely fallen off the trees, a mink coat is appropriate, preferably fingertip-length, and not too flashy, exactly the type of coat I bought last spring with my Christmas bonus. As for the rest of your body, anything Armani or Versace will do. My Upper East Side friend Marissa, who is elegant, solves the problem by wearing black at all times. Last time we had tea at the Mayfair Regent, she saw my spangled shoes from Maxfield Blue in L.A. and diverted her eyes, which is the Upper East Side version of a gag.

"Cam, phone on line three," says Sam.

It's Bruce.

"Cam, there you are."

"Hi, Bruce. How are you feeling?" We're both very polite, knowing how much is at stake. It's never good to hold a grudge in advertising. I'm not so naive as to think that this confrontation is over, but a marriage of convenience has been made, and I'm trying to go more than halfway on this. I even agreed to testify for Bruce if the Cream Puff case ever comes to court.

"They took out the stitches yesterday. I'm fit as a fiddle. Should be jogging in a week. Is the session happening now?"

"Yes. Durant is due soon for his vocals."

"Well, you may as well go ahead then and put him down."

"Why wouldn't I put him down?"

"There's been some thought around here of holding off, but I'll just tell them you're already in the studio."

"Who is 'they'?" The theme from *The Twilight Zone* rings in my ears, but I remain calm.

Bruce is vague. "Oh, you know. Feedback."

"We're going to finish this commercial, aren't we?"

"Well, that all depends."

"Bruce, help me out here. Who, exactly, has a problem with this?"

"Well, Simmons is not one hundred percent at this time."

"Where is Simmons? Maybe I should talk to him."

"In New York for a bottlers' convention. We can't reach him. So we'll operate on a best-guess basis for the time being."

I can almost see Bruce light a cigar.

"And your best guess is he's still not behind this campaign?"

"I didn't say that."

Sam signals to me from his seat at the console. "Let's go," he mouths.

"Bruce, I'll tell you what. Until I hear definitely otherwise, Juice and I are going to proceed on schedule. You know how the shifting sands operate."

"When can I tell Harold you'll be back in the agency? We have things to sit down and discuss face-to-face."

I'm thinking: *Can't we be pen pals?* But I say, "I should be back in a week, when this animation is finished. It's looking very good. But, Bruce, what's this in *Ad Age* about consolidating Koala and Spirit under one agency?"

His voice tenses up. "If the press calls you, your answer is 'No comment.' That is the agency position."

"But is it true? Do we have a leg up?"

"Who knows? The dust is still settling. By the way, did my lawyer call you about the deposition? They can do it over the phone. You have to testify that the dog was foaming at the mouth."

The dog wasn't foaming at the mouth, Bruce. You were

foaming at the mouth. But I'll do what I have to do as long as they don't put the dog to sleep. Anyhow, I'm sure that'll never happen. Lester has probably already taken it somewhere across state lines.

"I'm going to send Farfl to Pit Bull Heaven," Bruce says.

"You do that. Talk to you later, Bruce. The meter's running here."

For the next three hours I am happy to lose track of time while we lay down the tracks—first the percussion, then the strings, then the brass, the winds, and the synth.

We're in the middle of a rough mix, and I'm settling in with a bottle of Perrier, when Jed and his entourage arrive.

First, there's Chris, the bodyguard. Then a secretary with a tape recorder, making sure that Jed is not misquoted in the future. There's a guy in a T-shirt and leather bomber jacket carrying a case containing ten different varieties of water—Perrier, San Pellegrino, Volvic, you name it. This is not so unusual. I heard that George Harrison has seventeen kinds of water on the rider for his recording sessions.

Lawrence, the manager from L.A., and the gorgeous redhead who is referred to as "Mindy, Jed's trainer," file in. Also along for the ride is Jed's girlfriend, Tracy, the Soap Star.

"I'm so pleased to meet you," she says, extending a tiny white teenage hand. "Jeddie has told me so much about you. He really admires you, you know. You're like a mother to him, I think." She flips off her red shearling coat.

"Well, great," I say. Just great. "I've always wanted to be a mother."

154

Jed is friendly but completely businesslike, introducing himself to the engineer and to Sam, kissing me Hollywood-style on the cheek, and there's no way to tell what he's thinking behind his mirrored sunglasses. His T-shirt is rumpled beneath a red coat, the type you wear if you are riding to hounds. He grins and flashes the lapels, and I wish I could think of him as a trinket, a toy, but, actually, it's impossible not to genuinely like the guy.

"This coat belonged to King Edward. Myra got it at an auction in London. Check out the buttons. They're regimental."

That's the extent of any personal conversation, which is absolutely fine with me right now.

The entourage scatters around the room, which is, luckily, the biggest studio in the place, and Sam, Jed, and I huddle over the lead sheet, which has the lyrics and parts written out. Normally, a lot of very specific instructions would be given, but since Jed is a star, Sam just says, "Do what feels good to you."

Chris puts his feet up on the couch and disappears behind a copy of *The Hollywood Reporter*.

The intercom buzzes. "Cam, phone on line three."

"Hello, Cam," says the silky voice of Myra Durant. "I hope things are going well in the studio."

"Actually, we're just getting started, Myra."

"Well, I don't want to disturb you. I just thought we might get together while we're both in town. Say, tea tomorrow at the Palm Court?"

I know a command appearance when I hear one. "Four o'clock," I say.

"Perfect. It'll be fun."

I really like Myra Durant. If the circumstances were different, I'd actually look forward to having tea with her. But that's not something to dwell on now. Right now I have to finish this music track, and it has to be so phenomenal it wins a Clio this spring. Assuming I'm around to collect the Clio. Assuming we get the account.

It's impossible to think with these giant speakers blasting into my eardrums. So instead I psych myself to listen to Jed Durant sing the word Zing! in his trademark stutter voice forty-seven times, just for starters.

This is a purely professional session. I have no plans to meet or otherwise come in contact with Jed Durant again.

None.

Twelve hours later: Jed and I are walking down Madison Avenue, checking out the locked and grated store windows. By daylight, this street glitters like a brilliant-cut jewel, the windows teeming to overload with an expensive assault of luxurious fabrics, designer clothes, buttercream rainbow leathers, and gemstones the size of idol's eyes, but after hours it seems gray and vacant. A smattering of people, a few cabs and cars—that's about it. It's like the street is in hibernation till shopping hours begin again. There's not much to see, but we're walking off the energy that's left over from the recording session. You'd think we'd be drained after eight hours in the recording studio, but sessions always key you up, no matter how long they run.

The Teen Queen left early for an interview, and Jed and I ended up eating dinner with the entourage at the Lone Star Café Roadhouse on West Fifty-second, where the personal trainer frowned at us over a salad while we put away enough smoked ribs, fried chicken, and chicken-fried steaks to send the entire state of Texas into a cholesterol coma. A music group came on at eleven-thirty, and Jed and I sort of slipped out between numbers. We just wanted to talk, which is why we didn't go back to my room at the Carlyle. Jed and Myra have a triplex over Tower Records on Broadway, next door to Cher's, but we didn't especially want to go there either, since we wanted to be alone, but we didn't want to be *alone*.

"Are you planning to go to college?" I say.

"Not really. I learn more from being around people who know things. Like you."

"Me! What do I know?"

"You're a doer. Like my mother. You know how to turn things into opportunities. I'm not good at that. I just sing. If it weren't for Myra, I'd be singing to myself in the shower."

It must be close to zero out. I pull my mink coat tight around me. It's Umber Dusk, all female pelts. I remember the day I bought this coat—the first and only fur coat I will probably ever own. Of course, I don't believe in killing animals without purpose, but after all, minks are just rats in expensive coats, and besides, there was a major psychological purpose. It felt good paying for it myself, even if I did have a five-figure American Express bill the next month. The day I paid for the coat was the day I realized no white knight was going to come along and make things happen for me, as in unfurling apartments and cars and furs at my feet. I was going to have to do it for myself. That was going to be the way it was. And I realized something: it was okay to do that. It was even okay to pamper myself. Once I gave myself permission, every time I put on this coat, it makes me feel even warmer.

"When do they see the finished commercial?" Jed asks, and he hums a little phrase from the music.

"A few weeks—we'll actually have a rough cut now, but we want to wait till everything's tied up and all the effects are in. People expect a lot when it comes to TV these days. We want them to be knocked out."

"They will be."

We walk for a few minutes. Then Jed says, "What if something happens and they don't go for it?"

"You'll still be paid."

"No—what about you? And Juice? And everybody who worked on the spot?"

"We'll survive. We just won't get the account."

Jed frowns, and a little wrinkle appears on his forehead, probably the first one ever. "It seems like pretty serious cash to spend if nothing happens."

"Yes, it does. Very serious."

He shrugs. "I'm glad I'm not in your business. All I have to do is sell records."

"All I have to do is sell products," I say. "That's all there is to it. The selling."

"I'd rather let somebody else sell," he says. "I just want to sing."

"I just want to write."

He looks surprised. "Did you write this commercial? I thought there were writers."

"I wrote it. Sometimes I don't, but this time I did."

"You're a writer?"

"Well, I guess I am. About ten percent of the time, actually. The rest of the time I present work, or go to meetings, or go on shoots or recording sessions."

Jed nods. "Oh. Like a producer."

"Sort of." Nobody ever understands what a creative director does.

"If you like to write, you should write," he says.

I'm a little startled to hear it put so bluntly. Of course, he's right, but he can afford to be a purist. When I was in school, I thought the same way. If the aptitude test said you'd make a good forest ranger, that's what you decided to be. Period. If you got A's in English, you were a writer or an English teacher. It was black and white, even if you weren't a child star. It's pointless to discuss careers with an eighteen-year-old self-made multimillionaire teen idol. I change the subject.

Jed starts telling me what it's like growing up without a father, and I know exactly what he's saying.

"You know," he says, "growing up without a father—well, it's not easy."

"I know." And I do.

"I never had any men I could relate to. Myra had lots of men friends and boyfriends, don't get me wrong, but it's not the same."

"I never knew my father either."

He puts his arm around me, and we walk silently, contemplating whether this genuinely gives us something in common.

"I have a picture my father's family sent me, when they told me he was dead. A picture of me that was his. That's all I have," I say. "For a long time I thought my ex-husband looked like my father, and that's why my mother hated him. Then one day I figured it out. Saw it in her eyes. *I* look like my father. It's him she sees when she looks at me. That's why she's always running from me, I think. Because she's still running from him. And so"—I try to flip my hair back and sound undeserving of sympathy—"I lost them both."

"I only have Myra, but she's great," Jed says. "There's nobody like her. She kept us together. She kept us from starving just by using her wits. She never talks about my father."

"Do you know who he is?" We stop at a jewelry store to admire the weirdness of those headless velvet neck things from which the jewels have been stripped for the evening.

"Yes," says Jed, and that's all he volunteers. "But it doesn't matter."

"Is he still alive?"

"Yes." Then silence.

That rules out John Lennon.

"I didn't know my father at all. Then I found out he was dead. I wonder if it would have made a difference if he were alive. Would I have gone to him? Would I have loved him or hated him?"

"It doesn't matter," says Jed. "The people who matter are the people who are there for you. Whether or not you're related."

I'm wondering how I can relate so well to a teenager, talk to him about things Timothy never began to want to hear. And I realize at the same time that it really doesn't matter to Jed if I'm five or ten or fifteen years older than he is, or more. He likes that. It reminds him of Myra. The Soap Opera Queen was right. It hits me that this could probably become something if I'd let it, because it's sort of permissible incest.

I'm just putting this together in my head when I feel something in my back.

A gun!

"Got a wallet?" says a man's voice from behind some trashcans.

Jed turns around and freezes. "I don't have any money on me, buddy," he says. Jed's eyes are flickering up and down the street, but it's deserted. Not even an off-duty cab. I'm thinking: *Good God, why didn't I get this kid home and off the streets? This is all my fault. They're going to kill me, they're going to kill him, and it's all my fault.*

I can't see the robber because he's directly behind me, but I can sense that he's large. I try to stay calm.

"Take my purse. It's Chanel." Do New York muggers read *Women's Wear Daily?* I feel the chain yank off my shoulder, so I guess they do.

"I'll take this too," says the voice, and he grabs my coat by the collar. With one tug, it's gone, he's gone, and I hear his footsteps and I realize it's over.

Jed starts to chase the mugger and I grab him. "Come back here! He might be crazy, or a crack addict. Let's just get out of here before he comes back."

A cab cruises by and I push Jed into it. He's shivering and crying, "Oh, my God . . . oh, my God." But at least he still has his wallet.

In my room in the Carlyle, I sit on the bed, and Jed paces around, hitting his fist into his palm, but his voice is like a wounded kitten's.

"He could have killed you, and what good was I?"

"You did exactly the right thing, which was nothing. These types are lunatics. Drugged out. You can't control them."

"I was worthless."

I'm wondering if we call the police if it will get into the papers. I'm wondering if we don't file a report, will my insurance be good. I'm thanking my lucky stars that the mugger didn't recognize Jed and kidnap him for ransom.

Jed is shivering, so I tug a blanket off the bed and wrap him in it. He looks up at me with huge eyes and he's no longer a lover or a teen idol, he's a scared kid. I can never see him as a lover again. "It's okay," I whisper, smoothing his hair. "It was just a coat."

"And a purse. And they could have killed you. They could have shot me in the face. Oh, God."

"It's okay," I say over and over, until he sits down on the bed and then lies down and then falls asleep.

The blackout shades are down, the heavy curtains are pulled, the walls are padded with chocolate-colored fabric, and it feels like a flotation tank on the European plan.

This is not good. What if it got in the papers? What if Bruce got hold of it? Or Myra? As soon as light dawns, I'll get Jed out of here. Then I'll call the concierge and file a police report, without mentioning Jed. Then there are my credit cards—I'll have to cancel all of them before the robber has a chance to send his wife to Bloomingdale's or the Mercedes dealership. I'll have to borrow money from Juice. I'll have to call my insurance agent. His number's in . . .

My Filofax! This is the ugliest loss of all. I have a card in the front with my name and address, but I doubt the robber will use it. This is terrible, worse than the mink. Without my Filofax I feel helpless, stripped.

I get up, go into the marble bathroom, fill the tub, pull off my clothes, turn on the Jacuzzi, run a vent brush through my hair. I look like hell, but so what. You're supposed to look like hell when you've just been mugged.

I put on the white terry-cloth robe with the Carlyle monogram and tiptoe back into the bedroom.

Some message envelopes are on the floor, probably from yesterday.

Juice: Call him.

Bruce: No message.

Laurie: No message.

Marissa: Can I have dinner tonight.

Myra Durant: Confirming tea at the Palm Court at four o'clock Thursday. Today.

Her son is on my bed, shivering in his sleep. I pull the comforter up around him, tucking him in ever so gently, like a baby, lie down on top of the bed beside him, and turn out the light.

"Tea bags," says Myra Durant, wrinkling her beautiful nose. "You'd think the Palm Court, at least, would know how to serve a proper tea."

"You'd think," I say.

Myra is not doing anything but pouring tea, but half the room is staring at her, mesmerized. Her hair is down, shimmering over the pink-flowered back of the green velvet chair, almost touching the carpet. There is not one split end. I make a note to ask her what kind of conditioner she uses. She's wearing black suede pants, a heavy Bulgari gold chain around her throat, crocodile loafers, and a black vintage Chanel jacket looped with gold chains and medallions. Her nails are short, unpolished, and buffed, and I feel out of it in my dress, even if it is Ungaro.

On the chair beside her are three huge shopping bags. "I like to get my Christmas shopping done early," she says. "You'll have to tell me where you shop." She smiles, and I see Jed in her face.

I'm not hungry, but I order strawberries, just because the bright red fruit in the crystal bowl caught my eye when we came into the room.

"Now," says Myra. "I'll get straight to the point, so we can get the boring business matters out of the way and enjoy ourselves, because, you know, Cam, I like you. And my son likes you." She stirs honey into her tea. "And when my son likes someone, he's very open and friendly. Sometimes too open and friendly. He hasn't learned that balance yet."

My foot twitches under the table.

Myra leans over the table toward me and tosses the supermarket rag on the table. "You and Jed are seen together and photographed, people will get the wrong impression."

"Myra, I—"

She holds up a hand. "Not me, not our people, *your* people. That picture was unfortunate. It's not that it's not good for Jed—it's not good for *you*. Cam, as a friend I'm telling you, because I've been there. Don't give people . . . ammunition. They tend to use it against you." She stirs honey into her tea. "You're a bright lady, Cam, but if you don't mind a little professional advice, you're not political."

I find myself listening, not because Myra is Jed's mother. She's a woman who's turned disadvantages I didn't know existed into advantages. She pulled herself together and pulled her son along with her, and she managed along the way to keep her little family intact. I wish I could say as much. She has a child who loves her.

"We both have something at stake here," Myra says, and her eyes level me. "I'm telling you to stay away from my son."

"Myra, this was harmless." And over. It was just a piece of bubble gum that left a sweet, sweet taste.

"I'm telling you again. It's no good. For you. And I know you hear me."

I sigh. "Myra, just don't get the wrong impression—"

"Impressions count, haven't you figured that out?"

"Well . . ."

"Jed's image, for instance. What is it but an impression?" She sets her jaw and frowns. "You and I know that Jed is just a teenage boy, maybe not like all the others, more special, but still very human and very much a child."

I gulp.

"But I have spent ten years making sure the world at large sees something larger than life, and Jed has worked hard with me. We've created the Jed Durant that's onscreen and on records."

"A perceptual franchise."

"What?"

"Say, like Marlboro Country. An image that's created from what's really nothing that comes to stand for something in a category."

Myra nods, and her hair swings. "Yes, that's it exactly. Jed Durant stands for certain things—values. Good, clean values." She folds her hands on the marble table in front of her. "I intend to keep it that way, so we can't have any, shall we say, misperceptions. That's one issue."

"Of course."

"I like you, Cam, as I said. Don't misunderstand me. This is not personal. But don't set yourself up. You're playing with the big boys now, and they hit below the belt. They specialize in it. I'm sorry if I'm not mincing words here, but I consider us friends, and I'm telling you as a friend."

The violinists launch into "As Time Goes By."

"For now, for our mutual best interest, I am just going to suggest one thing: you are not to see my son alone on a social basis." She stirs her tea. "I don't think we need to discuss it, do you?"

"No, Myra. We don't need to discuss it." I should tell this woman that I got her son held up at gunpoint and he's in my bed at this moment.

"Good. Waiter? Can I have some more hot water?" She flashes me the whitest smile in the world. "Now, where do you do your Christmas shopping?"

Myra's right. Of course, I knew it all along. I keep asking myself why I got involved with Jed. I didn't even question it—I just plunged in. I suppose I was on the rebound, but why I couldn't have rebounded into the arms of a noncelebrity of voting age is a question unworthy of Socratic reasoning. I think the thing is sometimes I forget how old I am. I really do. From thirty-three to thirty-six, I was never clear on my exact age. My thirties seemed to blend together in a big beige blur, whereas every month of my twenties separated out like a freeze-frame. I guess that's why they call your thirties mid-life. It's just mid. That's all it is. The problem is, I don't *feel* any different from when I was nineteen. I'm still excited to get up in the morning, go out and get something done. I still want to make my mark. I still don't think I've made it yet. The problem as I see it is, success is a cloud in the sky. You look at it and you're absolutely positive it looks like one certain thing, but if you stare at it long enough, it changes shape. I'm not sure anymore what the hell it is I'm looking at.

As I'm heading up the elevator in the Carlyle, and back down the hall, I decide to leave Jed a note.

It's still dark as a tomb in the room. Jed is still a body on the bed. I stuff things into my suitcases and zip them up as quietly as possible, but I hear a stirring in the sheets. Then Jed sits bolt upright and snaps on the lamp.

"Where are you going?"

"I'm changing rooms."

"Why? You already have a room."

"True. But you're in it and I didn't want to wake you up."

"I am up. What's going on?"

He rubs his eyes and I notice he's even better-looking when he's rumpled like this. His eyelashes seem tangled, caught on each other. You want to comb them for him. "Let's order some food," he says.

I sit down on the side of the bed. "Jed, I have to get going. I just saw Myra."

That wakes him up.

"She's worried about you, Jed."

"God, she never lets me out of her sight." He pulls the sheet over his head. "I'm a prisoner."

"Come on. You go everywhere you want. But let's face it, you're not just a normal high-school kid." I yank off the sheet. "The point is, you've got to get going. And so do I."

"Yeah," he says, leaning over, and he kisses my cheek. He gets the picture.

I stroke his hair, like you'd pat a baby's head. He looks about thirteen years old, and I just want to protect him. "You were brave last night."

"So were you."

I know that now Jed's going to disappear back into the superstratosphere. Next time we see each other, he'll be on the cover of *People* and I'll be reading about it from afar. Very far.

Chapter Twelve

Marissa said it was necessary to go to this party at the Whitney. It's a benefit for AIDS, and she and Etienne are going, of course, and also an old friend of Etienne's from Le Rosey they want me to meet. My eyes are bloodshot even after two doses of drops, and I don't feel like going, especially after last night and then today's little tête-à-tête at the Palm Court. But they did send their car for me. Besides, I need a change of scenery.

So I'm riding along in the back of this limousine, hoping my black leather miniskirt and beaded thirties sweater set and rhinestone clips will look okay. Of course, I don't have my mink coat, but I've wrapped myself up in Jed's big cashmere muffler, which he left so I wouldn't freeze to death.

The Whitney is decked out in a Fourth of July motif. The theme of the party is "Independence from AIDS," so the place is slathered in red, white, and blue. A guy dressed like Uncle Sam on stilts greets you at the door and hands you a red-white-and-blue cardboard tiara if you're a female, a red-white-and-blue straw boater otherwise. I make my way downstairs. Red-white-and-blue paisley tablecloths, and the pillars are wrapped in red ribbons. On every round table, and there are lots of them, are flag-wrapped flowerpots with real apples, dried flowers, and flags. I scan the horizon for Marissa and Etienne and finally spot them against the back wall, in front of these giant paintings of Chairman Mao, which are artistically alternated with paintings of the electric chair.

"Cammie, we were wondering what happened to you!" Marissa, in her perfectly cut black, is fanning herself with her tiara. Her poreless skin has a slightly violet cast. Etienne always looks the same—like a banker, which he is—except for the curls tumbling down his forehead. With their curly jet hair and blackberry-currant eyes, the two of them look like brother and sister, which they're not; they've just gone through that transition that happens to people when they've been together for so long they start to look alike.

Etienne is French, from an old family with estates and vineyards and an investment firm in Paris, Switzerland, and Hong Kong. He's involved in international currencies, which gives him an aura of intrigue that matches his limousine with the blacked-out windows and the tinted glasses he wears indoors and out. The Mole would kill to be this guy. Marissa looks like a fashion designer, or maybe a decorator of the minimalist school; she's a comedy director, and she's directed two or three TV comedy series, including the hit sixties show *Hula Hoop*, but when you talk to her, she's serious beyond belief. You can tell her the funniest story or the best joke and she'll stare straight at you without cracking a smile and say, "That's funny." If it's really hysterical, she'll go all-out and say, "That's really *very* funny." To Marissa, life is a backdrop for a series of cold openings and blackout sketches; she can see humor in anything; she just doesn't laugh at it.

The thing about Marissa is that she works as hard as I do, maybe harder. She just doesn't show it. She's totally seamless, and I've always wondered how she does it. She never seems to rush. She never talks fast. She doesn't even put you on hold. I've decided it's in her background. Marissa was brought up in Swiss finishing schools and groomed to marry a title. Instead, she gave birth to a network TV show; she's the Countess of Comedy. There's a veneer that's more like a polished marquetry finish—on the surface, ornamental and smoothly beautiful, but behind it a very intricate intellect that's full of patterns, plans, and angles you'd never suspect.

Etienne, one of the most gentlemanly gentlemen in the world, pats my shoulder. "Ah, Cam. You are finally in New York." He speaks with an accent I've never been able to pinpoint—part French, part something else—the mystique only adds to his international aura.

"Is that from Sotheby's Duchess of Windsor auction?" A woman named Bryce, who is in the bow business, points to the jeweled panther pin clipped to Marissa's pearls.

"No," says Marissa, very low-key. I happen to know that the duchess was her godmother, but she doesn't mention it. Once I asked about a bracelet she was wearing—huge, chunky jewel-studded charms clunking from a thick gold chain, the twenty-two-karat kind, wrapped around the sleeve of her black cashmere sweater.

She just shrugged. "I found it in Mother's dressing room, wrapped up in an old piece of Kleenex," she said. "She was probably going to throw it out."

So you never know where her jewelry comes from, but you know it's real.

"How's the bow business?" Marissa says.

"Fabulous," says Bryce. "I have a new line—power bows, you know? For the feminine executive. I have an appointment with Bendel's next week."

"Power bows," says Marissa as she pulls me aside. "Coming next week in gray flannel and pinstripes for the woman who wants to dress her hair for success. That's funny. Now, listen, Cam. I'm not trying to play matchmaker or anything, you understand, but Etienne's friend Max over there is a very interesting man. He's in publishing." Marissa knows I've always wanted to write a book.

"Is that food?" I point to a long table in the opposite direction.

Marissa grimaces. "Hot dogs. Somebody's cute idea. It's not worth it. You'll get mustard on your face and God knows what in your veins. Max Max! Come over here."

A tall blond man in rolled shirtsleeves and suspenders materializes at her elbow.

"Max, this is our good friend Cam, from Chicago. She's in advertising."

"Yes, so I've heard from Etienne. I hear you have won many awards."

"Well . . ."

"Don't be shy. There's nothing wrong with awards. We must reemphasize excellence in this country. Tell me, what are your accounts?"

"Oh, a little of everything. Flakie Cookie Mix, Stratoglider Bicycles, Trendar Hair Products, Bridal Bouquet—"

172

"What's Bridal Bouquet?"

"A feminine-hygiene product."

"Oh. I see. I understand you're in town shooting a commercial."

"Well, the shoot is over. This is postproduction."

"My publishing house would like to do a book on advertising. Do you think anybody would read it?" Max looks over my head to see if anyone more interesting is in the room.

"Everybody's always curious about commercials—"

"Of course. We must talk at length. Would you like to dance?"

The band is playing a tango, and I have no idea how to tango, but I hate to be rude. We swirl across the floor, and while we're dancing, Max asks me where I went to school, what degrees I have, where I live, what are my clubs, whom do I know. I feel like I'm on a job interview.

"Max," I say, "is this how you interview people for a job?"

"Heavens, no. The personnel department does that."

"Tell me, Max. Have you ever gone hang-gliding?" Max is the last person in the world I could ever envision hang-gliding, so it doesn't surprise me when he doesn't answer. He's busy blowing a kiss to Bryce, the bow lady.

"We're going on from here to a book party for a friend of mine," says Max. "I hope you'll join us." He spins abruptly, dragging me along. "It should be fascinating. He wrote a biography of Cole Porter that puts his work in a whole new light."

I agree to go, which is how I end up back at Mortimer's.

"You didn't tell me we were going to Mortimer's," I say to Marissa.

"Well, a lot of book parties are held here. Glenn Bernbaum just does such a nice job, and the press loves to cover this place."

We check our coats and edge our way into the room, which is packed with people and topiary trees made of fresh herbs. A potpourri of rosemary and thyme perfumes the air.

"I won't know anybody," I say, surveying the elbow-to-elbow crowd.

"Of course you will," says Marissa, waving to Nancy Kissinger, whom I do not know. I hear the pop of a champagne cork, and someone is singing a Cole Porter medley in the next room.

Etienne hands me a glass of champagne. "I have been following the market, and your ad agency stock is going up very drastically. Could there be an acquisition on the horizon?"

I shrug. "Who knows? Anything can happen these days. The business is crazy."

Etienne nods sagely. "Somebody knows, I guarantee it."

I notice Cornelia Guest in the crowd, feeding the filet from her hors d'oeuvre plate to her little white dog, who is not a pit bull.

Max and I decide to brave the buffet table, and I realize that I do indeed know somebody at this party, and he is slicing Irish salmon onto rounds of black pumpernickel.

He probably won't remember me. I hope.

Just then he looks up, and his brow wrinkles.

"So," he says. "Have you learned to eat meat properly yet?"

"No," I say, taking some salmon. "That's why I'm

eating fish." He spoons capers onto my plate. One rolls off onto my foot, and I feel it squish inside my shoe as I hop away.

"Wait a minute," the chef yells. I turn around, and he's running after me with the knife in his hand, so I stop.

"Yes?"

"Did I get that on your dress?"

"No. Actually, it fell into my shoe."

"Hm. Let's see." And he's down on one knee, prying off my shoe.

"It's okay. Really. It doesn't hurt—"

He shakes out the mashed caper and carefully puts the shoe back on my foot. Everybody is staring.

"Why are you doing this?"

"I'm a leg man."

"Good for you. Now, will you please let go of my leg? Thank you very much."

"You're welcome."

I don't turn around.

I hurry back to where Marissa has staked out a table. "We're going to Elaine's after this," she says. "So don't eat too much. So what do you think of Max?"

I look around. Max is two feet from the table, surrounded by about five women. "Well, he's attractive."

"I'm glad you said that, because I think so too. And, you know what? He also has a very large interest in the publishing company. His grandfather founded it. This is the kind of person you need to meet, Cam. There's nobody like that on the West Coast. They're all so plastic. You're moving to New York, I hope. You belong in New York. It fits you."

Max sits down with us and lights a cigarette. "Cam, I understand you enjoy riding."

"Marissa must have told you."

"I used to ride, but I stopped. I had to have three vertebrae fused."

"Which three?"

I did a commercial once for a back-pain analgesic. We had a demo that showed a cutaway of the spinal column, so I know what he's talking about.

Max snaps to attention for the first time. "Twelve through fourteen," he says. "It took months to heal." He proceeds to give me a rundown of his entire surgical history, with microscopic attention to the lumbar region.

Mario Astor, the famous fashion designer, comes by the table to admire Marissa's pin, cutting off Max's dissertation in the lumbar region. "I knew the duchess well," he says. "Did you know they stole all her lingerie while she was in that coma? And her luggage too—that gorgeous luggage with the WW's. An outrage!"

"Ah, author?" Max waves over a short dark man. "This is Chris Graham. We were roommates at Harvard." He hands me a copy of Chris's book, and I look at it. I love new books, the feel of their covers, the crispness of the pages and spines.

"This is wonderful," I say, and I mean it. God, how I envy this guy who actually wrote a book. "How long did it take you to write it?"

"Forever. I was working as a magazine editor for years, and trying to write after work, and you know what that does for your concentration. Then finally, three years ago, I quit and just wrote until I finished the book."

"Good for you. Had you written much before?"

"Just a few articles. To be frank, I wasn't sure I could do it."

"Well, you did. Congratulations."

"Chris, darling," somebody yells. "You have to speak to the baroness!"

I sit with the book in my lap and thumb through the pages. What if it were my book? I would love to write a book, but I have no idea how to start. All I can think of, though, is *what if it were my book*? What if I could do something besides advertising? Could I?

"Marissa," I say. "Maybe I should write a book."

She nods vigorously. "You should. Of course you should. Talk to Max about it right away. But we have to get going now. We have reservations at Elaine's."

Elaine's is a soft-focus blur of red-and-white-checked tablecloths, funky little Italian Christmas lights, sepia murals, photographs of the famous, artwork, and Elaine herself, dominating the floor like a diva. We have a huge table—ten people—and everybody talks at once over arugula salad, pasta, and, after dinner, little tissue-wrapped macaroons and *poire* liqueur. I talk to Max about my idea to write a book, and he's encouraging.

"It shouldn't be too hard," he says. "You're already a writer."

"That's why I'm worried. I can't remember when I wrote anything longer than thirty seconds. But I know enough to know it's going to be hard. And I don't know what to write about. I'm really not certain if there is life after advertising. I mean, I've thought about it, but . . ."

Max adjusts his bow tie apathetically and stifles a yawn. Then he suddenly snaps to attention. The group is on the move again, social salmon swimming upstream.

"Where are we going?" I ask Max.

"The Sea Cruise," he says.

The Sea Cruise is awash in blue beach umbrellas and furniture that looks like slightly used flotsam that washed ashore at Miami Beach and was shipped north. A mirror ball throws sparkly reflections on the dancers, and the bar crowd looks like a combination of trust-fund junkies and postpartum preppies.

Everyone is young. Except us. Why are we here?

"Why are we here?" I ask Max.

"Well, it's still a little early for KK's, which is where we really want to go—if we can get in. I'm a member, of course, but there can still be a problem. One of those stupid things that happens when a club first opens."

"KK's," says Marissa. "Perfect. Let's go. We'd love to go to KK's."

"What's KK's," I ask.

"Everybody's writing about it. It's the new club in the Fifties that's just like a house. There's a living room, a dining room, even a bedroom. I hear the furniture is all imported from Madame Claude's in Paris. The owner bought the entire contents at auction."

"Marissa has to see this because it's her only chance to see firsthand how the elegant French courtesans lived," says Etienne.

"Look," says Max. "There's Sandy Culvers, the owner of the Sea Cruise. I want to ask him what he thought of the piece *Spy* magazine did on me. They concentrated on my political opinions and quoted me as saying the ACLU was a branch of *Pravda*, which of course is nothing short of irresponsible journalism. I'll just catch up with Sandy and we'll move on."

Max moves off into the crowd and I suddenly get the uncomfortable feeling that all these preppie guys in their bow ties are checking me out. I'm too old for this. Maybe I should just take a cab home. A guy in a tuxedo wanders up, looks at my legs, my leather miniskirt, my beaded blouse, and when he gets to my face, he snaps his head away. This happens again, and I'm figuring, what the hell, these people are weird, and then I get a funny feeling that somebody's behind me and I spin around and there's this huge six-foot-four person with a ponytail and a chipped tooth glaring over the top of my head at anybody who has the nerve to glance in my direction, and I realize it's the chef. The chef from Mortimer's.

"So," he says, lighting a nonfilter cigarette with a match from a box of Blue Tips. "Who's the piece of furniture?"

"I beg your pardon?"

"The dead wood. Grandpa." He shakes out the match in the direction of Max, who is heading back toward us with a short blond guy.

And so I am forced to make an introduction. "Max, this is—"

"Jamie Kelly," says the chef, his hand engulfing Max's.

"Jamie is a chef at Mortimer's. You may have seen him earlier tonight, slicing salmon."

Max introduces everyone to Sandy Culvers—everyone except the chef, that is. He already knows Sandy.

"We were both on the list of the ten sexiest guys on the avenue in *Avenue* magazine," says the chef. "I was the only one without any money."

The two of them toast this prestigious honor.

"Weren't we about ready to go somewhere?" I say.

"Well," says Max, "we can give KK's a try, but I'm afraid I can't guarantee anything. If we can't get in, though, we can go to Au Bar."

"No problem, Maxie," says the chef. "I know the KK's people. They eat at Mortimer's all the time. They love my crème brulée."

"Oh, my God," says Marissa. "You are responsible for that fabulous crème brulée? The best crème brulée in New York?"

This is how Jamie Kelly ends up in Etienne's limousine with us, reciting his secret recipe for crème brulée.

"One hundred egg yolks," he says. "Seven quarts of heavy cream. One quart of milk. Four pounds of sugar. What you gotta do is temper in the egg yolks. Put the sugar in last, or it'll burn at the bottom. Then you whisk the shit out of it. Then you put it in a bain marie—three hundred degrees, no more. And it takes three hours. But you gotta hit it. Boom! That's how you know it's done, it'll shake loose. Then you put sugar on top and you broil it and you're there."

Marissa looks as if he has just translated the Rosetta Stone for her. "That's fabulous," she says. "Incredible."

We pull up in front of KK's on lower Fifth Avenue and there's a mob scene. The street is teeming with rich, beautifully dressed, bejeweled people who are actively not being let past a velvet rope held by two thugs in tuxedos.

Max approaches a rope-holder, flashes his membership card, and is ignored.

"These people are impossible," he sniffs. "I should take their name and report them. They are having some kind of vulgar press event, apparently."

"No problem," says Jamie, waving to the thugs.

The ropes magically open. "You, you, you, and you," says one of the thugs, motioning to me, Marissa and Etienne, and Jamie. We are swept in by a wave of the crowd. Over my shoulder, I see Max in some sort of stranglehold, but the crowd moves too quickly for me to be precise about his fate.

"There isn't somebody waitin' at the top of those stairs for money?" says Jamie.

"We wouldn't do that to you, buddy," says one of the thugs, patting him on the shoulder.

Inside the fabled KK's we wedge our way through the packed ground floor, oozing our way around the gilt-trimmed Nouveau Regency furniture and pair of stuffed Dobermans, and ascend a paneled stairway to a series of drawing, living, and ballrooms.

A stream of people in black with pierced ears swarms by. "All people do here is walk up and down stairs," says Jamie. "You got your basic three floors of absolute decadence."

We follow the maze until we get to a vault where people are dancing in a cage. Moving up, we collapse in leather club chairs in the English library. A complimentary bottle of Taittinger materializes. "Thanks for the crabcake recipe," says Kevin, who is introduced as one of the K's.

"No problem," says Jamie. Even in this weird crowd, his outfit is unique. Actually, he is wearing what might qualify as a costume—a fifties turquoise-blue silk Palm Beach sport coat, Klondike boots, a Chicago Cubs shirt, and jeans. And, of course, there's the ponytail.

"There's a lot of serious money in this town, but they're such geeks. GUPPIES. Gainfully Unemployed Party Professionals," says the chef. "Want to see some real rock-and-rollin'?"

"Only if I can rock-and-roll in my sleep." It's two A.M.

"Honey, this is New York. The city of lights—"

"That's Paris."

"Well, you can't go to sleep. This town's just startin', and I just got off work and we just got together. Let me make a call."

He disappears and I look for Marissa and Etienne, but the crowd has a way of swallowing people.

The chef returns as I'm methodically searching the pseudo-bedroom with its canopy bed and harp and the pseudo-dressing area next door. "Eric Clapton's sitting in on a set over at Jimmy's Place," he says. "Let's travel." Being taller than almost anyone else in the room, he manages to spot Marissa and Etienne, and he motions them toward the door.

"Eric Clapton," he says, and you can see in Etienne's eyes that it doesn't matter if he has to be up in three hours to check the foreign markets, he isn't going to miss Eric Clapton.

"What happened to Max?" says Marissa.

Jamie shrugs. "It's a jungle out there."

Jimmy's Place is the opposite of every place we have been tonight. There is nothing stylish about it. The main attribute of the ambience is darkness—dark walls spattered with pictures and posters of rock stars, a few inscribed gold records, dark wood floors, a long, dark bar. I am introduced to the world of the Night People, the subculture of nightcrawlers who eat mostaccioli at three A.M., never see sunlight, and float in a current of socialites in strapless taffeta dresses, men in string ties who carry saxophones, and weirdos who will sweep your path for a quarter.

"This is an extension of my living room," says the chef.

"It's unique," I say.

"Well, you go to the Smurf Club, or Surf Club, as some call it, and that's where you got the WASP kids and girls looking for young stockbrokers. Then there's Au Bar. Au Bar is big."

"What's there?"

"Women. And it's comfortable, if you're into paneled basements. Then maybe on to Nell's, for highlights of Eurotrash. And then KK's, if you're into attitude people. The Universe usually goes pretty late too, but the sicko nuts go there. People who don't have jobs and just get blasted. Jimmy's is where you want to be."

He introduces me to Geraldo, who is a maître d' from another restaurant, Peter, who was a drummer with Paul McCartney, Sid, an off-duty cop, and Astrid, a performance artist. Peter shows me snapshots of his baby daughter.

"I just came from the Smokey Robinson gig," announces a curly-haired guy who is Chess, a sound-system specialist. He and Jamie discuss a charity benefit that's coming up, and Jamie talks him into donating a sound system. "This guy, he has a heart of gold," says Chess as Jamie stubs out his tenth cigarette of the night and socks down another brandy. "He's king of the causes. Somehow, he not only gets the top musicians in the country for charity gigs, he gets them to play for free. He gets me to give stuff away—and I'd cross the street to pick up a penny! Don't ask me how he does it."

"Hey, come on," says Jamie, ordering a Rémy and

handing me a Perrier. "It's for the children, the kids. It's a benefit."

Suddenly a glass breaks, and a scuffle breaks out at the end of the bar.

"Hey! Hey! Ouch! Let go of me, you asshole!"

"I'm just—"

"Let go of me!"

A young girl is trying to shake off a drunk. It takes Jamie about two seconds to materialize next to them. The guy makes the mistake of slapping Jamie in the face, and with one move Jamie grabs his head and bashes it into the bar. I sidle over next to Marissa and Etienne as Jamie escorts the drunk to the door by the collar of his coat, holding him in the posture of a used Kleenex.

"That was very good," says Etienne when Jamie returns. "Where did you learn that?"

"Championship wrestling," says Jamie. "Into the turnbuckle."

"I used to box," says Etienne. "Jab! Right cross! Upper cut!" He slugs the air, as Marissa and I stare in amazement.

"Or," says Jamie, "you can use the sucker punch." He turns to me and points to the floor. "Did you drop that?"

I look, and Jamie's fist whips by my face, missing me by centimeters. "Catch 'em off guard. Try to go for the nose, break it if you can. Mess up the face, and when they're down on their back, you get on top and stick your fingers in their eyes and gouge their eyeballs out."

"Absolutely," Etienne enthuses.

"Or else you give them a curb job." Jamie ticks off the moves on his fingers. "After you beat the guy up, you open his mouth and you stick it on the curb and you kick him in the back of the head."

"I like it." Etienne nods, displaying a previously hidden violent streak.

"Or then there's the blanket job. You wrap the guy up in a blanket and you whack him around. It doesn't leave any bruises. Supposedly."

"Where did you learn this stuff?" I say.

Jamie shrugs. "Six brothers," he says. "It was self-defense."

While he's talking, he hands me a bar napkin. There's a note on it: *I'm crazy about you.*

I head toward the ladies' room, and suddenly he's right behind me, pushing me into the room, locking the door behind us.

"You may be wondering who I am," he says.

"I know who you are. You're the guy who's into blanket jobs. You're the pervert who followed me into the ladies' room. What are people going to think—you following me in here?"

"Who cares?" He looks right at me, and his eyes are direct and clear and honest. "I just had to be alone with you."

"This is a fantasy of yours." I'm an authority on fantasies.

"No. My fantasy is girls in plaid skirts and knee socks."

"What! Why?"

"Catholic school. You have any knee socks? Plaid skirts?"

"No. No, I don't. So I guess you'll have to leave."

"That's okay. I have another fantasy—you in a black leather maternity miniskirt." He sits on the edge of the sink.

"That'll be the day."

"Come on, drop it."

"Drop what?"

"Honey, you know the rutabaga?"

"What about it?"

"The rutabaga. It's got a tough, waxy outside, and it's hard and cold when you touch it. But then you cook it right, and it's moist and soft and it melts all the way down your throat, it's so tender. And then you taste it and it's sweet and pure as honey. A little seasoning, and it's a beautiful thing."

"You sure know your vegetables."

"If I wasn't right, you wouldn't be standing here listening. You're a smart girl."

"And how do you know so much about me, Mr. Right?"

"You grow up on the South Side of Chicago with six brothers, you learn a few things they don't teach you in school. Besides, my father died when I was five. I had to catch on fast."

Suddenly I can see him, a little kid at a big dinner table, fighting for his place in the family, and I can't help but smile: he still seems like a little kid inside a six-four killer body. There's a vulnerability to him that doesn't match the ponytail and the chipped tooth and the sucker punch.

"It must have been hard for your mother," I say, "getting along without your dad, and all those kids to support."

"My mother? She's a saint. But the woman can't cook, to this day. That's why I had to learn."

"I'd say she is a shrewd woman."

Somebody rattles the door. We ignore them.

"So," I say. "What else do you know about vegetables?"

"I'm a gourmet, honey. I know right off when something's good. All it takes is a taste."

"Do you want to open your own restaurant someday?" I say, vamping to get a little less personal. "I think you'd be good at it. People seem to really like you. You'd get a following."

"Ahh, I'm more the peel-the-potatoes type. I'm used to taking the orders, not giving 'em."

"Really, you should think about it. You're forceful, you're a good cook, you know people, you're honest . . ." I recite as many traits as I can think of. But it's true. He would do well on his own. I really believe it.

"Don't you see me peeling potatoes? What's wrong with it?"

"Nothing. I'm just saying I see you doing anything you want."

"Maybe I should start thinking about it." He touches my cheek. For someone so huge, he's surprisingly gentle. "I like the way you see me," he says.

How do I see him? I don't even know him. But I do know he could have his own restaurant. That much is obvious. At least no one would argue with him.

"How does everybody else see you?" I ask.

He smiles, showing his chipped tooth.

"A sex symbol," he says. "Must be the ponytail."

We stand there staring at each other for a few more minutes.

By the time we leave the ladies' room, Eric Clapton is gone, so we don't get to hear him play. We do, however, get to hear Jamie sing. He jumps behind the microphone next to Peter Wolf and the two of them belt out a pretty respectable "Burnin' Love," and I have to admit he looks more like he belongs with the band, singing about burnin' love, than he did at the carving table.

"Well," says Marissa. "It looks like you've found yourself a rock-and-roll chef. That's very funny."

"I haven't found myself anything. I don't even know this person. Besides, he's violent."

She smiles. "I think he's . . . interesting."

When the applause dies down, Marissa and Etienne have disappeared, Jamie reappears, and I'm yawning.

"You can't be tired," he says. "It's an hour earlier in Chicago."

I briefly consider telling him how I worked twelve hours today, but forget it. Why would he care? "Aren't you tired yourself?" I say. "You've been on your feet all day."

"I get my second wind about now," he says.

"When do you get up?"

"Three, maybe four. Depends when my shift starts, if there's a party with a lot of prep."

"Well, I have to get up at seven."

He looks startled, as if he never realized that hour existed. Then he shakes his finger at me. "I think it's probably time you went home, in that case. Although I'll be a very sad man."

"Sad? Why?"

"Because, honey, I just think you're a baked potato with a big dollop of sour cream and beluga caviar on it."

This analogy is new to me, but I look at his eyes, and they're sincere, or at least there appears to be a real openness of heart, and it stops me because I realize it's been a while since I've seen a face, any face, with this kind of honesty written all over it.

The guy may be able to beat people to a pulp, but he actually looks like he's incapable of lying.

"Well," I say. "I have go go."

"But, baby. Aren't you hungry?"

Baby? "You were going to suggest cooking?"

"Please. I'm off-duty."

He leads the way out of Jimmy's Place and we are instantly accosted by a bum with his hand out. I jump back, memories of the mugger and the curb job still fresh. But Jamie reaches into his pocket and hands the guy a dollar. "Somebody's got to help them," he says. Two steps further, another street person comes up and Jamie hands out another dollar. Does this man keep any of his salary? At the all-night deli next door, he grabs bags of Cheetos, Hostess Twinkies, potato chips, Chips Ahoy!, plus a loaf of that soft white bread that's a cross between Kleenex and Styrofoam, and a jar of peanut butter. He eats this garbage on the way home in the cab. I find myself actually eating a Twinkie.

"Now, this is real food," says the man who makes the best crème brulée in New York.

We get to the Carlyle, and the sky is turning a pearly gray. "Good night," I say.

"Wait a minute," he says. "Do you think they have a glass of water in there?"

"Possibly. But I am not asking you up. So forget it."

"I just want a glass of water. The concierge can get it."

The concierge will probably take one look at this guy and throw him out, I'm thinking, but that's not my problem.

Jamie approaches the concierge. "Hi, Jerry. Got any water?"

"Sure, Jamie. Good to see you. Perrier? Evian?"

"Tap is fine." He turns to me. "That guy is one of the best jazz trumpeters in New York. I've sung with him."

Jamie takes his glass of water, his bag of junk food, and trails me to the elevator. "Just one more thing," he says.

"What?"

"Will you be the mother of my children?"

"What?"

"I'm crazy about you. Maybe it's because we have so much in common—I'm from Chicago, you're from Chicago. I'm a guy. You're a girl. I want you to be the mother of my children."

"You're not serious."

"Yes I am. You're beautiful, and I'm crazy about you, honey."

"I hate being called 'honey'! I'm not beautiful."

"Okay, so your eyes don't match. I'll give you that."

"You don't know anything about me." I notice the elevator man is watching this conversation as if it were a tennis match, his head snapping from him to me, me to him.

"What's there to know? You just escape from Joliet State Women's Penitentiary or something?"

"You're crazy."

"No I'm not. You'll see."

"Good night."

"Good night, Miss Right."

"Cam."

"Good night, Cam." He turns to the concierge, over at the front desk. "Take good care of this girl, Jerry. Take very good care of her." Then he says to me, "It's always good to know your concierge."

I get into the elevator and leave him standing there with HiHos and Cheetos and the stupid glass of water.

When I get to my room, the phone is ringing.

"Just remember," he says, and I hear the crunch of a corn chip, "with me around, you'll never have to slave over a hot stove."

"Good night," I say, but I'm laughing when I hang up. I can't remember the last time a man made me laugh at five A.M.. Or anything made me laugh at five A.M. I actually think I like this guy. He's got no relation to my life, but I like him. Maybe that's *why* I like him. He's a fresh slate. We have no past, no common ground. And he knows how to poach a quail egg, which is something.

I spend the entire next day at the video editor's, working on the commercial cut with Juice.

"There's some serious jungle drums," he says as we fine-tune the scenes to the music.

"What do you hear?"

"Three headhunters have called me, which means they have reason to believe I am or will soon be looking for work. Something's up."

"I've gotten the same kind of bullshit. And you know what? I'm going to buy us a little insurance. Just in case."

To do this, I leave a message at Simmons' office that we are in the middle of cutting the commercial and would love to have his input. When he calls back, I make sure we incorporate at least two of his suggestions into the commercial and suggest we keep communication lines open. I promise him a sneak preview, if he has time to stop by the editing studio.

By seven o'clock the commercial is rough-edited,

Simmons has come and gone, and we have a new ally. It's almost a sure thing that Simmons will go back to the bottling convention raving about the new campaign.

"Are you sure that was smart?" says Juice.

"Why?"

"When Brucie finds out you went around him, he's gonna flip."

"He's gonna flip no matter what we do, so we may as well do something that's going to sell this work."

"Whatever you say," says Juice, but he looks at me strangely, which I don't feel good about. We usually see eye-to-eye.

"Are you sure it's okay?"

"Sure. No problem."

I pull my chair up closer. "Listen, Juice. We're in this together. If this spot doesn't sell, if we don't get the Zing! business, we only have ourselves to blame at this point."

Juice gives a half-smile. "Waaait a minute, Miss Caméla. This is *your* action plan, remember? I'm not convinced we're not out on a thin limb here. I'm going along because *you* asked me along. For now. But I like being able to pay my rent, Cam. Remember that."

This is astonishing. Juice, the last of the red-hot rebels, never needs anything—or at least he never admits it. "I thought you always said, 'Let them fuck themselves,' Juice. Or did I hear it wrong? Or are you suffering from a fever?" I feel his forehead.

"For Christ's sake, Cam. There's millions of dollars at stake. Our jobs are on the line here. Get serious."

"Exactly. That's why we can't leave it up to Bruce.

You know it as well as I do—we have to make friends in the right places, and fast, or we won't be plugged in when the going gets hot."

"You ought to know about making friends." He's taunting me now, teasing.

"What's that supposed to mean? Let's keep this discussion on a business level."

"Like Jed Durant?"

Juice is fishing. He doesn't know anything for sure. He couldn't. "You read the *Enquirer* too much, you know that? Okay, I'll say it. Watch my lips. There is nothing going on between Jed Durant and me, if that's your insinuation." And it's true. Now.

"Okay. I guess we've both been working too hard." He reaches out and we hug each other, and that's that.

I go straight back to the Carlyle, order the operator to hold all calls, and fall asleep in my clothes until the phone rings.

It's the chef.

"I told the operator it was an emergency, and it is, 'cause I'm double-parked," he says. "Come on down. Somebody at work died. I have the night off."

The only reason I do is to once and for all put an end to this ridiculousness, but it seems like I blink my eyes and I'm at a Dominican wake in Queens. Apparently I am Jamie's date for the funeral.

The body is laid out, and to tell the truth, it looks very lifelike to me, with a rosary in his hands, very tanned and fit. This has to be makeup, because Jamie informs me that Ramon had worked with him at the restaurant on the night shift.

"How did he die," I whisper.

"Murder," Jamie whispers back. "Somebody offed him. Lead pipe."

"Jesus!" I look around uneasily.

Someone snaps flash pictures of the coffin, and I'm at a loss for words since I've never even seen a dead person before, but it turns out I don't have to say anything because, right there in front of the priest, the widow, the banks of floral tributes, and the coffin, Jamie kisses me, and somehow it doesn't even seem out-of-place. In fact, it seems highly appropriate and fits right in with the emotion of the moment—the widow weeping, babies crying, the rustled greetings and whispers, the prayers chanted in Spanish.

Jamie is dressed up, which is to say he's wearing a navy-blue turtleneck and pants. His eyes are huge and green and they show how sad he is, almost sick, really—I can see it in the way he frowns, the tightness of his gaze, the slight stoop of his shoulders, the way he walks, placing one foot carefully in front of the other on the blood-red carpet.

Ramon was one of the dishwashers at the restaurant, and they had been friends.

Jamie doesn't speak to the widow, he just holds her in his arms.

"What can I do?" he says to me, his fists knotted and white. "Me and some of the guys at the restaurant, we started a fund for the kids' college. Ramon was saving for that."

A priest comes in, and we sit in a line of metal folding chairs for the prayers. Jamie crosses himself and kneels on the carpet. The woman in the row in front of us holds a baby girl who peers over her mother's shoulder, and Jamie winks at the baby, and she notices, and she grins, and for a few minutes they're conspirators in a game of eyes. This man seems to be able to relate to anybody, from babies to celebrities, because he's like a tree with the bark stripped off, veneerless. He has no facade, no hidden agenda, his emotions sit right there on the surface, and you don't have to intellectualize, you just have to respond, like the baby.

I, for instance, am responding.

He holds my hand.

"Your hand is soft," I whisper.

"All chefs have soft hands. It's the fat from all the butchering." He inventories the scars. "This one is from cleaning a knife with a lemon. I had the knife backward. Really stupid. This one, I picked up a pan of rice for curry. Forgot it just came out of the oven."

"What about that one?"

"That's where my brother tried to kill me."

He loves his brother. I can tell by his expression.

After the wake we go to dinner at Sam's on the Upper East Side. Out of professional courtesy, the chef comes out of the kitchen and gives us a personal rundown on each dish. I order a hamburger. Jamie orders quail. Who orders quail in real life?

Suddenly Jamie jerks to attention. "There's my man," he announces, peering out the window. He stubs out his cigarette, bolts from the table and out of the restaurant. I figure he's spotted somebody who owes him money, but a few minutes later he's back, carrying a huge helium-filled frog with "Kiss me" stenciled on its side. He tries tethering it to our table, but it's too big, so he checks it with the coatroom.

"Are you a frog or a prince?"

"Honey, I don't know what I am, but I'm so happy with you."

"Please don't call me 'honey.' "

"Okay, honey."

We leave, trailed by the frog, and head downtown to pick up Jamie's friend Chess.

"You should have heard the Dead tonight," Chess says. "They were awesome."

I do not know the Dead. The Dead do not know me.

Tonight, it turns out, Jamie is driving Chess to pick up Bomber Jacket, an act he is wiring for sound. We stop at a hotel, where three girls get into the car. They are not normal girls, which is desirable, apparently, if you are Bomber Jacket. Two of the girls are white and one is black, but they look like triplets who have had a nuclear accident. They are all wearing skintight turquoise-fringed leather miniskirts with bare midriffs, and identical white wigs, teased up like inflated heaps of platinum meringue, which have been sprinkled with silver glitter.

We are on our way to a disco called Heart Attack, where Bomber Jacket will be performing their current disco hit, "Zap Me."

Jamie stands behind me in the crowd as we watch the girls gyrate onstage, lip-synching their hit, which consists of two words, repeated over and over—"Zap me, zap me, zap me, zap me." They shake their heads and showers of glitter descend onto the crowd.

"Hey, baby," Jamie says into my ear. "Come here often?" He starts singing along in perfect pitch.

Around three A.M. Jamie, Bomber Jacket, Chess, and I stop at the Pyramid Club. I have a Perrier as the girls and I discuss our one common interest— leather.

Nobody asks what I do. I guess I'm "with the band."

Dawn is once more breaking when Jamie strokes

my hair in the cab on the way back to the Carlyle. "You know what, honey?"

"What?"

"I'm hungry."

We go to an all-night restaurant, and he orders lasagne. You couldn't pay me to eat in this dump. We talk about the Vietnam war. "I'm glad I missed that," he says.

"I didn't miss it," I say. It occurs to me: This guy never wore finger cymbals or psychoanalyzed the cover of *Sergeant Pepper*. He probably thinks 4-F is a reading on a meat thermometer.

"Driver's license, please," I say. It turns out I'm eight years older than he is.

"I thought you were older," I say. Well, his hair does have gray in it.

"I thought you were younger." My hair has no gray in it.

He puts down his fork, and reaches across the vinyl booth and holds my hand tightly. "Don't go crazy on me, honey. I love you. Whatever."

"Jamie . . . think about this . . ."

"No. Let's not."

Half an hour later, we're at the Carlyle sitting on the floor of my room watching a rerun of *Green Acres* on TV. Jamie knows what kind of sunglasses Arnold the Pig wears. It gets later and later, and he's kissing my neck, my arms, and my shoulders, and that's it—not one place else. I love the feel of his lips, soft and exploratory, inquisitive but not intrusive, coaxing but never teasing. He's a big man, but his kisses are soft as petals falling off a tree. He tastes like brandy and smoke.

"Did your mother teach you to cook?" he asks between kisses.

"No. She taught me to peel a peach with a knife and fork. I taught myself to cook. I'm good at making garnishes."

He nods, as though that makes perfect sense. "I learned to grab what was on the table before somebody else got it," he says. And he reaches out and grabs for a bag of Oreos that's on the floor.

He misses the Oreos.

He gets me.

That's how we happen to spend the night kissing and hugging, and I can tell you: this man could bring back the Real Kiss. You forget sometimes what a Real Kiss is like, until you get one. I'm talking about a *Real* Kiss, when you take the time to run the gamut of each other's lips, the give-and-take of the soft flesh, the languid exploration of the bows and indentations, the humid heat of shared breaths. You forget what it's like to do this, and stop there, not because you're in high school and your parents will be coming home any minute, or because you're not precocious, but because you're a grown-up and you want to.

"You tell me when to leave," he says. His voice is all around me, a cashmere blanket.

"Leave," I say. But he doesn't, and we spend the night kissing and laughing, not necessarily in that order.

At six A.M. Jamie helps me pack and puts me in a cab for the airport.

"Take good care of this woman," he tells the driver. "She's going to be the mother of my children."

"I'm probably too old to have children," I say.

"So we'll steal some."

When I get home in Chicago, there's a message on my answering machine. "Hello, baaay-by," says Jamie's voice, sounding like the Big Bopper. "I know you're whooshin' somewhere over the country in an airplane right now, but I just wanted to tell you—I miss you, honey."

Funny. I miss you too.

Chapter Thirteen

Bruce isn't saying a word—he's just clipping the end off a new cigar. His office has a tomblike feel—every surface is cold and hard. The desk is granite. The conference table is stainless steel. The floor is marble. It used to be inlaid parquet, but when Bruce came on board he requested marble, and he got it. A stainless-steel coffee service is on one end of his desk, and after he lights his cigar, Bruce pours himself a cup and offers one to Juice and me.

"Play it again," Bruce says, and I rewind the videotape of the Zing! commercial and run it for the fourth time. Bruce squints, scrutinizing the monitor screen. Then he jumps to his feet. "Good," he says, "It looks just fine. Nice work."

"No comments besides that?" This is out of character.

"Juice," Bruce says. "What do you think?"

"I think it's better than they deserve. It's goddamn brilliant."

"Modesty becomes you, Juice," says Bruce. "Are you ready to show it to everybody?"

"Yes," says Juice.

"No," I say. "Not quite. Almost but not quite.

Juice, don't you think we need a little show business—some slides and videotape about Jed Durant and Cowboy Bob, some finished radio, maybe posters of the print? Show the spot in some sort of framework? Blow it out even bigger, until it becomes a real thing?"

"Well," he says. "Big we can always get."

"And maybe we can show it to some consumers—get their reactions on tape, to help sell it."

"That's fine, Cam," says Bruce, "except for one thing. We're out of time. They've moved the presentation date up two weeks."

"What! When did this happen?"

"You must have been on vacation."

"I wasn't on vacation, I was on production, as you recall. Why didn't somebody tell us this?"

"Well, I'm sure somebody tried to reach you. At any rate, the spot is fine. The production values are all there. Anything else is just icing on the cake."

"Sure, but the icing sells the cake."

"Whatever, Cam. If you can do it in forty-eight hours, be my guest."

Juice and I leave Bruce's office and regroup.

"Something's up," I say. "The fix must already be in."

Juice shrugs. "I'm not gonna second-guess. What's the difference anyhow? We got two days."

"That's just about enough time," I say, and we both smile, because in two days Juice and I can do just about anything.

And we do.

First, we gather the group in my office for a little pep talk. Everybody sits around the round table or lounges on the couch, scribbling on layout pads and yellow tablets. "Okay, everybody," I say. "This is it. The big shot. You've all done a great job so far.

Arnie, thanks for holding down the fort. Maeve, great work on those end frames. Brenda, the radio sounds terrific. Richard, the print is breakthrough . . ." I run down everybody's contributions, and then we all applaud each other. Everybody seems enthusiastic except the Mole, who of course is missing, and Clark, who is slashing layout paper into a pile of confetti with a razor blade.

"Now," I say, "here's the challenge. We have forty-eight hours to put together a presentation."

Juice pulls out his stopwatch. "On your mark, get set, go!"

We clip scrap art, we have slides shot, we make flip charts, we get every album Jed Durant ever made and blow up the covers into life-size posters, we pull in the Doc and he videotapes people's reactions as they watch the commercial for the first time. We rent special furniture for the presentation room, order popcorn from the office manager, and, as a final touch, buy Cowboy Bob bandannas to pass out after the presentation. We dot every I and cross every T, because we know that it counts. Nothing will be left to chance.

Arnie comes into my office as I'm rehearsing my flip charts.

"Cam," says Arnie. "I need five minutes."

"Sure, what's up? What's happening on Cakes for the Dead?"

"No, something else. I . . . I quit."

"No. You've got to be kidding." *He can't quit. If he quits, who's going to handle the day-to-day ongoing work while we finish up on Zing!? Juice and I are going to have to screech to a halt and interview fifty people. We're going to have to come in early and work till ten at night for weeks. Everything will be a mess. I can't let him quit.*

"You can't quit," I say.

"I'm going to Burnett. In two weeks. I thought you ought to know."

Lance stares in amazement.

"God. Don't do this to me. To us. We need you, Arn. You're part of the team."

"Cam, you know we're buddies, and the guys are all great and everything, but, well . . . Burnett's gonna double my salary."

"I can see your point." He's probably bluffing. "But, Arnie, what will you be doing? Creatively, I mean. You have to stick with us for Zing! If we get this launch, you're going to take over the brand, you know that. I'll turn it all over to you. That's major."

"What about the trade press? What if there's a merger or a takeover? The dudes are restless upstairs."

"Let's just deal with one thing at a time."

I debate with Arnie, negotiating extra vacation days, possible bonuses, new office furniture, a vice-presidency and the assumption of the Louisiana territories. Finally he agrees to hold off for one month before he decides definitely. So my finger is in the dike for the time being.

For the next three days, life is one continuous meeting:

8:00	Breakfast-meeting update
9:00	Group internal meeting
10:30	Research meeting with the Doc to review 150 overhead transparencies
12:00	Conference-call meeting with the production company re: overages
1:00	Update meeting with Bruce
1:30	Meeting with Juice at video editor's
3:00	Internal meeting with Arnie and group
4:00	Lunch at desk: one package Fig Newtons from machine

4:30	Client meeting with Bridal Bouquet
5:30	Meeting with Lance to review slide presentation
6:00	Begin real work

At ten o'clock the night before the presentation, Juice and I call the group together. In a battleground littered with cartons of half-eaten cold pizza, soft-drink and beer cans, crumpled layout paper and scrap art-magazine pictures tacked to every available space, we address the troops.

"Some of you may be wondering if all this is worth it," I say. "Well, the answer is this work." I tap the layouts and the stack of videocassettes. "It's great work. World-class work. Everybody here deserves a big pat on the shoulder."

Juice and I applaud, and the group joins in, clapping, except for Clark, who is skewering a piece of pepperoni with a pushpin. The Mole, who is in his after-dark element, is blank behind his sunglasses, but I can tell he feels like we do—exhausted, but good.

I probably should have camped out in my office, because the next morning we're back at seven-thirty, arranging storyboards and testing the sound system in the presentation room. I'm in my Ralph Lauren skirt and sweater, which is purple and clashes violently with the orange walls. But then, tell me a color that doesn't clash with orange. Juice has on a forties jacket and tie.

The audience/judge/jury files in—Bruce in the lead, flanked by Harold, Simmons, who has flown in for the screening, Lance, and Jimmy, and assistant Suit. There is also a woman I have never seen before.

"Cam, Juice, this is Marielle Moran. Marielle is ad manager from Trans-Corp, and she's joining us today. Today's meeting is highly confidential, so this is the extent of our group for now, and of course nothing leaves this room."

We all nod. The Invasion is on. And Bruce is Patton.

He begins by pacing the room, munching a croissant. "Gentlemen . . . and ladies," he says. "What we have here today is no less than our future. And a hard-won future it will be. Blood has been shed . . ." He points to his ankle. "But the enemy is clear: colas. We must seize our share of liquid stomach, and we must do it now. While there is an awareness of nutrition. While there is a crack in conventional thinking. New Age thinking is that crack. You have capitalized on it with an outstanding product—and we will crush the enemy here and now." He makes a fist and strangles the croissant in his hand. Crumbs fall at his feet.

Bruce has always been brilliant at visualizations.

Lance gets up and goes through forty minutes of charts on the overhead projector.

Juice then takes the floor and explains the visual concept, using the full complement of slides and music, ending with the overture from 2001, a trick he learned from Elvis Presley's comeback. The video monitors lower silently from the ceiling, and I stand to introduce the commercials.

"Let's look at the market today," I say. "Marielle, what do you watch on television?"

"Oh, everything. Old movies are my favorites, though."

"Harold, what about your kids?"

"Well, when they're home, which is not often, we hear an awful lot of loud music."

"Exactly. It's an eclectic market." I hold up a board

with a montage of magazine covers and newspaper headlines. "A mixed bag. But with Zing! we're going to capitalize on that by mixing the old with the new. The classic with the new wave. We're going to expand our market approach with the most exciting and creative spot in soft-drink history, and here it is."

Zero, in the video equipment room, throws the switch, and on go Jed Durant and Cowboy Bob. But I'm not watching the screen—I'm watching the clients' faces.

Simmons is beaming and tapping his foot. Marielle is smiling and nodding. When it's over, Simmons raises his hand. "Our people are going to say this is a masterpiece," he says. "It's the best commercial I've ever seen."

"A classic," Marielle agrees. "This agency certainly has the kind of work it takes to put this brand over the top, and I congratulate you."

We play the commercial five more times, and there's some discussion about repositioning one of the pour shots so the bubbles will be more prominent, but we know we have a winner. At the end of the meeting, I pass out the Cowboy Bob bandannas, and that gets a good laugh.

For a grand finale, I bring out the polo idea, winding up with Jed Durant's videotaped message. "This is an example of how we can capture the upscale end of the market," I say. "What do you think?"

Everybody agrees that it's a fascinating concept. Heads nod all over the room.

It's agreed that Simmons will present the commercial to the bottlers' meeting in two weeks, and after that, the committee will vote on the advertising budget and the final choice of the ad agency to relaunch this brand.

"But we don't see any problems, do we, Marielle?" says Simmons. "You people have done outstanding work. You deserve this business, and I'm going to do my darnedest to see that you get it."

Everybody beams. It seems like a done deal.

"Have a good Thanksgiving, everybody," says Harold, and I realize that there's a holiday this weekend, and I haven't made any plans.

It's always like this after a pitch or a presentation: reentry shock. You wake up with a jolt, realizing that you live in real life after all. The projectors are down, the monitors are off, there are no cameras running, no audiences to listen to what you have to say, no script or storyboards to create. It's just you and your life. If you have one left.

When I get to the elevators, Brenda is there. After five o'clock, the elevators seem to go into slow motion, you could wait till you freeze into a pillar of salt, but what's the alternative? Nobody's in a rush to walk down seventy floors.

"Going somewhere for the holidays?" I ask, just to make conversation.

"No. The family's coming here. Greg and I have our two kids, and there's my mom and dad. It's the baby's first Thanksgiving."

That's right—Brenda was pregnant last year. She has a baby. She has a family. Brenda is going home to her husband and child. I am going home to the Bird. Brenda may not have a Clio, but she has a life.

Corporations trick you. It's part of their charm. They lead you to believe you're part of one big happy family. They pat you on the head and reward you. They give you a title, an address, an identity, a parking place, and you think this is life, especially when you're on a roll—until the elevator doors shut and you're heading down seventy floors alone.

Well, I did get the Bird a drumstick-shaped seed bell. That's festive.

Driving home, I call Theo from the car phone.

"Your mother is on a cruise in the Baltic, but we're having dinner at home," she says. "Of course you'll come. It'll be the usual Thanksgiving people. The Williamses will be there, and the Kirklands."

Great. The Williamses and the Kirklands are pillars of society, but they're not going to take away the loneliness I'm suddenly feeling.

"Is there anyone you'd like to bring?"

I think about Jamie and I wonder what his plans are. I also wonder if I've blown this whole thing out of proportion.

"Actually," I find myself saying to Theo, "there is someone. You haven't met him."

"Oh? What does he do?" I can see Theo now, sitting in her teal-green bedroom, stacked with *Vogue* and *Town and Country* from ten years back, opening mail with an ivory letter opener while she talks.

"He's a chef. But he doesn't live here. I don't know if he'd come."

"A chef, how perfect. Ask him for his stuffing recipe when you invite him. If he comes, he comes, if he doesn't, you'll just come yourself. It's settled."

Now, why did I do that? Do I really want to ask him to fly in for Thanksgiving dinner? Maybe his own family has plans. Maybe he's cooking gosling at the restaurant for the swells. And then there are Theo's friends. They're used to me—they've known me from birth, so they made allowances. Maybe

Mrs. Kirkland, whose grandfather donated the French Embassy in Chicago, will faint when she sees Jamie's ponytail. He probably won't be able to come regardless.

At two A.M. the phone rings, and it's Jamie, from the pay phone at Mortimer's.

"Hi, dollface."

"Hi, Jamie."

"I miss you."

I don't say anything, even though I know what he wants to hear.

"We got slammed tonight," he says. "All the Euros, and some real heavy hitters, and all at once, I had to do an emergency vegetable plate for Bianca."

"What was she wearing?"

Jamie is better than *Vogue*. He always knows who's wearing what, since you have to pass the kitchen to get to the ladies' room.

"Romeo Gigli, I think."

Who the hell is that? I decide not to show my ignorance.

"Who else came in today?"

"Oh, the Duchess of York. I think she's pregnant again."

"How do you know? Was she with her obstetrician?"

"No. She ordered liver for lunch. No woman orders liver for lunch unless she's pregnant. Listen, honey, gotta run. I've gotta close."

"I was going to ask you for Thanksgiving at my grandmother's. If you were in town, but . . ."

"What's for dinner?" he says.

It's hard for me to adjust to Jamie Kelly sitting at our Thanksgiving table. The scene is so familiar, except for the fact that he's in it. The Napoleon Limoges service is on the table, Empress Eugenie's set which Theo's mother bought after World War I at auction in Paris. The huge blue-and-gold urns with their horseback battle scenes are in the center of the table, too precious for flowers, but Theo's collection of antique gold snuffboxes is strewn across the table-cloth like exotic jewels. I still remember the looks of horror when I was a little girl and I lobbed one across the table to my uncle. Gennie, in the starched black uniform she reserves for holidays, is clearing the crescent-shaped crystal salad plates, and out of the corner of her eye she's checking out Jamie.

"Now, Jamie," says Theo, radiant in pink Valentino, "you know Cam can't even boil water. She once tried to make Christmas cookies and she used the slice-and-bake type, and she put the whole roll into the oven. Of course, the wrapper caught fire."

"That's cool," says Jamie. "I can teach her to slice and bake."

"I should imagine. And why did you decide to become a chef?"

"I like to eat."

Mrs. Williams raises her wineglass. "To men who can cook."

Everybody toasts. Things are going better than I anticipated. Nobody even blinked an eye when Jamie showed up in a too-small sport coat and black corduroys with lobsters on them, even though we are not eating seafood. He *is* wearing a sport coat, a major concession. Since the sleeves end at his forearms, I suspect it is not even his sport coat, and I have a sudden desire to jump up and rip it off him. It doesn't belong. I know he wore this for me, and if he did this, he doesn't know yet: I like him just the way he is. Lobsters and all.

Gennie appears brandishing the turkey on a platter and places it in front of Russell. "Well, I don't know about this," he says. "We have a professional here tonight." He gestures to the carving set and steps aside. "Jamie? Will you do the honors?"

Everybody claps politely as Jamie moves to the head of the table.

"This turkey's kind of small," he says, surveying the group. "I don't know. It's gonna be close, and there won't be enough left for sandwiches. Gennie— how about an extra tray."

Everyone watches in rapt attention as Jamie takes two hot pads, grabs the turkey by the stuffing cavity with his hands, and rips it in half.

"Goodness!" gasps Delia Kirkland, whose bare hands have never touched grease in her life.

Russell stares.

Theo blinks.

Jamie drops the bottom half of the decimated bird onto the extra silver tray and proceeds to slash off the entire breast in one whack.

"That's not how I was taught to carve," ventures Ellis Williams III.

Jamie picks up a damask napkin and wipes off his hands. Then he takes off the sport coat and tosses it to me.

"Here—can you throw this on the bed with the rest of the coats?" He starts to dissect the breast. "You get all the meat off it this way and you can start your turkey soup right away with the carcass, instead of leaving it in the refrigerator for three days." The white meat falls into perfect slices. "This is how we do it at the restaurant."

He looks up and motions to the table like a conductor to an orchestra. "Eat, eat," he says.

And we do.

After dinner, we adjourn to the paneled library for coffee and rum pecan pie. Jamie sits on a tufted, fringed velvet ottoman with a cup of coffee perched on his knee. Ellis Williams III is arguing with Russell about the Chicago White Sox, of which he is an owner.

"You need a Walter Payton of baseball, that's what," says Russell.

Jamie perks up. "First you need them to do something about that work on the Dan Ryan Expressway," he says. "All that construction's gotta be hurting business."

"Exactly!" says Ellis.

"That thing's been under construction forever," says Jamie. "Nobody can get to the games."

Ellis nods enthusiastically. "Absolutely right-on."

"Nobody in this town has had the right attitude toward the White Sox since Commissioner Quinn turned on the air-raid siren when they won the pennant in 1958," says Jamie.

Ellis is laughing hysterically. "Everybody thought the Russians were bombing the city!"

A heated discussion about batting averages and most-valuable players ensues, and Theo smiles at me. She likes Jamie, I can tell. We wander over to the window and watch the traffic down on Lake Shore Drive.

"I think you could be very happy with this man," she says.

"Why do you say that?"

"Well, look at him. He's talking to Ellis and Russell. But he's looking at you."

"He tends to do that. But, Theo, he's a chef. We have nothing in common."

"When Russell and I got married, darling, we didn't have a checklist. Sometimes it doesn't matter.

You're a big girl, Cam. Old enough to know. It doesn't matter what I think, or what anybody thinks."

"Well, I'm reprioritizing things right now."

I should listen to Theo more often. It was Theo who took me to the opera when I was three, who showed me how to notice sounds and colors, who sang to me when there were thunderstorms and taught me not to be afraid. Theo never talked baby talk to me; instead she gave me a vocabulary. She gave me crayons and showed me how to write. In color. My mother—well, she gave me my life, but Theo gave me my self.

She throws up her hands as if Martians had landed on the coffee table. "Reprioritizing! You and your five-year plans! Good grief, keep your life and your business plans separate, Cam. This is Thanksgiving. Relax a little." She squeezes my hand. "It won't hurt, I promise you."

Jamie joins us at the window. "What are you girls up to? Getting into trouble?"

"I hear you sing, Mr. Kelly."

"I sang for the pope when I was in sixth grade."

"Really!"

"At the Vatican."

This is impressive information. Theo went to the Vatican too, but she had to pay to get in.

"Well! In that case, why don't you sing us an after-dinner song?"

"Theo!"

"No problem," says Jamie. And he strolls into the living room and sits down at the big grand piano that hasn't been played since I practiced my scales on it, and he pulls out a songbook left over from my piano-lesson days, when I used to practice at Theo's apartment.

"Here's something appropriate," he says. And he motions me over to accompany him as he sings "Over the River and Through the Woods to Grandmother's House We Go," and we couldn't have gotten more applause if we'd been Van Cliburn and Mel Tormé.

Later, we drive up the lakefront in Jamie's rented car. "Do you mind if we drop in on a buddy of mine?" he says.

"Who?"

"Jake. I always visit him when I'm in town."

We pass the Northwestern campus. "There's my sorority," I say.

"Oh, did you go to college?"

"Yes. I went to college." And graduate school and several courses toward my PhD too. *Oh, did you go to college?* For most of the people I know, going to college is tantamount to being born. Now that I think about it, I don't know anyone who *didn't* go to college. Except Jamie. It's part of the résumé, the credits you tally up when you meet somebody. College is worth so many points, then where you work, then what your job is. And it hits me: Jamie is not relating to me as a résumé, and this is the first time that's happened in as long as I can remember. It feels strange and wonderful. I unhook my seat belt and cuddle next to him in the car. We turn off at Central, and Jamie pulls into a driveway. "Let's roll, Kato," he says, and without knocking, we barge into the house and through the living room and he knocks on a door.

"Jake, you there?" he says as we go right in regardless.

I pull back on his sleeve. "What if he's out?"

"He's not out."

We go into the room and I'm introduced to Jake, who is lying in bed. Jake is a quadriplegic.

"Jake, I'd like you to meet Miss Right," says Jamie.

"Escape while you can," says Jake, but he's laughing, and Jamie keeps him laughing for the next half-hour.

"Thanks for the jacket," Jamie says, dumping it on the end of the bed. "She loved it." He knows I hated it, Jake knows it didn't fit, and we laugh some more.

Jake's parents come in, and his mother sits in the kitchen with me. "Jamie always comes by when he's in town," she says. "We're so glad to see him. A lot of people came after the accident, but now, you know how it is . . . But Jamie always comes."

While we drive back downtown, Jamie tells me the story of how he and Jake were swimming together one summer in high school, and they both dived into a pool, except Jake dived into the shallow end and broke his neck. "He's my best friend," Jamie says. "Besides you."

"I'm your best friend? Why? Since when?"

"Since I met ya, ba-by," he sings. "Honey, it's true isn't it? I can relax with you. You don't judge me. You don't bug me to cut my hair . . ."

"I like your hair."

"You like *me*. That's a best friend, isn't it?"

"You know, you didn't have to wear that sport coat. Why did you? Not for me, I hope."

"Honey, I wasn't sure who was going to be hanging around tonight, but I didn't want your family to think you were marrying beneath you. I wanted to be prepared."

"You were prepared. You were the only one who knew how to carve." *Marrying?*

He nods seriously. "You're right. I always knew we think alike."

"Twins," I say.

"Siamese twins," he says, and he reaches out and pulls me across the seat, as close as he can.

We're in front of my building. Jamie has to go straight to the airport from here because he has to work a double shift tomorrow at Mortimer's, which means being at the restaurant by eight A.M., and the last flight out is midnight.

"So will you marry me?" he says.

"Why would you want to do that?" I say, and I mean it. I may have degrees and titles, but I'm not half what he is as a person.

A Jed Durant song comes on the radio. I turn it off.

"Because you listen to me. Sometimes people don't, but you always do. To you I'm not just some blue-collar cook, some diamond in the rough."

"You're a ten-carat solitaire."

"You got a good eye. And you do things, you don't just talk about it."

"I'm divorced. I'm older than you. We have nothing in common." I'm ticking off the negatives, but I'm hoping he doesn't care.

"Honey, I just want to be with you. Do you want to be with me?" He makes it sound so simple.

"You're going to miss your plane," I say.

"Well, sometimes that happens." He parks illegally in front of the cardinal's house. "I know the pope," he says. "We ski together."

Upstairs, he pulls me down on the couch. "I want to give you something," he says. "Something that was my grandfather's, who I was named after." He reaches into his back pocket and hands me a flask. "My grandmother used to always carry it with her," he says.

Then he reaches into his jacket pocket and hands me a spoon. A tiny sterling-silver baby spoon. "This is for our future child," he says. "Elvis."

"Elvis." I am going to name my first son after the King?

"Only if it's a boy. You know, I was lookin' for a ring at my mom's house, but the other six kids must have cleaned her out."

"I don't know what to say." Which is an understatement.

He gets down on one knee, "Honey, I love you *this* much," he says, flinging his arms out. A Lalique plate crashes over. The Bird flaps hysterically in its cage. I could care less. I am irrational. I am emotional. I am flagrant. I am all the things I always try not to be.

I am in love.

So much for conversation. We make love instead.

We lean into each other, closer and closer, and I just want to press myself so tight against him that his imprint never goes away. He pulls off my stockings with one hand and massages my foot sweetly and kisses the arches and ankles. My dress disappears over my head, and he drapes it carefully on the floor, then lifts me and settles me on top of the silk and velvet. His huge hand covers my entire chest at once, both breasts and my throat, each of his legs is as wide as my entire waist, and I feel engulfed in a safe harbor, home.

"This is where we should be," I say, and I know I'll never go anywhere else again.

My head is buried somewhere in his chest when the colors start. Pale yellow, then tangerine, then hot, hot orange, embers sparking at my cheeks, the tips of my breasts, my belly. He seems larger than life, and I'm expanding, exploding to keep up. With two hands, he holds me around my waist, front to back, pressing into my hips, fusing us together. I have no past now, just a future with him, and I've never felt so stroked and soothed and secure. His touch is honest and sure, as if he knows, as if I told him, and we're not just making love, we're making a promise.

Later he says, "And I want you to be the mother of my children 'cause with your legs and my eyes we couldn't lose. And you got a great set of tits."

"Perfect reasoning."

"Honey," he says, arranging my hair around my face, "I'm just a guy going from day to day. I don't know what I'm doing half the time. But you think about things—you're so smart, people pay you big money to think. And you like being with me, so you must be even smarter. I won the lottery when I met you, and I knew that the first time, because you walked right in there like you owned the world. If we were on the trapeze, I knew you couldn't do the triple, but you'd try it. And I knew that underneath all that armor you were wearing, you were pure gold. You know what you want, honey, and if you want me, I'm the luckiest man in the world. Come on, baby." He pulls me closer.

"Where would we live?" I'm stalling.

"Wherever. If people eat, I can work there."

"Maybe after Christmas . . ."

"Is there somebody else? Let me know, I'll kill him."

"No. But that's not the point."

"The point is, I'm crazy about you." He looks at me and he's waiting for me to say something, but I can't really articulate what I feel. "What is it that you want?" he says. "Because all I want is you."

"I want to be with you." Now that I've said it, I realize it's true. This is a man I'm choosing with my heart, and because his heart is in the right place, I know mine is too. Finally. "But, really, we hardly know each other and we have to make sense."

"You'd never have to cook dinner again."

"That makes sense."

And he kisses my left hand, one finger at a time, and on the fourth finger he stops and traces the outline of a ring, and suddenly I know exactly what I want.

"Yes," I say, and I leap into his naked lap. "Yes, yes, yes."

Chapter Fourteen

I walk from a cloud into a bloodbath.

Nine A.M., the Monday after the Thanksgiving weekend, and the Xerox is still hot on the confidential management memo that will announce the hatcheting of six people in my group, a decision in which I had no part. Bruce and Harold are showing it to me for cosmetic approval. They sit there calmly, hands folded.

"What do you think of this wording? We want to do the best thing for morale."

"The best thing for morale would be not to fire anybody. Jesus Christ, look at this list! Arnie, for God's sake! I just talked him into turning down a job at Burnett, and now we're putting him out in the cold! Carrie and Clark. They've worked their tails off for us the past few months. Overtime, weekends . . . Richard—he's the best illustrator we have. Maeve—she just started. She hadn't even been here six months. The Mole—God knows how many times he's bailed us out. What's happening? Did we lose an account? Couldn't you have discussed this with me first?" *What was I, blind that I didn't see this coming? Is my name next on the list, in invisible ink? Was*

220

the Zing! presentation a success, or was I in the Twilight Zone?

"There's no need to get emotional, Cam," says Harold. "Nobody feels good about this. But we know you'll handle it like the professional you are."

"*I'm* supposed to handle it? *I'm* supposed to fire these six people who do not deserve to be fired?"

"Well, it's best coming from the immediate supervisor, which you are. We know you'll do it with sensitivity."

I put the memo in my lap. "I can't do this."

Bruce frowns. "Cam, you're a team player. There are certain business issues involved here."

I don't like the sound of this. "At least Brenda's not on this list."

"We tried to be as fair as possible."

"What about Fred? I don't see his name either, and he's not pulling his weight."

"He's a client's nephew."

"Of course."

"What about Dick Scully's group? Doesn't he have to absorb any of these cutbacks?" Scully is like the iguana, a creature that has survived since prehistoric times by staying the same. Somehow, Scully endures, no matter how lukewarm his group's work may be. This seems phenomenal, especially now.

"Dick won't be involved in this . . . transition."

"I see." But I don't.

Harold leans forward in his chair. "This is the beginning of a very positive opportunity for all of us," he says. "We've opened discussions with Soixant."

"The French?"

"It will be rough at the beginning, granted. Transition is never easy, but then we will see a major

221

move upward. An opportunity to become a mega-agency."

Bruce nods and flicks an ash off his cigar. "You have to admit, Cam, that with things as they have been, everyone's upward mobility has been limited. Now, the sky's the limit. How'd you like to think about working in Paris?"

Elba, in other words. "I can't speak French."

"Well," says Harold quickly, "that's all in the future. For now we have this reorganization to handle."

"When does this become effective?"

"Probably the first of the year. And you don't have to let people go right away. Between Christmas and New Year's is our target timing."

"What about the Zing! business? If we get it, can't we keep these people?"

Bruce shakes his head. "That's a deal point. The Soixant group wants to integrate their own people, so we have international strength on that business."

"And bottom line is always an issue," says Harold.

"What about Juice and me? It was our pitch."

"You're still key players. In fact, we plan to request a substantial increase for both of you. This coalition is committed to recognizing good work." Harold looks as sincere as I've ever seen him. Bruce looks at the carpet.

Harold stands up and puts his hand on my shoulder. "Let us think of a way to handle this personnel situation. We'll set something up with Human Resources. And you can put the word out to the recruiters if you'd like, to get a discreet head start."

"When will we get an official decision on Zing!?"

"Any day now. We see it as the crown jewel of our new coalition. If we keep a lid on the timing of the announcement, it could send the stock through the ceiling."

"So we're on hold?"

"I wouldn't say that," says Bruce. "There's the Bakery. Cakes for the Dead is taking off. Stratoglider is introducing a tricycle. Trendar Hair Care is talking cream rinse again. And media may have finally convinced Bridal Bouquet to get off the dime on that TV spot, provided they go for late-night fringe. There's plenty of new product opportunity there too. In fact, get on that right away." He makes a note with his pencil.

After work, Juice and I regroup at the Margarita. The mariachis are serenading us with "Don't Cry for Me, Argentina" as we try to make sense of everything.

"Here's how I see it," I say, tipping the mariachis to take a hike. "We got six lame ducks, two cases for euthanasia, and four live bodies, not including you and me."

"It's the typical political shit," says Juice, flicking guacamole off his fingers. "There's nothing we can do. We work at an expensive club, of which we are not members."

I eat nachos and contemplate this. It's true. And there's nothing we can do about it, except . . .

"There's still Zing!" I say. "We've done a great job with Zing! Simmons knows who did what there. We have equity. Supposedly it's in the bag, and that should give us some say-so, particularly if they open up Spirit. I have an idea." A wild thought surges through my mind. God! Why didn't I think of this before? "Listen, Juice. We can get out from under Bruce. We can make this merger work for us. It might even be good. Without the merger, we're stuck. Bruce gets promoted, we get promoted. The titles change, but we have no power—things stay the same."

Juice frowns. He doesn't get it yet.

"So what we do now is go directly to Harold with a proposition for the French. Here's the deal: if we get Zing! They set us up in our own new-products division, with Zing! as the cornerstone. Besides, aren't we the new product wunderkinds?"

"You believe your own press? Or are you talking coup?"

"Why not? Look what happened with the IBM account. Those guys who did the Charlie Chaplin work split off."

"They got their asses sued."

"Juice," I say, getting really excited now, "I think we could do it. We could pull it off. Between us we have . . . what, thirty years on soft drinks? Even if they just give us a retainer, we'd probably triple what we make now."

"That's true," says Juice. How can he be so blasé? He picks the salt off the rim of his glass. "Let me think about this, okay? A lot depends on my alimony situation."

"Okay, but don't think too long. We only have till Christmas. As I see it, we should get to Harold by"—I pull out my new Filofax and confirm on the calendar— "New Year's. And then we'd have to get Soixant involved up-front, too. But all we really need is a go-ahead from Simmons' people."

I'm thinking I could be president of this division. Free at last.

I call Jamie as soon as I get home.

"Honey, it sounds good, but, I don't know. Won't this new thing make you kind of crazy?"

"Sure, at first. But year one, we'd get set up, year

two, we'd start building the client list, year three, we'd maybe see a profit—"

"What year do I fit in?"

"You fit in now, Jamie. It'll all work out. You'll see."

Within twenty-four hours I am firing six people. I go from office to office to office, feeling like I have Bambi in my rifle sight. Firing someone is the worst feeling in the world, but even worse if they don't deserve it. There's no good way to handle it. What I do is go to their offices and tell them: policy. Corporate policy. I always go to the firee's office, ever since the time a baby art director burst into tears and spent an hour and a half in my office shredding Kleenex. Now, if the situation disintegrates, I can just slip out and close the door behind me.

I give the same speech to everyone, and everyone knows it's insipid. When it comes to an across-the-board cut like this, reasons don't add up. All you can say is, "Don't take it personally." So that's what I say. Everybody takes it pretty well, except for Clark, who throws a dart across his office into a target that, I realize with a start, is a picture of me.

Arnie storms straight into my office. "What the fuck is going on here? These people shouldn't be fired." He drops onto my couch and leans his head against the wall.

"I know. It's an across-the-board cut." Now comes the worst part. Do I tell Arnie he's next on the list? "Arn," I say, "this place is a zoo. Maybe you should rethink the Burnett offer."

"They gave the job to somebody else." He stares at me with venom in his eyes.

"Oh."

This is what I despise most about being in management—the ruining-people's-lives part. I walk down the hall and nobody will look me in the eye; word travels fast.

I'm sitting in my office picking at my fingernails with an Xacto knife when Bruce comes in.

"Tough day," he said.

"Yeah."

He swings the imaginary golf club. "It all boils down to this: the inner game. Some of us want to win more than others. Take your friend Lester."

"What's Lester have to do with it?"

"The chickenshit's settling out of court. He knows I'd bash his brains out in a jury trial."

"I think we acted prematurely. If-slash-when we get the Zing! business firmed up, we're not going to have enough people."

Bruce shrugs. "We can always hire. This is the Euromarket, Cam. Hardball."

"Eurotrash, you mean."

"Whatever. They've got the capital these days."

I decide to test Bruce, see if he has a shred of humanity buried under there. "Bruce, guess what? Not to change the subject, but I'm getting married. I'm engaged."

"Our little Cam! Well! Congratulations! Who's the lucky fellow? That broker?"

"No. Jamie Kelly. A chef from out of town."

"A chef. Now, isn't that great? Tell him about the French. He may go for the idea of living in Paris. Great food, great food. God, I remember the pressed duck at La Tour d'Argent . . . they number the suckers. He'll go nuts. This is wonderful, just wonderful. When is the wedding?"

"We haven't planned it yet, but after Christmas."

Bruce looks genuinely thrilled for me, and for a minute I soften toward him. The pressures of this business make people do strange things sometimes. Maybe that's his problem. He's under a lot of pressure.

"Do you speak French, Bruce?"

He grimaces. "Menu French, that's about it. I can barely speak *English*, you know that. But they got me in Berlitz classes."

This merger must be a done deal.

The minute Bruce leaves my office, I go to see Juice.

"Juice, sit down. Brace yourself."

"Nothing you say could ever surprise me. You know that. *You* sit down. You're a wreck." He starts raising his voice, getting dramatic. Juice should have been on the stage. "A wreck, goddamn it! A goddamn fucking wreck!" He grabs my hair. "Look at your hair!" He grabs my cheek. "Look at your . . . blood vessels!"

I sit in the pig throne, which is a wooden chair painted pink with hooves for arms and legs. "Okay, okay. Knock it off. I want to tell you about two future marriages which are going to happen."

"Don't say the word 'marriage' in this office. At least not out loud." He looks around furtively, as if two or three ex-wives and a palimony lawyer are lurking behind the storyboards.

I pick up a Slinky. Juice's office is a big toybox. "Listen. I'm getting married."

"Good for you. I hope not to anyone you've been married to before."

"No. To a chef."

"What chef?"

"Somebody I met when we were in New York. You'd like him."

"Great. Maybe now you'll be a housewife like the good Lord intended."

"Hah! President of a new-product division is more like it. Now guess who else is getting married."

"What is this, a pop quiz?"

"The company. To the French. A merger with Soixant."

"Is that why you fired six people?"

"Yes. They forced me to."

"They forced you not to tell me first? They pulled a gun on you?"

"Juice!" I can tell he's really upset. About the firings or about not being told, I'm not sure. "Juice, come on. I'm here now. We're talking about it."

"A little after the fact, wouldn't you say?"

"You should thank me. It was horrible. Why should you associate yourself with this shit?"

"Right, Cam. I should associate myself with storyboards and cutting and pasting, and leave the *executive* decisions up to you. After all, you're the executive in the group."

"That's not fair." But I know Juice is right. I should have shared this with him. I just was too preoccupied. "Juice, I'm sorry. It just got away from me. We're partners. The good news is, our new division is more viable than ever. With all this diversion going on, all this crossfiring, we can pull it off. It's almost time. All we have to do is lock down a few more accounts, and I know right where to start."

"Where?"

"Smartco. They live and breathe new products. We'll get a hearing, I'm sure."

228

Juice cuts out a string of paper sharks. "And what about your wedding? To this New York guy?"

"He's very supportive."

Juice nods. "He must be a saint." I can see he's taking this with a grain of salt. He's not even sure I didn't make the whole thing up.

"Come on. Cheer up. We'll be out of here in no time. Are you with me?"

He shrugs. "Whither thou goest."

"Hang in there, partner. It won't be long."

I go back to my office and look at the calendar. Christmas is four weeks away. I decide not to do anything drastic till then. No marriages, defections, or coups. After all, 'tis the season. I have too much Christmas shopping to do to have a nervous breakdown.

My whole career is teetering. So what do I do? I make out a Christmas list.

I used to spend weeks looking for just the right presents. I made gingerbread cookies in fantasy shapes and decorated them with silver sprinkles and candied violets, then gave them away in baskets I hand-painted myself. I stuck cloves into oranges. I needlepointed ornaments for the tree. I spent hundreds of hours on Christmas gifts.

Now I have distilled my Christmas shopping down to a two-point program: the catalog and the phone. At eleven-thirty I close the door, pretend I am inside making decisions, and circle items in Marshall Field's Christmas catalog. It doesn't help. I keep thinking about the people I had to fire, wondering how they're going to get through their Christmases.

At five-thirty I leave the office. I never get home this early. The Bird cheeps when I come home. I go back to his cage, change his seeds, and tickle his head. This Bird has seen a lot. They tell me birds in the parrot family live thirty years, so he's going to see a lot more. I'm probably going to have to provide for him in my will. He deserves it, he's been my only consistent living companion for five years. It occurs to me that I don't even know if Jamie has a pet. I don't even know what his apartment looks like. He's never seen my office, or my résumé, or my college yearbook.

How can we be getting married?

I wait till midnight, when the dinner rush is over at the restaurant in New York, and call him on their pay phone.

"I've been thinking, Jamie," I say.

"Me too, honey. I miss you. I wish you were here."

I wonder if he'll ever stop calling me "honey." "Was it a busy night?"

"Yeah. The Kissingers were here with a big party."

"You sound tired."

"I just finished cleaning Dover sole, and that's no fun at all."

"Well, I'll let you finish up."

Two hours later, he calls back. "Thank you," he says.

I'm half-asleep. "For what?"

"For what you give me, honey."

"What? I don't give you anything."

"Yes you do."

"What?"

"Oh, phone calls. Back rubs, sometimes. And making love."

"That doesn't cost anything."

"Yes it does."

"What?"

"A little piece of your soul."

I smile into my pillow. *That's* how we can be getting married.

"Are you coming home for Christmas?" I say.

"I *always* come home for Christmas. We all do. Mom expects us. She's expecting you too."

"I'm going to meet your mother?" I jolt up in bed.

"She's going to love you. Because I do. We always get together Christmas Eve—all seven kids, Mom, the husbands and wives and nieces and nephews. She has a buffet, we go to midnight mass. It's a tradition." He starts singing "Jingle Bells."

He's into "dashing through the snow" when I remember. *Christmas Eve.* The Smartco Christmas party, a.k.a The Prom, is Christmas Eve. Every year. And it's not so much a party as it is a command performance. Nobody likes it, everybody grumbles about it, but nobody bucks the system. I decide not to mention this now. Maybe the Smarts will economize this year and eliminate the party. Maybe I won't have to go— although this year it's more important to me than ever to keep up good relationships with the Smarts. Well, it's always held at a country club in the northern suburbs, and that's not far from where Jamie's mother lives; if we take the expressway, we can probably do both.

"Jamie?"

He breaks out of the chorus. "What, honey?"

"We have a slight conflict."

"You want to go to your church instead?"

"Actually, it's business."

"On Christmas Eve? What business is open?"

"Well, there's a company Christmas party given by one of my clients. A big bash. Maybe we could just . . . stop in."

"Sure, no problem."

"We won't stay long, I promise."

"That's good, honey, because my mom'll be waiting."

I'm wondering how we can pull this off, but it should work. Haven't I always been good at doing two things at once?

Chapter Fifteen

The hors d'oeuvres at the Prom are awesome. Clams casino, smoked ham, oysters Rockefeller, halves of embryonic new potatoes spooned with sour cream and caviar, three-inch nouvelle pizzas with trendy toppings like duck sausage and arugula, quiche, egg rolls, crudités, and microscopic chops of apparently unborn baby lamb ring three walls. If you walked the perimeter of the room with a pedometer, you'd probably rack up about a quarter-mile. An entire table is devoted to Tex-Mex: guacamole, nachos, tacos, the works. Another peninsula establishes a raw bar: enough bluepoints, jumbo shrimp, cracked crab, and mussels to populate a small ocean. In the center of the room, glacierlike ice sculptures with red roses and white poinsettias frozen inside encircle mounds of glistening caviar.

This is business entertaining at its best.

The black-tie crowd swarms in from the adjacent receiving room, where a mammoth fire blazes in a rough-hewn stone fireplace. It looks like about seven hundred people. The current governor, two ex-governors, the mayor, the head of an investment banking firm, a soap-opera star, forty or fifty Fortune 500 CEO's, the owner of a Kentucky Derby winner, the owner of Kentucky Fried Chicken, Ann Landers, and Jesse Jackson are in the crowd.

"Where will my driver eat?" someone is demanding.

Jamie glances over and shrugs. He is wearing a stage jacket from his rock-and-roll act, shiny and turquoise, sort of Palm Beach circa 1964, with a navy turtleneck and dark wool slacks. His hair is slicked straight back off his face into his usual ponytail, which is held by a pink terry-cloth-elastic band. A few pieces escape and hang over his eyes.

"Beatrice, you've really outdone yourself this year," I overhear the mayor, who is in front of us in the receiving line.

Beatrice Smart, who spent the last forty years teaming up with her husband in propelling a minor-league aerosol-can company into Smartco, a blockbuster conglomerate now worth God knows how many multimillions, smiles and jangles her diamond-braceleted arms across the décolletage of her jeweled caftan. The fabric looks like it was embroidered in twenty-two-karat gold thread by Imelda Marcos' personal seamstress. "Heh-heh-heh. Good!"

This is the big blowout business/society party of the year, and the Smarts are not shy about acknowledging it.

Only the *crème de la crème* of the Smarts' business associates are invited to mingle with their real-estate-tycoon crowd and personal friends. The party is always held on Christmas Eve at a fancy suburban country club. The Smarts are gracious, no question, but apparently they haven't thought that you might have other plans. At any rate, it wouldn't matter, since refusal is tantamount to a letter of resignation. Beatrice Smart considers it a personal insult if you don't show up, and this is a woman you don't want to ruffle, much less insult.

Jamie's family is having their traditional Christmas Eve eggnog party two suburbs away. The plan is, we'll sneak in late. It really feels good to have a relationship where the other person can actually compromise. Timothy always hated parties like this. He used to punish me for forcing him to go by sitting there looking elegant, like Jay Gatsby would have played it if he'd been forced to touch down in Schaumburg. Or he'd come to the party and wouldn't speak to anyone. Or he'd come to the party and yawn. Or, if he was really pissed off, I'd find a Water Pik and vacuum-cleaner-attachment variety pack under the tree Christmas morning. He was good at passive aggression. But with Jamie there was no argument. He did point out that he'd be missing the eggnog party with his six brothers for the first time in his life, but it wasn't like we were going to miss it *entirely*. We'd agreed to make it for the Christmas carols, around ten o'clock. I knew it would work out, since the Prom always goes like clockwork. Beatrice Smart could have coordinated the Normandy invasion with her eyes closed.

The huge doors to the dining room are flung open by tuxedoed waiters as Stanley Paul strikes up "My Kind of Town" from the ballroom stage. It's the big version of his orchestra. Eighteen pieces.

"Want to dance?" says Jamie.

I shake my head quickly. It's deadly to be seen dancing at a party if you're in top management. The party photographer will invariably get a candid shot of you with the front of your dress slipping three inches too low, they'll post it on the coffee-room bulletin board, and your career is dead in the water by Monday morning. Like any society, there are the rules, then there are the RULES.

"Here's the rules," I tell Jamie. "Be conservative. Talk politely. Work the floor; don't dance on it. We are here for one reason: to make a good impression. Not to have a good time. We should not drink too much, talk too much, or stuff ourselves at the buffet table. Any extravagance is suspect. You can almost hear them in the next management meeting: *"She porked down six desserts and we could see up her dress when she was dancing with Norton from R&D! Did you know she wears a garter belt? Quick! Pull the brand from her group."*

Jamie shrugs and tickles my elbow. Of course, he's seen much fancier parties than this at Mortimer's. The Smarts are big, but I don't see any First Ladies in this crowd.

Brucie's wife, Sarah, catches my eye from across the room, and we wave. I like her. God knows what she sees in Brucie; she must be a steel-belted woman. Of course, she doesn't have to put up with him all that much; he's at the office eighteen hours a day. I hear she makes him smoke his cigars in the garage.

"Sarah, this is my fiancé, Jamie Kelly. From New York." As if being from New York would explain why he looks more like he dropped in from another planet.

But she's gracious. "Hello, Jamie, and congratulations. Welcome to M&M. We're like one big family here."

"Well, I like big families."

Jamie looks at me, and I can see he likes my vintage forties dress too.

What you wear is important: nothing too revealing, too flashy, certainly nothing remotely sexy. At internal company parties, the younger secretaries often show up in bare midriffs or strapless dresses or lace gloves. That's how you know they are not executives, even if you've never met them. The managerial women try to blend in with the woodwork, which means a dress that won't compete with the boss's wife's. The older executive secretaries, the kind who are corporate fixtures, have the best strategy: they skip the party scene altogether. They can afford to. They have real power. Of course, at the Prom, the guest list is limited to top management.

Me, I always wear the same thing when it's business-black-tie—a jet-beaded black forties bias-cut dress that I got from my grandmother when she was cleaning out her storage locker. It hits me mid-calf and has a deep neckline and short sleeves. Nobody can ever place it, which is good. I love this dress. Theo has a four-generations portrait: me as a baby, my mother, my grandmother, and my great-grandmother. In the picture, Theo is wearing this dress. It's my secret, and it makes me feel very superior, no matter what anyone else is ever wearing. Ralph Lauren can give you Heritage on a Hanger, but money can't buy a dress like this.

Brucie sidles up. "Cam, Cam, good to see you." A robust kiss intersects with my cheek, leaving a damp spot, like I was smacked with a sponge.

"Bruce Berenger." He extends a hand to Jamie, and he's smiling really happily now that he's seen him and realizes that this guy is not ideal corporate-companion material, unlike if I had showed up with, say, Lee Iacocca.

Brucie waves a blue-cornmeal corn chip. "Great guacamole. Just great. Jamie, you gotta try this stuff." Bruce gives Jamie's shoes the once-over and I know he's relieved beyond relief that I'm not quite high enough on the ladder to rate sitting at one of the Smarts' personal tables.

Jamie could care less. "They got a pretty good crowd here." He sips his Beefeater's, and his huge green eyes skim the room, and I know he's not missing a thing.

Bill Abbott materializes at my side. He leans over and I notice a madras cummerbund and matching suspenders.

"So who's this?"

"My fiancé."

I introduce Jamie. Off to the left, I see Charlie Ness peering at us with arched eyebrows.

"So," I hear Bill Abbott say, "what did you say you do?"

"He's a chef," Bruce answers for Jamie. "Thank God, because who would want to eat Cam's cooking?"

"I would," says Jamie.

We search for our table in the dining room, which is straight out of *Babes in Toyland*. The Prom has a different theme every year. Two years ago: snowflakes. Last year: American country. This year, it's bears. Cute, fuzzy stuffed bears. Big bears, little bears, mama bears, papa bears, baby bears, miniature bears, life-size bears with triplet bears riding them bear-back, bears in pinafores, bonnets, uniforms, and mittens, bears perched on branches of trees and reindeers' backs and staggered four deep over the backdrop of the band stage. At each table, centerpieces of giant gingerbread houses are populated by bears. Perched on the service plates are boxes of jelly beans and thimble-size bears in little microscopic T-shirts. These swiftly disappear into pockets and purses.

Jamie is talking to Marilyn Arthurs, the senior brand manager on hairspray. She's wearing a poison-green satin Christian Lecroix knockoff, and she has a cold.

"What you need is some chicken soup," Jamie suggests.

To him, with the right recipe, you could cure cancer.

"I can't make chicken soup unless it's Campbell's," she says, drumming her champagne glass with French manicured nails.

"Honey, wake up. All you do is cut up the chicken and vegetables."

He's right. This would be easy for Marilyn, if she thought about it. Her specialty already is slashing things—like budgets.

She sneezes and gropes for an antique lace handkerchief that's tucked into the pocket of her satin jacket. "I tried it once. It tasted like dishwater."

"How long did you leave it on?"

"An hour."

He shrugs. "That's your problem. Good stock takes six hours."

"Who has six hours to watch stock boil?" enunciates Marilyn.

"Just leave it on low and cut out, honey," Jamie says. "No problem."

Suddenly all the women are asking Jamie for culinary advice. So is Bill Abbott, who turns out to be a gourmet cook. "There's an art to a wok," I hear him saying. "But when it comes to bok choy . . ." Julie edges into the conversation by asking Jamie how to roast a pig in the microwave.

"Good for you, Cam," says Sarah Berenger as she

checks her place card. "You've found a man who can cook."

I look at Sarah, and I wonder if she knows what I'm thinking: In the ad world, everybody is a caricature. Her own husband borders on one. So do I, I admit it. Call it an occupational hazard. We are forced to exaggerate ourselves, position ourselves like the products we sell, then sell ourselves. Jamie is not a caricature. He's a real person.

Beatrice Smart ambles over, diamond bracelets ajangle, dress wafting like a metallic spinnaker, and everyone snaps to attention.

Jamie pulls a red-and-white-striped candy cane out of the chimney of the gingerbread-house centerpiece and starts eating it. "The problem with these things is, they always put on too much icing. You can't taste the gingerbread."

"Jamie's a chef," I tell Beatrice Smart as he breaks off a corner of the roof and pops it in his mouth.

"How nice."

Jamie snaps off a spun-sugar shutter. Is he going to eat the entire centerpiece before the first course hits the table?

"At Mortimer's in New York."

Her eyes light up. "Mortimer's! My goodness!" She must read *Women's Wear Daily*.

"Their eggs Benedict!" She rolls her eyes in ecstatic memory. "How *do* they do it?"

"You can't cook the eggs more than two minutes, twenty seconds. And I make a great hollandaise. Forty egg yolks, three hundred and twenty ounces of clarified butter . . ."

Beatrice nods attentively. She's shrewd, she's probably figuring out a way to formulate hollandaise in an aerosol can. Spray-on hollandaise sauce. I start writing the commercial in my head:

VIDEO	AUDIO
A CAR CRUSHER DESCENDS AND PULVERIZES A DOUBLE BOILER.	ANNOUNCER (V.O.): Say goodby to messy hollandaise. Say hello to new
CLOSE-UP OF HOLLANDAISE CAN.	Smartco Instant Hollandaise. Brunch can be a
CAN SPRAYS EGGS.	breeze.
	Music up: "Sh-Boom."
GARNISH WITH A TRUFFLE.	ANNOUNCER: When you cook the *Smartco* way.

"A daring chef will cook the hollandaise over an open flame," Jamie is saying, "not in a double boiler. You'll whisk the yolks till you can do your initials in the bowl with the whisk—that's the consistency you're after. Then take it off the flame."

Sarah Berenger is taking notes on a cocktail napkin.

"Slowly drizzle in the clarified butter, a cup at a time. When it gets shiny, add the warm lemon juice. And voilà—hollandaise."

Beatrice Smart grabs Jamie's sleeve and pulls him aside. I follow. "It's so *nice* to have a friend at Mortimer's." She drills him with a look. "They say it's the *rudest* restaurant in America."

"Only if you're not a friend." He smiles. "Heh-heh-heh."

"The next time we go to New York, Ronald and I will go to Mortimer's," she announces.

"Sure, honey. Ask for Jamie. They'll take good care of you."

Honey. He just called Beatrice Smart, one-half of our biggest client, *honey.* I drift into the crowd. Maybe she'll forget I'm with him.

No such luck.

I'm checking out Juice's green bow tie with little red dots. Or maybe they're not dots. I squint.

"Pigs," Juice says, tilting his head back and surveying the crowd with a superior glance. I look closer. He's right. There are miniature hand-painted pigs all over his bow tie. I've never seen a person who can come up with a pig for every occasion. Juice doesn't mind being identified with pigs at all. "They have superior intelligence," he reiterates, apparently oblivious of the fact that they allow themselves to be sliced into strips, fried, and eaten on toast with lettuce and tomato.

The band launches into "My Way," and Beatrice Smart sashays up, forging a wake across the dance floor.

"Woo-oop! Woo-oop! Dive! Dive!" Juice does a great imitation of a submarine diving for cover as he disappears behind a pyramid of bears in aprons and T-shirts.

"Cam!" Mrs. Smart waves at me, and I'm blinded by a diamond solitaire, or is it a skating rink on her left hand? "Cam, your friend Jamie says the new trend in food will be mashed potatoes. Imagine it! Mashed potatoes!" She throws back her head and laughs, and a scalloped cabochon emerald the size of a baby's fist bounces on her bodice. Then she grips my arm and stares straight into my eyes. She has the smallest pupils I have ever seen. "Come over here," she says. We walk to the edge of the dance floor.

"Mashed potatoes. Instant mashed potatoes. We have that technology." She is silent for a second. "But so do others. Mashed potatoes are as old as . . ."

"The nursery," I say. "That's just it, Mrs. Smart. Nursery food is the new trend. People are fed up with nouvelle cuisine and food they can't pronounce. They're going back to what's familiar."

Beatrice Smart nods vigorously. "Trends," she says. "We have to go with the trends."

"It's not what's new," I say. "It's how we position the product. The identity we give it in the marketplace. Look at Stovetop Stuffing. Stuffing had been around since the Pilgrims. They just showed us a new angle on it. We can do the same thing with mashed potatoes."

Mrs. Smart wheels around to Jamie.

"Exactly!" Mrs. Smart announces. "We'll have to discuss this seriously with Ronald." She checks her watch, which has an opal face, ringed with pavé diamonds. "You'll join us after the party? A few close friends. Family. We'll talk mashed potatoes then." She whirls around like a tank on a turret and rolls through the crowd, commandeering the closest ex-governor for a fox-trot charge. "Fame!" she sings along with the band.

Jamie and I make our way back to the table as some sort of pink mousse is served. "God," I whisper. "You must have really made a hit."

He grins. "Nursery food, honey." He pulls out my chair, and I notice I'm sitting next to Bob Shatola, V.P., Smartco R&D. He's very intelligent, black, and a research chemist. The last time I talked to Bob, he was carrying a big round ring with a set of varicolored scalps attached to test the effectiveness of cream-rinse formulas. "She invited us to join them tonight."

"When?"

"Tonight. After the party. To talk mashed potatoes. Do you want your picture on a box of freeze-
dried mashed potatoes? Sort of like Chef Boyardee?"

Jamie shakes his head. "No good, honey. My mom
doesn't like to stay up late on Christmas Eve. Santa's
comin' early over there."

Oh, God. His mother's! Don't ask me how, but it
slipped my mind. Jesus! All the nieces and nephews
and the six brothers. "Listen." I touch Jamie's turquoise sleeve. "I know we said we'd stop by, but
Beatrice Smart is really serious. And it's so hard to
get one-on-one with her."

"This is Christmas Eve."

"You don't know her. She never stops working.
She thought up the idea of aerosol lint remover
when she was in labor. It's a famous story. She was
timing the contractions, and . . ."

Jamie is just standing there staring calmly at me.
Bob Shatola has finished his mousse by this time,
and he looks up. "Saved your place," he joked,
gesturing to Jamie's empty chair.

The waiters clear the table for the next course.
Suddenly there's a drumroll, and Ronald Smart leaps
onto the stage to a smattering of applause, his steel-
gray hair and Italian custom-made tuxedo giving
him an air of authority that he doesn't especially
need at this party. I flicker my eyes at Jamie. This is
the holiday toast. No talking.

Mr. Smart holds up his hands, palms out, like a
politician, or maybe the pope. "Friends," he says,
tapping the microphone, "and everyone here tonight is a friend of Beatrice's and mine—welcome,
good health, happy holidays."

I notice Brucie across the table applauding enthusiastically. Jamie is still standing next to my chair. I look up at him with my most pleading expression. Sure, I'd like to meet his mother and the brothers and nieces and nephews, but they'll always be around—in fact, I'm sure they'll be there Christmas Day—and I'm not sure when I'll have another shot at Beatrice Smart.

"What if we call them and then go over tomorrow?" I whisper.

"What is this? 'Let's Make a Deal'?" Jamie doesn't even lower his voice, and everyone at the table looks pointedly at us. Mr. Smart is speaking.

"This year will long be remembered as . . ."

Dramatic pause.

"The year of the Hairspray." He pulls a can of Smartco Super-Hold Hairspray from his tuxedo pocket and spritzes the air. "Why? Because of you. Our friends."

Everyone raises a glass.

Jamie still won't sit down. He leans across the table and cracks a six-inch-square corner, complete with icicles, off the gingerbread house and downs it in two bites as the frosting wall collapses.

The waiters bring in grilled veal chops and start setting them around the table.

"Excuse me," I mutter. I look up at Jamie. "I'm going to the ladies' room." I'm hoping that when I come back, he'll be sitting there eating a veal chop.

Luckily, our table is close to the back of the room, so I sneak out between a life-sized stuffed bear in a starched calico apron and a Christmas tree decorated with strings of popcorn and Life Savers. I whip into the ladies' room, and when I turn to close the door, it bumps on Jamie's shoulder.

The ladies' room is huge at this club—complete

with dressing tables, chintz-upholstered chairs, and an attendant. It's empty, except for the attendant.

"Take a break," says Jamie, and hands her a five-dollar bill.

She leaves and Jamie locks the door and leans against it. Then he reaches out and folds me into his arms.

"I know," he said, and his voice is very low. "You're a big shot. You know all about company politics. Okay, I'll give you that. But I know all about Christmas Eve and how that should be. So we're even. And Christmas Eve is the night Christ was born and all, and it's when you should be with your family."

He's right, of course, in the logical sense. But we're not dealing with Rudolph the Red-Nosed Reindeer here. A major new-product assignment is at stake. What am I going to do? Drop the ball? Miss my chance?

"Jamie," I say, somewhat muffled from being buried in his arms, "I know it shouldn't be a priority—it's not, it's *not* a priority, I promise you, but Beatrice Smart really likes you."

"So when she comes to New York, I'll make sure I help her get a good table at the restaurant," he says evenly.

This is not going well. Not well at all. I know Jamie knows exactly what's happening here. He doesn't need to say, "You'd rather spend Christmas Eve discussing box copy for a new and better potato flake than with my family, like we agreed." I search my mind for a logical argument. No dice.

"Well," I finally say, "I think I have to go with Beatrice Smart. We can see your mom tomorrow, right? On Christmas Day. That's the important event, isn't it?"

"Baby, you gotta do what you gotta do. I'll see ya later."

"No, no, Jamie. *We'll* go with Beatrice Smart. We will. Because it was your idea, the mashed-potatoes thing. It's both of us. Come on."

He drops his arms and leans over, touching my forehead with his. He imperceptibly shakes his head no, and I can see his beautiful alabaster skin, so close I brush his face with my eyelashes. BANG! BANG! BANG! Somebody is trying to pound down the door. "Who's in there?" a woman's voice bellows.

"Who wants to know?" says Jamie through the door.

"This is Security. Please clear the powder room." I can hear walkie talkies.

Jamie throws the lock, the door swings open, and the First Lady of Illinois, surrounded by a feminine entourage, enters the ladies' room. "This is the *ladies* room." A woman bodyguard glares. You don't mess with her. She's probably packing heat in her beaded bag.

Jamie shrugs. "Young love," he says. "We just can't seem to agree on a china pattern. Right, honey?"

He walks out so nonchalantly you'd think this was the lube bay, not the powder room. Much less the governor's wife. I follow, and we walk back to the table without saying a thing. The air around us seems to have crystallized. Ice crystals.

We go through the motions of eating the stupid veal chop, and Juice breezes by the table. "Nuclear missile strike your centerpiece?" he asks. I've been nuked, that's what. I'm either going to be blown to bits or die of radiation: now, *there's* choices.

If I go to Jamie's mother's, I will miss out on a chance to get a real leg up with Smartco. I have the scenario laid out in my mind. Beatrice Smart will take me under her wing and fit quite neatly into my plans for the new-product division. Jamie will do the commercials and become a media mashed-potato celebrity: the Idaho Chef. All this is about to be blasted to smithereens so I can assist in the assemblage of sixty-two miles of Lionel train track. I should have a major talk with myself right now.

VIDEO	AUDIO
HUGE CHRISTMAS PARTY.	MUSIC (under): "Dance of the Sugarplum Fairy"
I AM SEATED AT TABLE. GIANT XMAS TREE TOWERS OVER TABLE.	
ONE ORNAMENT IS ABOUT TO FALL OFF ONTO MY HEAD. A GIANT AX. THE AX TALKS.	AX: If you meet Beatrice Smart after dinner, you will blow this relationship and be alone for Christmas, New Year's, and the rest of your life.
	ME: Okay. But will I get promoted?
THE AXE FALLS	SOUND EFFECT: WHAM!
CUT TO BLACK.	

Dessert is served, and I pick up a spoon and tap at a thin peach-colored candy shell, which breaks open to reveal coffee ice cream surrounding a center of coffee liqueur.

Juice swoops by the table again. "I don't get this relationship," he mutters on his way past, with a look in Jamie's direction. The Success Junkie won't let go. I'm hooked on the adrenaline, on the ready-set-go of it all. I want to walk away from it, but it's like the man you love to hate. Worse. Success is the pit bull of achievement. You touch it, and it clamps bear-trap jaws around your ankle. You can't shake it off, even though you know you're being maimed. And so I'm sitting here talking to Bob Shatola about potato-flake technology.

"Our freeze-dry facility is highly underutilized," he is explaining as coffee and after-dinner drinks are served.

"But couldn't we incorporate some flanker products into the freeze-dry line without great expense, since we already have access to the technology?"

I flash on a name for the line: Roadhouse-Style Potatoes. There will be plain mashed potatoes, and cheese mashed potatoes, and chili mashed potatoes, maybe New Orleans mashed potatoes and black-eyed peas. This is how my mind works. Show me a salt shaker, I'll spawn you fifteen new products in five minutes. Give me overnight, and I'll have the national rollout down to the last test market. It's a sickness.

The question is: Why can't I handle my life with even one-tenth the finesse that I launch a new product? Why can't I get off it and get on with it? Maybe Bill Abbott was right—what do I know about women? I know all about being Superwoman. *Right, Cam, and that's going to take you a long way in this life. Maybe they'll engrave a graph with your sales increases on your tombstone.*

Jamie is talking to Bill Abbott, who is across the table. They're discussing the Wisconsin Dells, and Jamie is picking fat green and red sugared gumdrops off the roof of the gingerbread house and eating them in lieu of his dessert. Bill is smiling broadly. He's very happy that I have a date, *i.e.*, living proof that I know something about women. Suddenly I am more qualified than ever for the fem-hyge business.

Every once in a while Jamie looks up at me. It's not an accusatory look at all, although I admit it, I'm feeling guilty. Jamie always accepts things as they are. It's me who apparently isn't capable of that. I glance across the room and notice Ann Landers two tables away, wearing a floor-length silver gown. Maybe I should ask her for advice.

A ripple of applause escalates to a thundering ovation: Beatrice Smart has stepped up to the podium. "Everyone, everyone," she says into the microphone, her words punctuated by a drumroll, "if you'll look under the poinsettia plant that's on every table, you'll find a number. If your seat corresponds to that number, you'll win a little something to take home. . . ."

Cymbals clash.

"The number is six!" announces Bill Abbott, peering under the silver-gilt-wrapped poinsettia pot.

"Six!" whispers Mimi Shatola excitedly. "That's the number on my place card. I win . . ." She bounces in her seat. "I've never won anything before."

"The prize is your very lovely and perfectly delectable centerpiece," announces Beatrice Smart.

Mimi Shatola blinks at the remnants of the gingerbread house at the center of our table. It's more like gingerbread *shards:* Hansel and Gretel after a terrorist attack.

Brucie frowns. "Aw, look at that sucker." He starts to laugh and I know he's planning to eat out on this story for the next month.

Stanley Paul launches into "Winter Wonderland" and I hear a rustle at the next table: a famous fashion designer in a glittered turban is unfurling a Hefty garbage bag, lawn and leaf size, from her evening purse. She leans across the table and sweeps her table's gingerbread house into the bag. While she's at it, she sideswipes in the poinsettia plant and a few stuffed bears from the surrounding decor. *One. Two. Three. Four. Five.* Perhaps she is endowing an orphanage! *Six. Seven. Eight and nine (twins).* She drops the bag to the carpeted floor and drags it toward the front door.

Every year, the Prom seems to set off the crowd's Attila the Hun instincts. Two years ago they stripped the country club, right down to the last wreath. Only because Ronald Smart built the place were repercussions minimal.

Jamie is checking his watch. What does he think? Santa is waiting on his mother's rooftop with a meter running? Just then, Ronald Smart Jr. leans over my chair. "Ronald and Beatrice are expecting you," he said. "And your . . ." He looks skeptically at Jamie. "Friend. A car will be waiting for you in the driveway in five minutes."

I smile a thank-you, but inside I'm miserable because I know that no matter what happens, I'm going to lose out tonight.

Jamie comes over and pulls out my chair.

"See you later, okay?"

"Let's see how things go tonight. I might end up staying at my mom's."

"Oh." I feel like someone squeezed all the confetti out of me. But I can't do anything different. I can't change. I feel my spine tighten; my stomach is in a slip knot. I get hot all of a sudden, and I'm smoldering slowly, slowly, and then: *Why should I? Why should I always do all the changing? You said you loved me because I am me, Jamie. Well, I'm not just the lady who feeds you half-melted marshmallows from the top of your hot chocolate with a spoon! This is me too. What you see is what you get! If it's good enough for me, it should be good enough for you too.* God, I'm sick of justifying myself. I fold my arms tightly across my chest.

Jamie walks me through the crowd to the coat check and over to the front door. A uniformed driver slides around the side of a navy-blue stretch limo. "Miss McKenna?"

Beside us, the heiress to a meat-packing fortune is stuffing a fully decorated Christmas tree into the trunk of a Mercedes station wagon. Several people are rolling out luggage carts heaped with stuffed bears. One man seems to have worked out a relay system—he makes three trips to and from the entrance portico, racing back inside each time to load up on bears.

It's freezing cold, about fifteen below zero, more with the wind-chill factor. Jamie is not wearing a coat. Mine seems nonexistent, regardless of the fact that it's Ungaro. Or maybe I'm suddenly cold because I'm leaving the warmth that Jamie creates in the crook of his arm, which is . . . *Shut up! You're being ridiculous!* Wait a minute—didn't I make a New Year's resolution that I'd find someone meaningful this year, someone who cares about me and I can care about, and now that I have, I'm climbing into a navy-blue stretch limo and being driven farther away from him than ever. *Give yourself a break, Cam. This is a career breakthrough. Jamie understands. He's had—what has he had?—hollandaise sauce like this.*

Jamie shoves a stuffed bear in a Chicago Bears helmet into my arms.

"Later," he says, and it's there in his eyes: the disappointment. I've let him down. He throws his cigarette onto the ground. Jamie can say more with a cigarette than most people can with their entire vocabulary and a thesaurus.

Okay, goddammit. I didn't say one thing when he ate the door prize. Not one fucking thing!

We don't kiss, which feels like being struck, because it's the first time since that first dinner in New York that there wasn't a kiss good-bye, and a hug in which he would stroke my back and the curls on my neck. I slip into the limo and the driver closes the door behind me. It's dark inside, and "Silent Night" is playing on the radio. I push the button and the window glides down.

"Merry Christmas, Cam," Jamie says. "Ciao, baby."

Then he walks away from the car and I am alone.

I hate the week between Christmas and New Year's. Everyone at the office is in limbo—everyone else is out on vacation. You can never get anything done. There's a gray, colorless feeling in the air, a warp between all the red and green and confetti. The days seem long and dark. We're supposed to get word on the Zing! business, the final decision, any day, but until then we can only sit and wait. Now more than ever I need work, to be busy, to be diverted. Beatrice Smart loved my ideas and is waiting for a follow-up. I've done some concept boards on the mashed-potato idea, but my heart's not in them. My heart is smashed, stomped, and weeping. I know I hurt Jamie, but I hurt myself even more. He's never hurt me—even though he hasn't called me since the Christmas Eve party, I know he never meant to consciously disappoint me. He just couldn't deal with me, and how I blame him? He's not in advertising, he doesn't have seven-figure clients. He doesn't understand about being in a client-service business, and how important certain accounts are. If a soufflé falls, he can always crack some more eggs. What do I expect? I barely knew Jamie Kelly, when it comes right down to it. And he didn't know me at all.

Yesterday I called Jamie at the restaurant. All I did was ask him if he got back to New York all right, to which the obvious answer was yes, since I was talking to him and he was in New York. "Don't you want to talk?" I said.

"Sure. Have you been enjoying yourself? How's that job going, huh? You unhappy?"

"Yes," I said.

"Good," he said. "You're dealin' with a bunch of bloodsuckers and leeches and you're the only one who doesn't see it. Unless you're one of them. Open your eyes. What are those people doing to you? What are you doing to yourself?"

"I happen to earn a very good living this way. And I do a pretty damn good job of it."

"You're a sorry little loser, honey. When instant mashed potatoes are more important than family, something's wrong. You're a nice girl, but you don't know a thing about life."

"I think that's a pretty chauvinistic approach."

"You're stupid too. Just don't be messin' with my heart." Something crashed in the background and he hung up, leaving me feeling even worse, because I think he may be right.

So I'm sitting here peeling my forty-dollar manicure down to the quick, wondering how I'm going to face New Year's without him. Why is it that relationships always seem to fall apart just before the major sentimental holidays? But I can't let it get to me like this, especially now, because we're on the verge of hearing about Zing!, and the second we do, I plan to pitch my new-product-division idea to Harold. I've worked up a plan on paper that would put six new products in the division for starters, and I drew up an organization chart with me as president and Juice as executive vice president. I showed it to Juice this morning. He didn't have much to say, but I know I can't count on a lot of cheerleading from him—he's not the organizational-chart type.

"So what do you think?" I said.

He just stared at it.

"Nothing's going to change," I told him. "We'll still be partners, like always. But we'll have power."

"*You'll* have power," he said. He gathers a marker and draws a crown at the top of the chart. "Queen Cam and her loyal subjects."

I can't figure this out. After all my plans and hard work, I expected a little more enthusiasm, but men always seem to have trouble dealing with women in authority, no matter who they are. I know the pattern—Juice will get into it later, when the ideas start getting creative, like he always does. I'm just going to have to lead the charge for now, but that's okay. I'm used to it.

I walk out into the hall and drop by Arnie's office.

Empty. He took a two-week vacation, but I know he's not exactly off in the islands—he's putting his book together and interviewing for a new job. I still hate this whole reorganization thing. It makes me feel sick, but what can I do? Mergers defy rationality, but they seem to be the wave of the future, and I'm caught in the undertow.

Sally flags me down. "Could you go to Harold's office?"

I pick up a pad and pen and head up to Heaven. First thing off the elevator, I see a catering company setting out fancy appetizers and champagne on white tablecloths in the reception area. This can only mean one thing. We got Zing! *We got it!* Harold has obviously called me up for a congratulatory toast, before he brings up the whole agency to make the announcement. That's usually the way we do it.

I'm really excited going into Harold's office, or, more appropriately, suite. The entry room is done in a combination of brown suede and Biedermeier. He has a Biedermeier conference table, a Biedermeier tiger-maple secretary that he uses as a bar. Harold's actual office is paneled and has an English-library feeling, warm and homey. It's one of the few offices I actually like in this building, where everything tends to be cold and severe.

Bruce is sitting there with Harold, on one of the leather couches, and the feeling in the room stops me cold. Nobody is drinking champagne. Nobody is smiling. I feel like I've walked into an execution or something.

"We didn't get it," I say.

Bruce stands up. "Well, Cam, actually, yes. We did get the Zing! account. Simmons called me this morning with the decision."

"That's great! Are they going with the reposition-ing and everything? The commercial?"

"Yes, they bought into the entire program. Even the polo sponsorship. We become the agency of record as of January 1."

"That's just the best news. Congratulations."

I notice nobody's congratulating me here.

Harold lets out a sigh. "Cam, please sit down. We have a few things to discuss."

"Okay." Much as I like Harold, he tends to be overshadowed by detail. Here we are in the face of a major win, and it looks like he's caught up in some petty minutiae. The time-sheet issue, probably, for God's sake. Maybe now is not the best time to bring up my reorganization plan.

"Cam," says Bruce, leaning forward in his seat and frowning, "there are certain . . . inconsistencies on the Zing! budget that need to be thoroughly explained. Especially since we're going to be submit-ting the bills to the client right after the first of the year, so we can roll out the commercial." He opens a folder. "Exactly what do you know about the pur-chase of an Hermès riding saddle for Jed Durant, which was billed to this production?"

"Saddle? I don't know anything about a saddle."

"We sincerely hope that this is the case, because this is a three-thousand-dollar item which cannot be justified as a production expense." He pulls the bill out of the folder and hands it to me. "Somehow your signature got on this. Do you know how?"

"This isn't my signature. I don't know anything about it."

"It was billed to our corporate account, which you are authorized to use."

"Well, I'm authorized to use it, but I didn't. I have

257

no idea about this. None. In fact, I'm pretty confused. What's all this about?"

"This is a serious situation," says Harold. "If this saddle had gone through the billing to the client, there could have been repercussions."

Bruce lights a cigar. "I'll put it in black and white. Somebody—you, unless we prove otherwise—charged this saddle to the company and sent it as a Christmas gift to that kid singer."

"What!" I can't believe it. I can't believe *they* believe it. I thought this was America—land of the innocent until proved guilty. "I didn't do this. I don't even know what you're talking about. Why would I send Jed Durant a saddle?"

Bruce leans back in his chair. "Personal reasons," he says, his voice bland.

"What personal reasons?"

He shrugs. "Only you would know."

Harold jumps in. "Let's not get personal about this. Whatever the reason, an unauthorized expenditure was made. And apparently approved. Cam, finance tells us that when the receipt came in, you signed for it."

"No! I never saw a saddle, I never saw a receipt. How could I have signed for it?"

He puts the piece of paper back on the desk, like it was Exhibit A. This is close to my signature, but it's not. However, I don't see any handwriting experts in the office that can prove it. "What is this, some sort of witch-hunt?"

"Cam," says Harold, "I want you to know, we didn't go looking for this. Nobody is trying to single you out. We received . . . complaints."

"From whom? About what?"

"That's confidential, but suffice it to say, the allegations were serious. And they were not made in an incriminating fashion, I want you to know. Nobody is out to get you. They arose as a matter of constructive concern, that's all."

"But," says Bruce, looking as sincere as his suit, "you are an officer of the company. As such, you are responsible for your actions. Even if they do not always make sense."

"What are you saying?"

Harold looks very sad. "Cam, you know I like you. We all do. This is not personal. And you've done excellent work. So it's not professional. It's ethical. We are in a very unfortunate position here."

I try to be calm. "Are you saying that you believe I charged a three-thousand-dollar saddle to the company and sent it to Jed Durant?"

"Possibly," says Bruce.

"It's not true. Period. Point-blank."

"I believe you, Cam. I really do. But the facts point in another direction. It would be best all around if you resigned. Effective immediately."

My head is spinning. *The bastard framed me!* Good God! I feel like a character in a Jimmy Cagney movie, the innocent schmuck who just got the chair.

"Harold," I say calmly, "may I speak to you alone?"

He nods at Bruce, who leaves, swinging his cigar and wafting smoke in a figure-eight pattern.

"Harold. You know I did not do this. It's crazy. It's stupid. Why would I?" There's a lineup of antique paperweights along the front of Harold's desk, and I pick up a green one, just to have something to do with my hands, so he won't see that they're shaking.

He nods. "I believe you. But don't ask me to back you up on this, Cam. I can't back you up because to believe you and back you up would mean firing two senior people, and with what's gone on here last month, I can't do that. It would break the back of this agency."

"And this wouldn't? You don't think this is just a tiny bit unfair and unjust?"

"Cam, we are going to announce the Zing! business, and what's more, this is not public yet, but they are going to move Spirit into our agency within six months. We can't risk the consequences. I won't do that to this agency."

I jump to my feet. "What is this? Are you throwing me in? Harold, somebody set me up, I know it, and you probably know it too. I have no idea who did it, but I have my suspicions, and all I can say is that Bruce has been less than supportive of me ever since we began this project, and now I see why."

"You're wrong," Harold says, very quietly. "Bruce has been one hundred percent behind you. I know you two have had your differences, but believe me, he is just as stunned and upset by this as I am. Cam, listen to me, as a friend, because I am your friend."

My eyes burn, but I can't cry, I can't let them see me cry. "What's the big picture here?" I say. Because I know there must be one. "Who's going to run this business if I don't?"

"We are a team here," he says, his arms folded across his chest. "No one person is indispensable, not even me." He picked up a piece of paper and scans it. "I will, in fact, be moving to Paris to work in Soixant International headquarters. They will be sending a representative here to take over as chairman. Bruce will become president."

"Who's going to run the creative department? Dick Scully?" The thought makes me choke out a laugh.

"John Jusinski."

I freeze. Did he say *Juice?* Well, I suppose he did. It makes sense. But it's such a shock, I feel like I've been shot. "Well. It sounds like you've got a done deal here. Except for one thing. You are maligning my career and my reputation and I refuse to accept it. This is not even legal, and it's discriminatory."

"Cam, don't blow this into more than it is. Take it as an opportunity. You've been here five years. It's time you got a fresh perspective. I'll help you all I can. References, letters of recommendation—anything you need." His look is saying: "Please don't rock the boat."

"Thanks." *What an incredible coward. He knows I've been set up, that's why he won't look me in the eye. But he doesn't want to risk a confrontation. I'm expendable. He's going to go to Paris and forget I ever existed, wipe me off his conscience.* "It's clear to me that appearances are more important here than any shred of truth."

"That's not so, Cam. If you have any evidence to the contrary on this, Bruce and I would welcome it. Nobody's happy about this sort of thing. Call me at home if you'd like. Meanwhile, this conversation is completely confidential."

"Does Juice know about this?"

"Not yet. We thought it would be best to speak with you first."

"Well, Harold, I just want to say this, and I'll say it to Bruce too. This is the most inequitable thing I've ever heard of in my entire business career. It's a railroad job, and I'm not going to stand for it. You don't know what's involved here, but I'm going to show you. I should hope you'll give me the courtesy of an open mind."

261

I think I detect Harold softening a bit. He has to know he's being a total bastard. "Of course."

I look at the receipt from Hermès with my so-called signature approving it. "Do you mind if I take this and copy it?"

"Until we come to a final determination on this, we'll keep this conversation between those of us who were in this room," says Harold. But I know the grapevine. It should take about ten seconds for this to spread like a grease fire.

I stalk over to the elevators with the sound of champagne corks popping in the lobby. Back in my office, I sit there stunned. I can't believe this is happening. It's like something out of *Dynasty*. But since it's a lie, I can fight it. I'm not upset anymore, just lividly furious. The first thing I do is throw on my coat and go straight to the Hermès store in the Hancock Building.

The saleswomen are all perfectly calm and serene amidst their jewellike silk scarves and soft pigskin leathers when I show the copy of the receipt for the saddle. Everything seems so genteel, so uncutthroat. Maybe I should have gone into retail sales.

"Excuse me," I say as calmly as possible, but I know my voice is shrill. "Does either of you remember this order for an Hermès saddle?" How many people order three-thousand-dollar saddles, even for Christmas? We're not talking stocking-stuffers.

The two women behind the counter scrutinize the receipt. The one with a blond geometric haircut nods pleasantly. "Oh, of course. I remember. I helped the gentleman myself."

"Gentleman? Do you remember anything about him?"

"No—actually, it was a phone order." She looks

up the transaction in her file. "Yes, here it is. He specified a rush delivery to Los Angeles, but it had to have a monogram, so we turned the order over to our L.A. store."

"Did the man give his name?"

"No. Just that he was ordering it on the request of the person whose name went on the card."

I thank the woman and take her card. From a pay phone I call Juice and ask him to meet me at Billy Goat's.

I order a double cheeseburger, but I can't eat. "Juice," I say. "You have to help me."

He looks worried. "Sure, Cam. What's happening?"

"They're trying to set me up for some kind of a fall here. Bruce and Howard think I tried to slip something through expenses and give it unauthorized to Jed Durant. A saddle."

"Did you?"

I want to slug him. "Of course not!" I'm almost screaming. Luckily, Billy Goat's is so noisy, nobody notices.

Juice shakes his head and drains a Heineken in one gulp. "I warned you not to mess with Brucie. You're in the shark pool now, and you know sharks never sleep."

"But, Juice. I didn't do it." I enunciate each word slowly and carefully, so he can read my lips. "Juice, you saw the expense requisition forms. You went over them with me at the end of every day of this production—the overages, everything. If I had put through this bill, you would have seen it. It couldn't have happened."

"You're right," Juice agrees.

"So will you tell them that?"

"Let me think about how to handle it."

"Will you write a memo about it?"

"I'll take care of it this afternoon. Relax. Eat your cheeseburger."

The next morning, I go straight to Harold's office.

"Did Juice send you a memo?"

"No. And, Cam, we have to start putting the team together. We can't wait. The press expects an announcement today."

"Hold on."

I grab Harold's phone and punch Juice's extension. "Juice! Did you get that memo up to Harold yet?"

"No. I didn't."

"Juice, can you do it now? It's important."

"Actually, Cam. I can't help you out on this. I want to but I can't. It's messy. I had drinks with my lawyer last night, and he frankly suggests it would be a very bad idea for me to get involved."

"What do you mean, a very bad idea? You are involved."

"No, Cam," he says softly. "You are."

I stand there staring at the phone. Something is terribly the matter, and I'm not sure what. I pick up a garnet-colored paperweight and turn it over in my hand. "Juice seems to have some sort of problem," I say.

Harold stares at me. "I know," he says.

Words are insufficient. I smash the paperweight down onto the glass desktop and it shatters, smashing blood-colored splinters of crystal across the desk, which cracks like a broken windshield. What the hell. I have nothing to lose.

I'm out of there and down the hall in seconds, pounding at the elevator buttons. Nothing comes, and it seems like I'm waiting for hours. It's intolerable, I'm going to explode. I run to the fire stairs and circle down, down—ten floors. By the time I get to Juice's office, I'm completely out of breath. He's calmly going over a layout with an assistant art director.

"What the fuck is going on? Tell me."

Hector makes himself scarce.

"I told you, Cam. My lawyer said—"

"Forget the lawyer. What is *really going on here?*"

"Cam, sit down. If they want to frame you with a monogrammed saddle, they can do anything."

How did Juice know it was a monogrammed saddle? Bruce or Harold might have told him it was a saddle, but even I just found out it was a monogrammed saddle, and I never mentioned it. Oh, God . . . Oh, God.

The picture at last comes clear. Bruce didn't know it was a monogrammed saddle. Neither did Harold. The only person who knew it was a monogrammed saddle was the salesgirl. And, of course, the person who actually ordered it.

Juice.

I want to lay into him, slice his guts open on the drawing board and string them up in the fluorescent lights.

"You're doing this to me? *You?*"

"Drop it, Cam. I know you're upset. You should be. But face it. You're doing this to yourself. You always were the star of the Cam McKenna Show, and you still are."

His eyes are narrowing and all I see is pent-up anger and frustration. I look around the office and it's got all the clip art and toys and videotape reels and art books and type books and everything that's so familiar, but this man is a stranger.

"Juice," I say, "we've been a team for seven years at two agencies."

"No. I've been your backup band for seven years at two agencies."

I draw a quick breath. "Is that how you saw it?"

"No, that's how *you* saw it. Cam McKenna, ace creative, with the press to prove it. Cam McKenna, with the corner office, the big title, and the executive bonus."

"Juice, we were in this together."

"Uh-uh, Cam. I'm sick of picking up cloaks around here. *You* called the shots. *You* made the decisions. *You* fired six people, as I recall. *You* wanted to be queen for a day in your own queendom. Yes, ma'am. I just did your bidding. And the work."

How could I have been so blind to this? When did it start? What did I do? How did I let it pass by me? I'm more upset by this than by the saddle incident or anything else.

"Juice . . . I'm so sorry. I really thought we were together. Without you . . ."

"I know that and you know that. But, believe me, my paycheck doesn't know that."

"I was trying to get us our own division."

"With *yourself* as president. Sure, we started as a team, and we were great. But that was then. Something happened. Cam, I defy you to think of one sentence you've started in the past twelve months that doesn't start with the word *I*."

I can't help myself now. Tears stream down my face and splash into my lap. I really can't take it. Because he's an asshole and a traitor, but he's right.

"*You*," I say, but I can only whisper. "It was you."

"No, it was you. As usual, you deserve the credit. You did it all by yourself."

"With a little help from you."

"Believe what you want." He shrugs.

It's hard to accept that Juice wants to get ahead so badly that he's willing to do this to me. But he is. I feel all the air seeping out of me, as if I'd been pricked by a sharp pin. The tears stop. Suddenly I've lost my taste for the fight.

I think of Jamie. *Those people don't care about you*, he said. And he was right. Or else I made them not care. Probably a little bit of both. The point is, I've got to get out of here. I feel like I'm sealed in a sarcophagus.

I stand up. "Good luck, Juice." If he wants it that badly, he can truss it up and have it on a silver platter with an apple in its mouth. It's not worth it to me; not anymore.

Chapter Sixteen

I wonder if the headhunter notices I'm wearing an Armani jacket. At any rate, he's impressed by my reel, which is rewinding on the VCR now. A five-digit commission is in the air. His swivel chair inches closer.

"That's just incredible," he says. Richard Jacoby is one of the top creative recruiters in the business. He came from Ogilvy himself, so he knows the business and the people. Richard has direct access to the grapevine, probably via his former associates who have since dispersed across the country. Before I'd even gotten my résumé revised, he was on the phone to me.

Not that I'm in any rush, but I am very bad at being unemployed, although you'd never know from my Filofax that I'm out of work. Unemployment is exhausting: culling files, making calls, editing your reel, typing notes, juggling networking lunches, breakfasts, and drinks. After two weeks, I know I'm just fooling myself, going through a charade of being high-powered and efficient when it really doesn't even matter if I get up in the morning.

Richard Jacoby adjusts his gold Rolex. "You're

clearly an A-level professional," he says. "Now, I'd like to bounce an idea off you. How would you feel about a CD position, creative-driven agency, blue-chip accounts . . . in Atlanta."

"Atlanta." The outback of advertising.

"Well . . ." He riffles through a deck of index cards on his lap. "There's a reorganization going on here, it's not as immediate a need, but at Scanlon in Dallas—"

"Dallas?" Did New York, Chicago and San Francisco fall off the map?

Richard frowns. "Cam, as you know, the industry is in a major slump right now. Budget cuts, cutbacks, mergers—forty percent of the advertising work force is out of a job. Atlanta and Dallas are two good opportunities. They'd be thrilled to have you! We're talking Soapy Bleach in Atlanta, Cheeze-it Chips in Dallas. Major pieces of business. You could make an impact. Of course, you'd have to somewhat lower your salary expectations . . ."

"I'll think it over."

Is this what it feels like to be out of work at six figures? Sitting there listening to a guy whose fingernails lost their grip on his agency job ten years ago tell you that you've just joined him in Advertising Never-Never Land? Wearing an Armani jacket to be told that you will never be able to afford one again?

Back at the apartment, I make myself a bowl of Cream of Wheat, which I eat standing up, and try to think things through.

It shouldn't be too hard to get a good job. I figure I can hold out two, maybe three months. I was fully vested, so when I cashed in my profit-sharing, I got fifty thousand dollars. Hardly a golden parachute, but enough to tide me over. Or is it? My Platinum

Card has seven thousand dollars on it from last month—I bought two Armani outfits. Visa has four thousand, but I can pay it off monthly. Flipping through my checkbook, I can see that most months I make five thousand dollars in card payments. I get the manicure scissors out of the bathroom drawer. One by one, I pull my credit cards—which I just replaced after the mugging—out of my wallet and cut them into pieces.

I feel like I have to remind myself to breathe. *What happens if nothing happens?* Will I have to take a fast real-estate course, get a license, and sell condos for a living? Will I stay in "advertising," sentenced to write two-color brochures for local drugstores? Will I end up in the communications department of some second-string company that's too cheap to hire a real ad agency, writing newsletters and speeches? Will I turn into Richard Jacoby?

I open my closet. Five-hundred-dollar sweaters, thousand-dollar purses, four-hundred dollar blouses, three-hundred-dollar shoes stare back, challenging me to wear them and make a fashion statement. My apartment is filled with items like this—art-deco mirrors, Jensen sterling flatware, antique lace pillow shams, Egyptian-cotton sheets, handmade Amish quilts; my savings account has three hundred dollars in it. I own the condo, but the payments are fifteen hundred a month plus maintenance. Fifty thousand dollars doesn't seem like so much money anymore.

I think about Jamie, who lives in a loft I have never seen, but I know he sleeps on a futon, and how much can Chicago Bears T-shirts cost? Could I live in a loft and sleep on a futon? Where would I store my Lalique collection?

It seems to me for all I played by the rules, the

rules changed. If I could just hate Bruce, that might help, but I can't even see my way clear to that. As for Juice, I feel more sorry for him than anything else. He's got to go down to the office every day and deal with those people and their fuck-up mentality. Okay, I was egocentric. But he's twisted. Let him trash himself. Let him put pigs in every layout from here to kingdom come. Let him speak in tongues. Who the hell cares?

The phone rings. So far, I haven't gotten too many calls. Zero communication from Juice. Juice—my partner, my pal, my compatriot. My Brutus. My Judas. I read in *Ad Age* that he'd gotten promoted—a half-page article in last week's cover story on the merger.

"Cam. How are you doing?"

It's Brenda Parker—the last person I expected to hear from.

"Hi, Brenda. I'm fine. Thanks."

"I wanted to say good-bye. You left so suddenly, I didn't have a chance."

I can picture Brenda back at the office pecking away on the manual typewriter she refuses to give up. I remember how I used to pity her for not being hip and quick and with-it, and I feel ashamed.

"Well," I say. "You know how it is."

"Yes, I think I do. We'll miss you, though. I want you to know. I really respect you and your work. Maybe we'll work together again."

"Brenda . . . tell me, how do you do it?"

She knows what I mean, and she sighs. "All these years, so many times I've wanted to quit. But I didn't, and now I can't. Where would I go?" She laughs, but not bitterly. "They're not hiring too many forty-five-year-old copywriters. You did it right, Cam. You made a name for yourself."

"And you have a family. As for me, I'm leaving the business." As I say it, I know it's true.

"Well, you know what you have to do."

"I guess we all do."

We promise to meet for lunch, but I know we never will.

The phone rings again a half-hour later. It's Bruce. "Cam," he says, "how's it going?"

"Oh, great. I have lots of interviews lined up. If I want them."

"That's good." Do I detect concern in his voice? Is he capable of concern? "I'm here to help, you know," he says. "Maybe you didn't think so, but I am."

"Thanks."

"Let me explain, Cam. You and I—we're two different types. I'm pretty emotional about this business. You have to be to survive. Sometimes it hurts others, sometimes you're the one who gets hurt. Nobody means it. It's just . . . the business." He sounds uncomfortable. "You're good at what you do, Cam. You care. Let me give you one piece of advice: don't lose that. It's worth more than the job."

"I appreciate that, Bruce. Can I give you one piece of advice, in return?"

"Sure."

"Quit smoking."

He laughs and so do I.

"I'll work on it," he says. "Good luck, Cam. If you need anything, call."

I'd sooner call Timothy, but I get his point. I've seen Bruce as my nemesis for so long, it's hard to believe he's being so decent. Of course, I'm no longer a threat, he can afford to be magnanimous. But he didn't have to make this call, I'll give him that.

I know I have to rethink a lot of things, starting with myself.

Juice—he was an asshole to do what he did to me, but when and how did I let it happen? When did he stop being my friend? When did I stop listening to him? When did he start thinking he didn't matter to me, that he wasn't valued? I flop down on the couch and stare at the ice on the windowframe. Something has happened to me. Jamie was right. Sometime between my divorce and now I turned into a self-centered jerk who talked about herself, bought herself presents, and decorated herself. Maybe it dulled the pain when the marriage ended—who knows, and who cares? It happened, and I let it happen. I can't even blame the business. I can only blame myself. Maybe I'll just be here and flagellate myself with guilt for two or three months. Self-pity feels therapeutic, like a seaweed wrap.

The phone rings. I let the answering machine pick up this time. "Cynthia," says Timothy's voice. "I've been trying to reach you for a week. Now they tell me you're no longer with the agency, whatever that means. Listen, we need to talk. You know we do." The machine clicks off.

How different my life would have been if things had worked out with Timothy, assuming Timothy had been a normal human being. I picture myself going to Junior League luncheons, telling the women in their St. John knits about my husband's latest promotion, or celebrating my own promotion with him with dinner at a window table at Ciel Bleu. I see myself getting diamonds by the yard and kisses by the dozen for anniversaries and birthdays. If I had a husband, I could thumb my nose and go back to my Lincoln Park town house or my acre in Lake Forest.

If I had a husband, I wouldn't be sitting here now. If I had a husband, I might have a child. Suddenly I hate all women with husbands. Not that I'd trade places with them. It's just so obvious that now I don't fit in anyplace anymore. I'm free now, but free for what?

I'm Magellan at the edge of the earth, but the earth is flat, and I'm teetering out there, and if I don't watch my step, I'll go over.

I yank the vacuum cleaner out of the closet. It's a Kirby, an institutional-type monster somebody gave me at a bridal shower when Timmy and I got married. Once a week, the maid makes a go of it, but I haven't touched this pterodactyl in years. Where the hell are the hoses and attachments? How the fuck do they go on? Do you have to change the bag? Screw it, I'll just do the carpet. I cover the entrance hall mindlessly for about ten minutes, staring at the carpet nap, till I hear the front-door buzzer. Pulling the living-room blinds apart, I look down and see Timothy letting himself into the building. He's coming up the stairs as I race to the front door to throw the chain on. "Cynthia, don't be so immature," he yells through the closed door. I hope the chain holds.

"Go away!"

"We have to talk. I knew you were home. Why do you always do this? You're being a baby about this. A crybaby."

"So what? Let me alone!"

"Cynthia, that woman in L.A.—"

"I don't care. About her or you. I'm busy. Vacuuming." I vacuum like a fiend.

"Please." He's shouting over the noise.

"No."

"Cynthia."

"No!"

I turn off the vacuum cleaner and listen to the silence outside the door. I walk over and talk between the door and the chain. "Timothy, I am going to marry somebody else. Please go now."

"Who?"

"You don't know him. He's from New York."

"Do you have a ring?" I can only see Timmy's shoulder and right side.

"I have a . . . a spoon." Since I haven't given back the baby spoon, are we still engaged?

"What?"

"On second thought, wait there." I go to the bedroom and rustle through the basket on my dresser where I keep my jewelry until I find the destestable amethyst bracelet.

"Here." I toss it through the door crack onto the hall carpet. Then I close the door.

Suddenly I'm hyperventilating, short, shallow breaths, no oxygen. I feel dizzy and sick. *What is it you're supposed to do? Breathe into a bag?*

I remember this from high-school cheerleading tryouts, when I would hiccup and hyperventilate and Miss Manning, the gym coach, made me breathe into a bag. I flash on feeling like a nerd, sitting there puffing into a bag, my hair frizzy and damp, while all those girls with straight, smooth hair shook their pom-poms. I didn't make the squad. In the closet is a small Gucci shopping bag, from when I bought a wallet. I put it over my face and breathe in and out, watching the red and green stripe inflate and deflate.

I'm really glad I breathed into that bag. It made me sit and think and collect myself, and after a while I didn't care about Richard Jacoby or Dallas or Atlanta, because I knew I never wanted to write or edit another headline, pitch another commercial, or edit another inch of tape. I never want to sit hour after hour in another windowless conference room, or write copy about crotch rot or split ends, or try to convince everybody that what this world needs is lemon-scented paper towels. I no longer want to swim with the sharks, soar with the eagles, or get slaughtered with the sheep. I have no shred of desire to bounce off, run by, wave past, or touch base with anyone regarding anything related to selling a product or a service.

Breathing in and out of the bag, it suddenly became so blatantly clear, I couldn't wait to stop hyperventilating so I could get out a pad and pen. *Write.* I haven't done that in years—written with a pad and pen. Jotted down, yes. Written, no. When I write, it's usually a memo on the computer, or else I dictate, and it's no more than sixty seconds' worth of words.

I will write a book. Or maybe a short story. Or an article. Or a play or a script. I will go back to my roots, to what I was always best at.

The pen feels clumsy, I'm not used to it, and after a while it starts to gouge a dent in my third finger. Over and over on the page I am writing the same thing: the date. Nothing else comes out. No ideas. No images. I don't know where to start. I used to be able to sit down at the kitchen table, and before I'd finished waiting for my nail polish to dry, I'd have a story down. I forget exactly how I did this.

Tears are splotching the page now, running the ink. Whatever I've lost, this hurts the most. I throw the yellow pad and the pen on the floor and cry myself to sleep on my Egyptian-cotton sheets.

In my file cabinet are some big manila folders stuffed with stories I wrote years ago, in my other life—charming little stories about trains with faces, snowflakes that dance, stuffed bears that come to life and lead little girls and boys to treasure troves of gumdrops. I fan them out around me on the floor. It's hard to believe I wrote this stuff. Writing used to be as easy as flipping a switch. My mind is unexercised and overdisciplined. I can frame a marketing strategy, but not a paragraph. I can name a lawn mower, but not a character. The more I try to force myself, the harder it gets. I don't even know where to start.

The computer is no longer my friend. Its keys glare up at me like evil teeth. The chemistry between us is gone. I banish it to the closet and get out legal pads and felt-tip pens.

I have to face it: I'm not a writer anymore. I'm . . . what? A professional conceptualist. I'm something that doesn't even have a place in the dictionary—a person who thinks up ideas for a living. I'd have a better chance of changing careers if I were a supermarket checker. At least it's a skill that people understand.

I make scrambled eggs and feed some to the Bird. I clean his cage. I calk the bathtub. I let down a hem. I clean out the refrigerator and put a box of baking soda in back of the top shelf. I arrange my sweaters by color, dark to light. I put shelf paper in the dresser drawers. I flip through the *Wall Street Journal*. In the classifieds, there's an ad: *"Restaurant. Prime space for lease."* And a number. I decide to rip it out and send it to Jamie—with a letter.

"Dear Jamie," I start to write. I tell him about the saddle, about Juice, about getting fired. I tell him he was right, and I apologize for missing his mother's Christmas Eve party.

I tell him I really do wish I'd gone to his mother's party. I can't remember the last time I went to a big bosom-of-the-family thing like that. It would have been fun. Now that I'm cut off like this, I remember the need to be enfolded—by family, by love, by traditions.

The letter goes on and on. I tell Jamie how I have the baby spoon by my bed and how I picked it up last night and stroked the engraving, how it calmed me and made me smile—imagining him as a baby. Maybe if I'd gone to his mother's on Christmas Eve, she would have showed me his baby pictures.

I write about how I miss him, about the space in my soul that is his now. I tell him about my father and The Picture and I write a long description of the house I grew up in. I tell him about my mother, who is always on a cruise, and Theo, who is always right. I even tell him about Timothy and the amethyst bracelet. I tell him he should open a restaurant. When I put the pen down, I have written fifty pages and I know I can still write, that I still have ideas, that there is still something there, maybe a lot. The letter is a beginning, but I don't want to send it to Jamie, I want to give it to him myself.

I need to be with him. Not just now—for a long time. I need him in my life. He is more important than a job, my apartment, anything. Maybe it's not so bad to be out of work. It'll give me a chance to think about my life—our life. Nothing's really keeping me here. I can go to New York, move there. Work it out with Jamie—if he still wants me, which I know he does. You don't give your grandmother's flask to a woman you never want to see again.

I call Laurie. She's not there, but her answering machine picks up. It's been weeks since we've actually spoken in person—we've been communicating by machines.

"Hi, Laurie," I say to the machine. "I need you to Bird-sit. Just for a while. You have the keys, and the seeds are on the table, and once every three days, scramble him an egg and feed it to him with tweezers."

BEEP!

I pack a suitcase. It's the first time in two years I've gone on a trip without my computer and my briefcase; I feel like I'm traveling naked.

But I know I'm not. I'm taking along something better—me, myself, my own ingenuity. What's so bad about that? Am I any less of a person because I don't have an embossed business card? Am I any less talented without a nameplate on an office door? Years ago, when Timothy left, I felt like I'd fallen into a black hole, the emotional void between the world of the salad bar and singles bar. I sold myself short then; I can't do it now.

I'm on to something bigger, something better. I call Jamie from a pay phone at O'Hare Airport.

"Who?" he says. "Who is this? I vaguely remember."

"It's New Year's Eve," I say.

"So it is."

"I have a resolution."

"What's that?"

"Spend it with you."

"That could be one of your better resolutions."

We're both silent for a few seconds. Nobody's blaming anybody for anything. Nobody's begging forgiveness. No tears, no recrimination, just the simple fact that we want to be together.

"I quit," I say. "Or they fired me."

"Probably the best thing that ever happened to you. Maybe we could get together for a drink tonight. Watch Guy Lombardo."

"Guy's dead."

"Okay. Sammy Davis Jr."

"Should I call you when I get to La Guardia, or when I'm in the city?" I say.

"Both."

I'm flying now, I'm leaving Chicago and my apartment and advertising and the hype. I'm leaving a life, but actually I'm not leaving at all. I'm coming.

Honey, I am coming home to you.

"They got some nice 109-A's," says Jamie, knocking on the glass case.

"Whats?" A herd of antlered elks' heads are peering down at us from the wood-paneled walls, along with a stuffed chicken, a knife set framed like an old master, a rack with cleavers and saws, and a clock flanked by a plastic cow and sheep.

"Prime rib. They don't have a bad piece of meat here at Lobel's. We can't go too wrong."

Jamie is making New Year's Eve dinner at his loft, just for us. He has the night off, and we're together. There's a lot to talk about.

A butcher in a red-and-white-pinstripe shirt and white apron tosses a piece of meat on a scale. "Chef," he says, "I got something special for you in the back. I was gonna take it home, but since this is obviously a special lady . . ."

He can figure this out because Jamie keeps kissing the top of my hair. He leans over and whispers into the nape of my neck, "There are eight bones to a rack of lamb."

"There are?" In my past life as a housewife, I

never got into the mechanics of cuts of meat, never touched any raw food that didn't come wrapped in plastic or frozen in a box. It feels so good to be there with Jamie, nestled into the damp snowflakes still clinging to his huge overcoat, feeling his long hair tickle my cheek.

The butcher returns with a piece of meat.

"See?" says Jamie, counting. "One, two, three, four, five, six, seven, eight. And you want an eye about the size of a fist." He makes a fist and it's huge, the hand of Goliath.

"Anything else?" says the butcher.

Jamie peruses some books for sale along one wall and pulls out something titled *Meat*. "This looks interesting. I want to start making my own sausage. Mom gave me a meat grinder for Christmas." He tosses the book on the counter.

We head down Madison Avenue with the rack of lamb. I still have my carry-on bag from the trip from Chicago, since I met Jamie directly at Mortimer's.

"Let's stroll," he says.

It's only six o'clock, but it's dark. People are dashing around with the sense of anticipation you always get on New Year's Eve.

"What if I moved here?" I say.

"That's the way to go, honey," says Jamie. "But only if we get married right away. My mother wouldn't want me living in sin."

"Tell her I'll make you an honest man." I put my hand in his pocket, and it feels rough and tweedy.

We cut over to Fifth Avenue at the Plaza. The Christmas decorations are still up, the horses and buggies are decked out for the holidays.

"I'm not getting another agency job," I say.

"I'll bring home food from the restaurant and we'll

survive," says Jamie. "Paris is out this year, though. Maybe next. If the restaurant business is good."

"I wish I knew more about the restaurant business," I say. I do, however, have something to contribute. I have an idea. Something I've had in the back of my mind since I saw the ad in the *Journal* is coming clear now.

"Jamie," I say, "let's talk about this restaurant thing." Even as we talk, the idea is taking shape, getting bigger, growing. And for once, it's not an idea for a soap flake or a cereal box. It's for us. And I'm not waiting for somebody to issue a memo *re: the brass ring*—I'm grabbing it myself. "What if you opened your own restaurant?"

"It's a lot of work. And I don't know anything about the business end."

"I do." And it all falls into place, in a rush. "I know about business, and you know about food. We could do this together."

Jamie starts walking faster. I can tell he's excited. I run to keep up, his legs are so long.

"To open and run for the first year," he says, "you're talking a million bucks—licenses, equipment, staff. You have to have a license to open, a liquor license, you gotta have everything checked out—ducts, vents, drains—that costs money. Then there's your stoves, ovens, steam tables, Fryolators, iceboxes, freezers, your lowboys, your reach-ins, your walk-ins. Then you got your pots, pans, spoons, plastic containers, knives, plates, bowls, monkey dishes. Racks. Storage—everything's got to be off the floor. And that's just your kitchen." He shakes his head. "A million bucks."

"Listen, Marissa and Etienne think you're the best chef in New York. He's an investment banker. Maybe he can help raise money. And the Smarts—God, they were so impressed. I can draw up a plan, with visuals, even. A professional presentation. And we can take it to them. Maybe they'll put up some financing. It's not impossible." This could actually work. I feel the adrenaline rush.

"I could do the ads," I say.

The crowd on the street has gotten worse—holiday revelers, laughing, bumping, everybody rushing somewhere. Jamie has to yell so I can hear him.

"You know, honey. You sort of got me thinking restaurant a while back. And what I'm thinking is, something this town doesn't have is a good pancake place. In Soho, maybe. Near my place."

"Pancakes? I thought you were a gourmet chef."

"Gourmet pancakes. Corn, and stone-ground wheat, and gingerbread—with real maple syrup and crème fraîche, and at night, caviar—two kinds. And for breakfast, real, honest pancakes, real butter and lots of it—banana pancakes, pumpkin, blueberry, Swedish . . . and German apple. The town would go wild."

"You'd have no competition," I say, and I start to get really exhilarated, like when I think of a great commercial. "There is absolutely nothing like this in New York. It could work. You could call it . . . Babycakes. "

"Babycakes! Well, you're the writer. But I'm thinking about something more basic—Mom's Pancake House."

Jamie picks me up, crunching the shopping bags between us. "My baby," he says, and he kisses me. "You're a smart girl, honey, and I always said so."

"It was your idea!"

"*Our* idea. But, honey, when you open a restaurant, you got to be willing to do everything from sweeping the floors to cleaning the grill. You may lose that manicure."

"Can't we hire somebody to do that?"

"Eventually. But we'll be putting it all back in when we just open up, so we can retire real quick."

"I can't see myself cleaning the grill."

"No problem. You can do hostess work. You got nice legs, I saw that right off. You'll look good in a short skirt."

Ex-groupie graduates to hostess.

"You can still write," Jamie says. "You can work at the restaurant, and work on your writing the rest of the time. It'll work."

"I'll be a published hostess." The idea is not so bad. If the restaurant catches on, we can franchise it and retire. I can envision the menu, right down to the type face. I can see the logo on T-shirts, bumper stickers. I know this isn't going to be easy. I may even hate it sometimes. But it's exciting. I believe in Jamie, and in myself. If I can sell a soft drink, I can sell a restaurant. We can pull this off, but no way I'm going to scrape any grills. Compromise can get you only so far.

For the next few blocks I'm figuring out how I can put my furniture in storage and get myself moved here. Will I miss my art deco collections, my silver tea services, my Viennese secessionist chairs and table?

No. I'm not going to miss a thing. Especially not my job.

"Bloodsuckers," says Jamie. "Audiovisual perverts."

"It had its moments." How can I explain the good parts to Jamie? It's like explaining an old relationship to a new man. In spite of all the craziness, and before things went wrong, there was the attraction, the seductiveness, the intoxication, the intensity, and passion too. All burned out like a supernova, a combination of elements that can never be again.

"Can we live in your loft?" I've still never seen it.

"As long as you make the bed. And I don't do the dishes."

"We'll get a dishwasher. Or eat off paper plates. You'll learn to make the bed. I have a duvet. It's easy."

"What's a duvet?"

By now we've been walking for what seems like miles. "We're not walking to SoHo, are we?"

"No. We're stopping here."

"Tiffany's?"

In we go. It's fifteen minutes before the store closes and the place is winding down. The guard looks suspiciously at Jamie as we approach him.

"Wedding rings," Jamie says, and we're pointed to the left, past case after case of dazzling stones.

Jamie puts the rack of lamb on the counter, points to the plainest tray in the case, the simple bands, and in fifteen minutes we each have a white-gold wedding ring, wrapped and boxed in powder blue, tied with white satin ribbons. He drops the Tiffany's shopping bag into the bigger one from the meat market.

"Hang on to that baby spoon, though," Jamie says. "We may need it."

I wonder how much longer it takes you to get pregnant when you're closing in on forty. For so long, I've relegated this part of myself to a little interior core, swaddled into oblivion by my career. Now I feel like I'm unwrapping a package, and inside is something wonderful that I can't wait to

285

discover. I'm looking forward to being the oldest person in my Lamaze class.

An ad-hoc chamber music group is playing Handel in the subway station. The music is bright and perfect.

"What are you guys doing on Friday at noon?" Jamie asks the young violinist. "Want to play a wedding?" He takes their phone number. "You know how to get to City Hall?" He gives each of them a subway token.

When Timothy and I got married, there was a huge pipe organ and a brass section, there were ten ushers, ten bridesmaids, a flower girl, a ring-bearer, and bows on the pews. My mother and I spent a month coordinating the matchbooks, the napkins, and the color of the tablecloths. Now I know: perfect matchbook covers will not get you a perfect marriage.

Jamie and I have no plans at all. We're improvising as we go along, together.

White Street, where Jamie lives, is industrial, bare, and charmless—you expect a factory to be around the corner. On one side of the block, a street person sleeps in a doorway, newspapers blowing around his ankles. Peeling posters are plastered in faded layers on the side buildings. Across the street in the middle of the block is a wide green door with chicken wire on the transom.

The elevator with its huge steel sliding door, appropriate for loading a flatbed truck, shimmies up two floors and opens right into his loft. I'm expecting disaster, but it turns out to be pretty slick. Messy, and not *Metropolitan Home*, but nice: polished pine floors and a big white room the width of the building. Over a thousand square feet. A rounded wall of glass brick partitions the room, and there's simple black furniture clustered at each end—couch, chairs, platform bed. Unemptied ashtrays, socks, and T-shirts are everywhere, but I'm thinking that my Viennese secessionist table and chairs will look fine in here. And high ceilings. The Bird will like this.

"Rent control," says Jamie. "I got this place from an artist friend when I came to New York. He went to Milan for a show and decided to stay. Nice of him."

"It's great." I check out the kitchen, which is minute but has every imaginable gadget tacked on a pegboard, while Jamie takes the lamb out of its butcher paper. He drops the powder-blue Tiffany boxes in a colander for safekeeping.

I wash and snap the green beans as Jamie pulls pots and pans off the wall. "That's not how to prep *haricots verts*," he says. "I'll show you." He stands behind me and puts his arms around me and holds my hands as the cold water runs over our wrists and between our fingers.

"What about the lamb?" I say.

"You gotta salt and pepper it," he says, turning my palms up under the water. "Then you put a mixture of garlic and shallots on."

He takes my hands and dries them gently, rubbing between each finger.

"You don't put the mustard on till later, with the garlic, parsley, and bread crumbs."

My back is still toward him; I can't see his face as he unbuttons my sweater.

"You cook it fifteen minutes, pull it out and put the mustard on the fat, and the bread crumbs."

He turns me around and starts kissing his way downward.

"You jack the oven up." He lifts me up and sits me on the edge of the counter.

"Put tinfoil over the bones." A kiss on my shoulder.

"A high oven will make the bread crumbs crisp." A kiss on my left breast.

"Then you give it another ten minutes, and you're talking heaven." One long kiss travels down from belly to hip to knee to ankle, and I drop my shoes to the floor, and this is how we end up not eating on New Year's Eve.

I've never made love among ingredients before. I'm pushed up and across the counter, knocking pepper grinders, garlic cloves, slotted spoons, strainers, and a jar of crystallized ginger onto the floor, as he becomes my will, my wants, my wishes. What can I do to make him feel this? How can I please him, be right for him? If I open myself wider, will we fuse together?

"I missed being with you, honey," he says.

I feel the water from the sink, still pouring full force, splashing on the small of my bare back. I grip his huge shoulders as they push me down into the cold marble counter, and feel him rock into me, forward and away and forward and away, our chests slipping on each other, salty and sweat-slicked, my skirt still on, pushed around my waist, my yellow satin tap pants looped around one ankle, and I know that this is the husband of my heart.

"It's ten o'clock."

"Are you hungry?"

The raw rack of lamb sits naked on its roasting rack.

"I'm thinking we should celebrate. It's New Year's

Eve. How about a pig sandwich and a bottle of champagne?"

"What?"

"House specialty of the Hard Rock."

Before we go out, we make a battery of phone calls and tell everybody the news. If they're not home, we tell their answering machines. I cable my mother in the Dominican Republic.

"What took you so long?" says Theo.

"Marriage," says Laurie. "Well, that's wonderful. Finally, the perfect excuse to blow off Timothy. He's calling me all the time to find out where you are. Getting to be a real pest."

"Just tell him I'm at the Hard Rock eating pig sandwiches and toasting my groom-to-be."

"God, you sound so happy. What are you going to wear?"

Jamie is unwrapping his ring and trying it on for size.

"Knee socks," I say as he waves at me with his fourth finger, left hand. "A plaid skirt and knee socks."

"There must be static on the line," Laurie says.

"You gotta spend about ten minutes when you first get here just looking at the memorabilia," says Jamie as his buddy the Sheriff opens the rope for us and we push through the line that's four deep to the end of the block. The Hard Rock is the Smithsonian of Rock-'n'-Roll.

Jerry Lee Lewis' "Great Balls of Fire" is blasting, and the place is up for grabs. There are yuppies in suits and satins, girls in masks and feathers, guys in tuxedos and T-shirts, New Year's noisemakers, paper hats and crowns and balloons everywhere. A woman in sequins and a tattoo toasts in our general direction.

The bar on the main floor is shaped like a giant guitar. "Fifty-seven Stratocaster," says Jamie. The bartenders are in a six-deep frenzy.

"Prince's *Purple Rain* coat," Jamie points out. "Over there, Elvis' original tour jacket. Ringo's drums used to be there, but they moved them. Gold records—John Lennon's for 'Let It Be,' Elton John, Peter Townshend, Pink Floyd. They got a curator here. Check out the ax-shaped guitar: Gene Simmons of Kiss."

We dive through the crowd to the bottom of the staircase, where the hostess recognizes Jamie. "Chef! Where you been?"

"Happy New Year, Tina. This is the wife-to-be. You got a quiet place for us to celebrate an engagement here?"

Tina claps, kisses us both, and motions us up the stairs and around to the back of the balcony.

"The VIP section," she says.

"There's Isaac."

Isaac, tall and thin, with a beard and piercing blue eyes, throws his arms open. "Chef!"

Jamie yells across the din, "How's the wife? How's the kids? Where's the champagne?"

A bottle of Taittinger materializes, and we are wedged in at Isaac's table along the balcony. I recognize Dorry Swope, the legendary rock-folk singer, who is supposed to be a recluse, and I'm introduced to Mac Haskell, a record producer, and Bill Murray and his high-cheekboned wife, Mickey. The other people at the table are probably famous too, but I don't know who they are.

Jamie leans over, says a few words to Isaac, and

minutes later I hear our engagement announced over the loudspeaker, and the entire restaurant cheers. Everything is a blur of noise, music, and voices. I haven't eaten all day and the champagne is going to my head and I'm seeing things. This must be the explanation for the fact that I see Timothy coming toward our table. I blink to clear my head. He's still there, only closer. *Oh, my God, he must have been calling Laurie from New York.*

I can't hear a word Timothy is saying; his mouth is opening and closing like a ventriloquist's dummy's; no sound seems to be coming out. He edges through the tables and leans over my chair, at the edge of the balcony railing.

"What are you doing here?" I say it through gritted teeth. He may not be able to hear me, but I'm sure he gets the message.

"Cynthia! I talked to Laurie. Don't do this. You're being infantile. What do you want? To get even with me? To hurt me? Fine! You did it. I'm hurt. I'm bleeding. But you know, and I know, that we belong together. We're flip sides of the same coin. It doesn't work when we're not together. Come with me. Now. Leave these assholes."

His hand is hurting my arm, and I look frantically around the room, feeling trapped. I catch Jamie getting up and coming around the table in one move.

"This is a private matter. Excuse us," says Timothy. His hand is under my arm, pulling me out of my chair.

"Excuse *me*," I say, and I yank Timothy's arm away from me.

"Did you drop that hundred-dollar bill?" I point to the floor, and when Timothy looks, my fist clenches up, my elbow straightens, and I hit him as hard as I

291

can. I could kill him, but I don't want to do time. Something crunches as I connect with his nose. I think it's my hand, but I don't care, it feels good anyhow, and, astonishingly, as if in slow motion, Timothy reels backward and disappears over the balcony. I cringe, waiting for the crash, but all I hear is screaming, and Jamie is leaning over the railing shouting. Timothy is hanging from the railing, blood smeared under his nose. Jamie shakes his head, disgusted, reaches out, grabs him by the sheepskin coat, and hauls him back up, slamming Timothy back onto his feet with a jolt. He says something to Timothy; I can't hear what. Timothy wipes his bloody nose and glares, but he shrinks back. I can tell he thinks Jamie's crazy. He looks at me in shock, and I shake my head. *No.* That's all there is to it. I can't even move, there are so many people pushing and shoving. Isaac has Jamie by the arm and security is pulling Timothy away and someone is shouting, "Call the police!" Dorry Swope has managed to flatten herself beneath a chair. The only person unaffected by the chaos is Bill Murray, who just keeps on eating his fries.

In the middle of this, the clock hits midnight, a huge cheer thunders out, and it's pandemonium. Somehow Jamie is back at my side. He grabs my hand and we run the gauntlet down the stairs, shoving against the tide of the crowd until we're outside again.

"Nice upper cut," says Jamie. "A little more practice and you'll have that sucker punch down."

"Is he going to be all right?" I open and close my fist. The knuckles are swollen.

"I hope not."

"He's my ex-husband."

"Really." Jamie's looking at me intently, anxiously, reading my face, hoping he won't see anything in my eyes, and he doesn't, because there's nothing there at all for anyone but him.

"My hero," I say, and mean it, and we kiss in the middle of West Fifty-seventh Street, with horns honking, people singing "Auld Lang Syne," police whistles blowing, and snow falling on our shoulders and our hair.

"Honey," he says, "let's go get some Twinkies and go home."

By the year 2000, 2 out of 3 Americans could be illiterate.

It's true.

Today, 75 million adults...about one American in three, can't read adequately. And by the year 2000, U.S. News & World Report envisions an America with a literacy rate of only 30%.

Before that America comes to be, you can stop it...by joining the fight against illiteracy today.

Call the Coalition for Literacy at toll-free **1-800-228-8813** and volunteer.

Volunteer Against Illiteracy. The only degree you need is a degree of caring.